TURNING THE LETHAL TIDE

His would-be killer had managed to struggle back to the platform, but had not found the strength to climb the steps. He was hanging on to a railing support half out of the water, his head drooping, breath rasping loudly in the gloom. Every so often, it was punctuated by a hacking cough as he tried to clear his throat.

"Gallagher!" It was a long, drawn-out plea with barely any strength in the voice. "For God's sake, don't leave me here!" Another hacking cough echoed within the chamber.

Gallagher said nothing, the twin lights of his helmet fixed upon the drooping form. He felt himself shiver slightly. The man's posture reminded him of a tableau in some bizarre religious painting; a vision of a condemned soul forever doomed to remain in an eternal purgatory.

"Gallagher! Have mercy, for Christ's sake. Have mercy . . ."

Gallagher lowered himself beneath the surface once more. The weak cries came muffledly to him until, as he went deeper, they faded completely.

Also available from HarperPaperbacks
by Julian Jay Savarin

Trophy
Target Down!
Wolf Run
Windshear

Coming Soon

The Quiraing List
Villiger

NAJA

JULIAN JAY SAVARIN

HarperPaperbacks
A Division of HarperCollinsPublishers

This is a work of fiction. The characters, incidents, and dialogues are products of the author's imagination and are not to be construed as real. Any resemblance to actual events or persons, living or dead, is entirely coincidental.

HarperPaperbacks   *A Division of* HarperCollins*Publishers*
10 East 53rd Street, New York, N.Y. 10022

First published in Great Britain by Alison and Busby Limited.
This edition published by arrangement with St. Martin's Press.

Cover photo by Herman Estevez

First HarperPaperbacks printing: March 1993

Printed in the United States of America

HarperPaperbacks and colophon are trademarks of HarperCollins*Publishers*

10 9 8 7 6 5 4 3 2 1

For John, Keith and Ian,
wise men all

PROLOGUE

i

"It's all set."

"What is, Fowler?" Sir John Winterbourne, former Admiral, looked up at his subordinate from his high-backed chair. "What's all set?"

Staring down at the face which strongly reminded him of a petulant cherub, Fowler suppressed the distaste he felt. Winterbourne had recently been made Head of Department. Anything less than ten years was, to Fowler's mind, recent. Winterbourne had been installed for just under a year. There had never been a honeymoon period.

Fowler said, patiently: "The operation to entrap Naja."

Winterbourne pursed his lips thoughtfully, making Fowler wait. Fowler maintained his own expression of benign imperturbability, knowing that would annoy Winterbourne. The entire Department knew who was really in command.

At last, Winterbourne said: "If this blows up in your face, Fowler, you're on your own. I want nothing to do with it."

"Of course, Sir John."

Winterbourne's expression was now one of open suspicion, not wanting to trust Fowler's apparent willingness to carry the can.

"I'm quite serious, Fowler."

"I'm certain you are, Sir John."

"And keep our people out of it as much as possible. Use outside help."

It was a dig at Fowler. Winterbourne liked using outsiders; Fowler preferred to keep everything within the Department. Things were less likely to go haywire.

"I'll be using Gallagher," Fowler said.

"Does he know?"

"By the time he does, it will be too late for him to get out."

Winterbourne actually smiled. There was a look of pure malice in his eyes. "Oh, well," he said.

ii

Naja. The genus Cobra, one of the deadliest snakes on earth.

The man relaxed on a deckchair in the bright Greek sunshine and felt good. He was clothed only in shorts and his darkly tanned muscular body had two parallel weals that went from left to right across his torso from beneath his armpit, before disappearing like burrowing worms into the forest of dark hair upon his broad chest. The weals were a permanent reminder of the closest he had ever come to the termination of his lucrative and dangerous career: they had been caused by two rounds from the Heckler and Koch sub-machine gun of a very accurate German policeman. The policeman had not lived through the exchange.

The man was known as Naja, arguably one of the deadliest people on earth. His associates in the many businesses he ran as a cover for his real activities knew him by many other names. Countries knew him as their citizen, or the citizen of other countries, but not that he was Naja. Their police forces and their intelligence services would have pounced with alacrity had they been aware of his identity. Yet many of those very countries had availed themselves of his services. Unfortunately, he was known to keep detailed records of his transactions, powerful tools of blackmail. He had told each of his clients so. Many therefore wished him dead . . . if only they knew who he was and where he could be found. Many had sent agents in quest of him. None had survived. So the countries he had served lived in fear of a man they did not know, and whom they hated. Others continued to seek him out . . . for his invaluable help.

Naja stared out at the glistening blue of the Gulf of Lakonikos and meditated upon the cupidity of his fellow beings, for whom he had little love but much contempt. To the islanders of Kythira which nestled at the southernmost tip of the Peloponnese peninsula, he was the rich businessman-owner of the imposing walled villa on high ground to the north of the island, with its commanding view of the gulf. Some thought him Greek, since he spoke the language with an impeccable Athenian accent. In other countries, people thought him Italian or French, German or Scandinavian, all of whose languages he spoke with a subtle regional accent. In England, he sometimes chose to speak with an American accent. Ninety per cent of the British, he knew, could not differentiate between the many regional variations of the vast American landscape. To them, Americans were all alike.

Naja grimaced briefly. He would soon be favoring Britain with one of his visits. A new job had come in, requiring meticulous planning. He felt a cold admiration for the intelligence-gathering capabilities of his newest principals. He himself had not known of the existence of the weapons he was expected to steal. Nonetheless, he looked forward to the exercise with some pleasure. It made a welcome change from his recent series of political assassinations.

He stretched himself luxuriously, a big hunting cat basking in warmth of the bright sun. He was beginning to miss his London club, anyway. A year was long enough.

A stunning blonde woman came out of the house, wearing a scant bikini. She plunged cleanly into the deep swimming pool. Water was pumped from the sea far below to fill the pool and was changed every day.

The woman surfaced. Her startlingly black eyes stared at him. "Are we leaving?"

"Yes," he said.

iii

Jack Donlan was powerfully built. Not very tall, he more than made up for his lack of height by his width of shoulder. He prided himself on keeping fit, which was just as well. He had one of the most dangerous jobs in the world, as a diver in the North Sea.

Donlan's idea of a relaxing weekend was a quiet sub-aqua swim in the watery darkness of underground rivers and flooded mine tunnels. His partner on such occasions was usually Tom Millar, a slim younger man who, while not as skilled as Donlan, was nonetheless an expert diver. Donlan would not have tolerated him otherwise.

On a bright, late spring day, they stood at the edge of Vicar's Pool, just north of the mining town of Mansfield, adjusting their gear in the last seconds before beginning their dive. The pool was itself a flooded mineshaft that went straight down for 105 feet. The water was so clear, they could see the silt-covered bottom.

They both knew the shaft well, and the tunnels that radiated from it. They knew that the silt layer was over six feet deep and they would descend cautiously so as not to disturb it. The resultant cloud would hang in the still water, impenetrable even to their powerful lights. In addition to the underwater lamp attached to the close-fitting caps of their wet-suits, each carried a hi-power torch at his belt.

Satisfied that the demand valves of their breathing equipment were working properly, they lowered themselves into the water. They waited for a few moments to allow the water permeating through their suits to form a warm layer between skin and suit, then Donlan went steeply down, legs moving with strong, measured strokes. Millar followed, tagging him from a safe distance.

They switched on their cap lights just before reaching the silt level. Donlan swam into one of the four tunnels leading off from the shaft. It was one he frequently used whenever he dived here. Abruptly, light from above was cut off; but his own lamp pierced the darkness brightly. The water was unbelievably clear.

Millar followed him.

They swam through the series of branching tunnels that Donlan knew so well, which was why he paused uncertainly when he came upon a tunnel he had never seen before.

Anchoring himself with one hand against the wall of the tunnel in which they had been swimming, he motioned to Millar to stop. Donlan then removed the torch from his belt, played its light on the entrance of the strange tunnel. Why, he wondered, hadn't he seen it before? It did not seem new. There were no fresh scourings in the earth.

He moved closer, cautiously. The light was now illuminating deeper into the entrance. Then he saw why he had missed the tunnel before. The light was playing upon an encrusted door. Its shape told him that, when closed, the door would be flush-fitting. Only exceptionally close scrutiny would have betrayed its presence.

Motioning to Millar to follow, he entered.

The tunnel was narrower than the others and, though there was plenty of room, Donlan thought that turning round could prove difficult if not done with care. With that caution in his mind, he swam along the tunnel, knowing Millar was not far behind.

The tunnel ended abruptly and Donlan suddenly found himself in an enormous chamber. The tunnel had spilled him out, taking him by surprise.

He barely had time to register that he had popped to the surface when an excruciating pain took him in the chest. His mouth opened wide with the suddenness of it and he felt blood pouring out. He began to choke. Then someone had ripped his mask off and was holding him beneath the water. He was dying, and he knew it, but he fought mindlessly for survival.

Displaying remarkable presence of mind, Millar switched off his light. Donlan's death-struggles echoed through the water to him. He began to move backwards along the tunnel, praying no one was coming up behind him. As he moved, he deliberately stirred up as much silt as he could to spoil the vision of anyone who might have decided to look for Donlan's partner. No diver went down alone.

Millar made it to the entrance of the tunnel feet-first. He had not dared turn around in case he got stuck. He felt panic rushing at him. His breathing rate increased; he fought that down. The last thing he wanted was to fall victim to a novice's most common mistake, especially not in such circumstances.

He began to retrace the route back to Vicar's Pool, fighting his panic continuously as he kept up his disturbance of the silt. Once or twice, he blundered into a tunnel wall and his air tank clanged against something. He felt his heart stop. Sound traveled far under water. In these tunnels it would be amplified, virtually telling them he was there.

It was the worst of all nightmares coming true. He tried to increase his speed, felt he was barely crawling. He could handle diving emergencies with a calm head. Trying to swim away in the pitch-black waters of flooded tunnels from people who had murdered your partner was something else entirely.

He banged into the wall again. His breath was coming too fast. *Too fast.*

He decided to switch on his light. As the light came on, he saw the two figures coming toward him.

A terrible despair seized him. The sob he'd been holding in burst involuntarily out of him, blowing his mouthpiece away. Water rushed gleefully into his opened mouth.

Then the figures were upon him.

1

Gallagher powered the gleaming black Audi *quattro* along the A25 toward Dorking in Surrey. The rain poured down, slamming into the road surface with a vengeance, bouncing briefly up again with the force of the impact. He stared through the windscreen, cleared by the fast sweep of the wipers. The rain did not worry him. If anything, he enjoyed the way the turbo-engined four-wheel-drive car treated the appalling conditions with disdain. Behind him, a high tail of spray, thrown up by the fat wheels, billowed in his wake. He had partially lowered his window so that he could hear the swish of the tires as they bit into the streaming surface of the road. He smiled, having a good time of it.

The road swept downward in snaking bends. The car took them with ease. The big green digits of the glowing speedometer readout sat at 100. Gallagher knew the car could take the bends at an even higher speed, but chose not to. Even so, the way the *quattro* hurled itself through the bends, its 275 bhp Treser-modified engine roaring with what sounded like gleeful abandon, sent the adrenalin pumping through him. The entire car pulsed with a power that begged to be unleashed.

"That's enough, Lauren." He spoke softly to the car. It seemed to growl seductively in response.

Gallagher smiled again, put gentle pressure on the accelerator. The digital readout flicked rapidly upward, settled on 110.

"All right," he said. "You win, but that's it for now."

The car hurtled round a steeply descending bend without drama, seemingly glued to the road. Gallagher's eyes swept the six digital instruments with an unconscious ease that went back to the days when the instruments before him would have belonged to the infinitely more complex cockpit of twenty-nine tons of Phantom screaming across the upper reaches of the sky. In the left-hand corner of the instrument binacle was the quarter-circle of the tachometer with the multi-function timer set at its center. In the middle was the speedometer readout, flanked on the right by the twin horizontal lines of the boost and water-temperature gauges which were measured by cursors. Beneath them was the digital fuel gauge.

The cursor on the boost gauge danced with manic frenzy as Gallagher changed down into fourth to take a sharper bend. Sometimes he felt a brief twinge of nostalgia for the Phantom cockpit; but brief it was. He did not yearn for the old life. There were other aspects of his past that he tried to avoid, though he was not always successful.

He liked his new profession. He had little to complain about. Mercifully, his past had left him alone for a while and, despite the dark and swollen sky with its overload of water, he felt good.

The bend changed into a sweeping right-hander and Gallagher pulled back into fifth gear. The digits briefly shot up to 115 before settling down to 110.

The road began to level out. A car going the other way hooted querulously and needlessly. The *quattro* had held its line, never once deviating from its side of the road. The other car, Gallagher knew, though traveling at perhaps half the speed, was in far greater danger of going off the road in those conditions. He shook his head slowly in resignation.

He began to slow down, saw the sign he was looking for: "Silent Pool, 100 yds." In moments, he had reached the entrance to the big lay-by. He pulled off the road, eased the car into the parking area. He steered the *quattro* round until its nose was pointing toward the road, then reversed until practically at the bush barrier. He stopped, shut down the engine. The car whined into silence. The rain hammered at its bodywork.

There were four other vehicles in the lay-by: two Jaguar saloons, a Bentley Mulsanne and a big white Mercedes van the size of a small coach, with smoked side windows. The Mercedes was parked nose-in. The other cars had been reversed into their positions. There was no one in the cab.

Gallagher had parked the *quattro* close in to the Mercedes, away from the other cars which were empty, and all grouped together on the opposite side of the white van. This placed him closest to the exit from the lay-by. He remained momentarily in the car, listening to the drumming of the rain. He had a clear view of the road to his left where it disappeared toward Dorking. To his right, the stern of the van hid approaching traffic. Every so often, cars swished past, in both directions.

He opened his door to climb out. As he did so, a door in the side of the van slid open and a man in jeans and a pale blue T-shirt was looking at him. The man moved aside as Gallagher, not wanting to get his own jeans and shirt wet, quickly locked the car and entered the van.

The man looked at the *quattro* appreciatively. "Nice. Very nice." He scowled at the rain. "Flaming June," he added.

"I thought this was what everybody wanted," Gallagher said. He turned from the man, who pulled the door shut, to look about him.

The interior of the van was decorated in a way that would have made the lounge of an expensive flat look positively slumlike. There was wall-to-wall pile carpet and wall-to-wall stereo. Comfortable armchairs with seatbelts were bolted to the floor. The chairs could be swiveled and there were six of them, three placed along each side. In the middle was an oblong table of dark green marble. There was a radiophone, television screen and a cocktail cabinet. Drinks were on the table. Soft lights glowed from the ceiling. The ceiling and sides were plushly upholstered in hide of the palest cream. The carpet was a deep red, the chairs white. The compartment was sealed off from the cab, but had a door for access. This barrier, too, was richly upholstered in cream.

In addition to the driver who had opened the door, there were six other people in the van. Two casually dressed men were perched on each of the wheel arches that had been upholstered into bench seats. In the nearest pair of chairs were two other men, in neat City pinstripes. The furthest pair contained, on the left, a beautiful woman dressed like a medieval princess; but the slim cigar in her elegant mouth effectively killed the image.

The man opposite her was dark-haired, with a strong face and lively eyes. He looked, Gallagher thought, like a soldier. Perhaps it was the haircut, or the fact that he was track-suited.

One of the men in City suits said: "About time too. We've been here for over half an hour." He had a roundish face, black hair distinguishedly graying at the sides, and wore light-reactive sunglasses. He looked like the kind of man who hated being contradicted or kept waiting for more than two seconds.

Disliking him on sight, Gallagher said neutrally: "I had to pick up my car in Cobham. It was in for a service."

"Couldn't you have done that afterwards?"

"I had to get here," Gallagher said with the patience of one talking to a backward child. He saw the man's lips tighten as he turned to the other man in the pinstripes. "Who's paying me? You or. . . ."

"I am," Pinstripe answered.

"Good." Gallagher turned back to the one in glasses. "We'll begin this early. If you're going to remain here while I'm working, you keep out of my hair."

The woman leaned forward slightly, expectantly. She even took the cigar out of her mouth, which remained slightly parted.

The eyes behind the sunglasses seemed to narrow, but Gallagher was not sure. "Do you know whom you're talking to?"

"Yes. An idiot."

The van itself seemed to hold its breath, waiting for the expected explosion. Instead, there was a continuing silence as they locked eyes.

There was a quiet cough, and the man who was paying Gallagher said: "Mr. Tramm is Miss Luce's manager, Gordon."

"That's right," Tramm said, still glaring at Gallagher. "So watch it, or I can make sure you don't even get to take pictures of piccaninnies in Brixton."

Gallagher knew he was going to hate Tramm.

The cough came again. "My advertising company is responsible for Miss Luce's publicity, Mr. Tramm. Mr. Gallagher has worked for me on several occasions. I respect his work. If he says he wants you out of his hair, that's what he gets. And as to the taking of pictures of . . . er . . . piccaninnies in Brixton, publicity campaigns can go dreadfully wrong."

The sunglasses turned upon the speaker. "Are you threatening me, Nellis?"

"God forbid," Charles Nellis answered mildly. "You are my client."

"Just keep remembering that. I pay you, you pay Gallagher. Therefore *I* pay Gallagher."

"Wrong, Tramm," Gallagher said. "The Nellis Advertising Group pays my checks, and I can turn down any assignment I don't like. I'm beginning to think this is one of them."

Nellis stood up, crouching to clear the ceiling. He was taller than Gallagher's own six-foot-one, and had the benign air of a bemused bloodhound. The sad brown eyes tended to enhance that resemblance, as did the luxuriant tufts of graying hair that drooped behind his ears from an otherwise bald head. His colleagues all knew him, however, as one of the sharpest business brains around. Under his helmsmanship, Nellis Advertising had grown from nothing to a high-profit concern in record time. Nellads, as the group was more commonly known, had some of the most lucrative accounts on its books. They had recently picked up the account of one of the prestige car manufacturers, worth millions, in the face of some of the most savage competition that the advertising world could mount. So when potential competitors looked at Charles Nellis and saw a sad bloodhound that enjoyed a tipple perhaps just a little too much, they never realized they were looking at a carefully cultivated façade; until too late.

Nellis turned his most defeated look upon Tramm. "I would advise against upsetting the applecart at this stage. I really don't think we could organize another session without extra funds and more time. That would ruin your schedule, wouldn't it?" He smiled apologetically. "Let Gallagher do things his way. Photographers can sometimes be a little touchy, can't they, Gordon?" The bloodhound turned slightly, eyes signaling: *Humor the idiot.*

Gallagher said, "As long as he keeps out of my way."

"There we are," Nellis said brightly. "All sorted out. Shall I introduce everyone?" Not waiting for a reply, he continued: "Goordon, I'm sure you've seen Miss Luce on television."

Gallagher nodded at Doria Luce, who gave him a speculative, half-amused smile.

"Next to her," Nellis went on, "is Christopher Jameson, who'll be doing the diving. These two gentlemen on the benches are from Astra Video. They'll do their shooting when you're finished and won't get in your . . . er . . . way. Phil Clegg you met at the door. He drives this penthouse on wheels. And of course, last but certainly not least, Jerry Tramm. OK, everybody?" He didn't seem to expect comment.

Gallagher knew that Nellis had personally booked the whole team, including the Mercedes, complete with driver. The Mercedes was one of a fleet of vehicles specially rigged to suit the tastes of aspiring stars. Somewhere on this motorized magic carpet there would be a small changing compartment with washbasin and toilet. He had seen the ads. It wouldn't surprise him to find that Nellads represented the firm that made the conversions. Nellis would not have missed out on that.

Tramm was saying: "Doria is going to be big, very big. This is a crucial point in her career. She had better not catch a cold today." He was looking at Gallagher.

"Mr. Tramm, I'm just here to take stills. If I've got this right, you were the one who asked Nellads for something medieval, with lots of atmosphere. Nellads presented the idea, which I believe you accepted without reservations. That's what I've been told. Now, unless I've got it all wrong, that's how we're going to do it. If Miss Luce catches a cold, it's your affair, not mine. When I've taken my pictures, that's my lot. I'm off. Astra Video then takes over." Gallagher looked at Nellis. "Charles, have I got it right? I'd better know where I stand."

"You've got it absolutely right," Nellis said. A firmness in his voice brooked no contradictions from Tramm.

Gallagher said: "Right. I'm going out to check the location. I won't be long."

Jameson picked up a bright blue plastic anorak from behind his chair, stood up. "I'll come with you." He began to put it on.

"Right," Gallagher said again.

"Care for a drink first, Gordon?" Nellis offered. "Warm the insides a bit."

Gallagher declined. "Never drink when I'm working."

Clegg drew the door open for him. The sounds of the rain and the traffic, held at bay by the sumptuous upholstery, suddenly burst into the van. Gallagher climbed out quickly, unlocked the *quattro*. The rain beat at him as he reached in to pick up his Nikon, a light-meter, and a voluminous, hooded creation that looked like a small tent. He slung the camera and the light-meter round his neck, put on the large anorak. The camera was safely out of the rain. The size of the anorak also enabled him to change films within its shelter during inclement weather; he had bought it for just that purpose.

There was a noise behind him. Nellis stood there, blinking in the rain.

Nellis said: "I'm sorry about Tramm. His crack about Brixton piccaninnies was uncalled for."

"Does it worry you?"

"Frankly, yes. No client of mine. . . ."

"It doesn't worry me. Get back in, Charles. You're getting wet."

Nellis hesitated, then reentered the van. Jameson, on his way out, paused long enough for Nellis to get by. Then Clegg pulled the door shut. Gallagher walked toward the exit, followed by Jameson.

Silent Pool was in fact two pools. Gallagher and Jameson turned left out of the lay-by, walked up the short track to the first pool. It was shallow, with a surface coating of thick patches of algae. The rain pummeled them, tearing them to pieces.

"Ugh!" Jameson said. "You're not going to put me in there, are you?"

Gallagher stared at the sorry pool. "No. Let's check the other one."

The track, barely fifty feet long, was wide enough to take motor vehicles and was in fact an access road to a farm that hugged the right-hand edges of the pools. It turned right, toward the farm. A sign warned that way was private. Gallagher and Jameson turned left off it, on to the soggy earthen path skirting the lower pool. They came to a rough wooden barrier with an unlocked gate in it. They went through, came up to the second, larger pool.

The first thing that hit Gallagher was the over-
whelming stench that assaulted his nostrils above
the smell of the wet earth.

"Trippers," Jameson said.

"What?"

"This is meant to be a beauty spot. People come
here."

"Smells like an open-air toilet."

Jameson smiled at the comment. "There's supposed to be a ghost too. The usual beautiful maiden
who drowned herself."

The pool itself was roughly a hundred feet in
length and about fifty across. They were standing on
a tarred path at the lower end of the pool. Here, it
was shallow, but not still. The swelling brought by
the rain caused it to pour into the overspill and down
into the second pool.

Midway along the path, a small rough boathouse had been constructed out of stripped saplings
and branches. The house perched outward, just
touching the surface of the water. Next to it was a
small boat, painted to look like a medieval funeral
barge. Plastic sheets protected it from the rain. Gallagher assumed Nellis must have obtained permission to use it on the water. The boat was tethered to
the log-cabin boathouse which itself let in copious
quantities of rain. The boat had grounded itself
broadside-on to the path, its prow pointing away
from the log structure. Water spilled past the prow
and on to the path, to stream across and down into
the second pool.

The path continued, encircling the pool in an
untarred, undulating route. At the far end, the
ground rose perpendicularly for about twenty feet,
its face scoured by countless rivulets brought into
being by the heavy rain. A fine mist hung there,

spreading out over that part of the water. Huge trees at the top formed a dark canopy with their branches.

The surface of the pool was less covered with algae than its twin and from its bottom several colonies of plants grew in furry stalks toward the dim light.

Jameson said: "We're going to use it."

"Yes."

"I was afraid you'd say that. It doesn't look any better than the other one. Oh, well. At least the boat's here."

"You must have dived in worse places."

"I find that hard to believe."

Gallagher smiled. "Let's go round. I want to check some angles."

They began walking. Here and there, a rough wooden railing bordered the pool. It looked fragile.

Gallagher said: "How did they get the boat up here?"

"It traveled on top of the Merc, then we humped it to this pool." Jameson grinned. "We hoped you'd use it instead of the other."

"When did Tramm arrive?"

"About two minutes before you did."

"Then what was all that about my being late?" Gallagher asked.

Jameson's eyes were amused. "Playing his manager-to-the-stars role. You handled him quite well. Impressed his sexy starlet."

"Doria Luce? Oh, come on. She eats people like me for breakfast."

"Well, I wouldn't mind being eaten by her."

"You've got a dirty mind, Mr. Jameson."

"Oh, definitely," Jameson said unrepentantly. "And the name's Chris."

"Right." Gallagher decided he was going to like Chris Jameson.

They walked right round the pool, stopping now and then as Gallagher worked out the best places from which to take his pictures.

At last he said: "I've seen enough. Let's go and get Mr. Tramm's precious starlet wet."

"You're going to enjoy that, aren't you?" Jameson remarked, looking forward to it himself.

"You should worry. You'll be in full diving gear. Anyway, doesn't she have a wetsuit underneath those fancy clothes?"

"No. She wants the clothes to cling to her lovely body properly," Jameson said with relish, "and I'll be the one holding on to it."

"Down, boy," Gallagher said. "Tramm will be watching you like a hawk."

"Not out here he won't. He's not the kind to get his feet wet."

Gallagher changed his mind about Jameson having been a soldier; at least, not a squaddie. He said: "You don't sound as if you like him."

"I don't have to like him. Nellads pay me, just as they do you."

As they continued back to the lay-by, Gallagher marveled at Doria Luce's refusal to be put off by the state of the pool and the weather. The things people were prepared to endure for publicity. The rain still pounded.

Jameson banged on the side of the Mercedes when they reached it. The door slid open and they climbed in, leaving muddy footprints on the wide strip of rubber matting that had been laid across the van from the entrance. Water dripped off them and on to it.

"The sooner we get it done," Gallagher said to

everyone, "the sooner we'll be out of here. I'm ready to roll."

Jameson said: "I'll get my gear on." He disappeared through a door at the rear of the compartment.

"Ready when you are, Gordon darling," Doria Luce said. She had a throaty voice with a marked trace of the East End that belied her patrician looks.

"Fine," Gallagher said noncommittally. He looked at Nellis. "The flowers and the candelabra?"

"We'll bring them up."

"Right. I'll see you up there." Gallagher turned to go.

"Wait for me," Doria Luce said. She had stood up and was putting on a black hooded cloak.

As Gallagher went out, Doria Luce joined him, holding her long dress off the ground to reveal bare ankles and black slippers on her feet. The slippers were soon dirty.

"Cheap stuff," Doria Luce said as they walked. "The slippers, I mean. You put Jerry in his place," she went on, glancing at Gallagher.

The eyes were black with a greenish tinge to them that was so faint it could be observed only when light played upon her eyes in a particular way. Her face was delicately shaped, with a fine nose that curved very slightly, narrow and haughty. The mouth was equally delicate, gently upturned at the corners. The firm chin spoke of determination. She walked with a grace that was enhanced by the length of the dress.

Gallagher wondered why she bothered to hold it off the ground, considering it was soon to get soaked. But she was doing so unconsciously, he decided. As an actress, she would have had plenty of practice.

When she had stood up to put on the cloak, he

had noted the curving shape of her body, to which the medieval gown did full justice. No wonder Jameson was looking forward to the part he had to play.

Her face was devoid of makeup, giving her an unnaturally pale look, yet adding a haunting mystery to it. It was exactly what Nellis wanted to come across in the photographs. As they walked, Gallagher found himself toying with the idea that the ghostly woman of the pool was at his side. The hooded cloak, glistening with rain, served to strengthen the impression.

She glanced at him again. "Penny for them?"

"I was just thinking about what you said," he lied.

"About Jerry?"

"Yes."

"Well, you did put him in his place. He didn't like that."

"You could have fooled me."

She gave a laugh, a light, tinkly one, almost like that of a child. It was full of mischief.

"God. His face!" She paused, added: "You're very sure of yourself. Many people quake in his presence."

"That's their problem. Is he a good manager?"

"He's ruthless. In this business, that means a good manager."

"Until he turns on you."

The eyes were fathomless. "What a funny thing to say."

"I don't see that it was. If Jerry Tramm were my manager, I'd never turn my back on him. Call it instinct."

The eyes remained speculative for brief moments, then she smiled, daring him. "Think you could be better?"

"You'd be too much for me, Miss Luce, even if I knew how to handle the job."

"Oh, I don't know," she said, thoughtfully. The delicate lips curved into a tiny secret smile. "And enough of the 'Miss Luce.' Too bloody formal. Call me Doria, darling."

"If you wish."

"I wish. Strange one, aren't you? Miss Luce this, Miss Luce that. . . . Most photographers I know can hardly wait to paw me—under the excuse of showing me the right way to pose, of course."

"It sounds as if you don't like posing for photographs."

She appeared to shrug. "Part of the job."

They had arrived at the boat. She stared at the pool. "God. Look at it. Yechh!"

"Just remember to keep your mouth closed when you go under. I hate to think what the water's like."

Gallagher took a few quick readings on the light-meter, shielding it from the rain as much as possible. He had thought of using a transparent plastic bag as protection for the Nikon, with a hole for the lens, but had decided against it. Too cumbersome. If he worked quickly, he wouldn't get much moisture on it. The light had improved, though the rain still fell heavily. He had loaded with fast film to give him the effect he wanted.

"And here come my burial flowers," Doria said. She was looking back toward the lay-by.

The others were on the access road, laden with flowers and wreaths. Nellis, in a raincoat, carried the candelabra with the inevitable plastic bag over it. James was in his wetsuit, a small air tank on his back, hoses and mouthpiece dangling on his chest. His face mask was raised and he carried his flippers in one hand. Clegg and the two Astra Video men carried the flowers. There was no sign of Tramm. Nellis had covered his bald crown with a floppy hat.

"So where's the great manager?" Gallagher asked.

"Too delicate for this sort of weather, darling."

"I thought he was worried about you catching a cold."

"Had to make the right noises, didn't he?"

"Christ," Gallagher said in disgust.

Doria Luce smiled. "I'm beginning to like you."

"Yes, well. . . ."

They fell silent. The rain had eased slightly now, but it still came down with some force. Oddly, there was no wind at all.

"I like the rain," she said. "Even here."

No accounting for taste, he thought. He was here because it was a job that paid well.

"What is this session all about, anyway?" he asked. "What are you promoting?"

"Isn't it obvious? Myself. No . . . that's not strictly true," she went on. "Jerry has an idea for a film. He wants stills and a video to help him sell it to a company. It will be a vehicle for me, he says."

Gallagher said nothing. It was none of his business.

The others arrived, began preparing the boat. Jameson had come barefoot. He dipped his feet in the water to clear them of mud, then put on his flippers.

"I'll need all kinds of shots after this," he commented to Gallagher. "I'll be lucky if I catch typhoid." He grinned, pulled down his mask, secured his mouthpiece and waded out into the pool. After a while, his black-clad form disappeared smoothly beneath the surface.

Looking around suddenly, Gallagher found Doria Luce's eyes upon him; then she turned to study the preparations on the boat. Out of their wrappers, the flowers gave off a multi-perfumed smell that took away some of the disagreeable stench from the pool.

The boat was soon ready, and Doria Luce removed her cloak, handed it to Nellis. She climbed in, settled herself in a reclining position among the flowers, while Clegg and one of the video men held the craft steady. The rain washed her face and her clothes, etching the outline of her body in sharp relief within seconds. The gown was of the thinnest material. The candelabra had been fixed to the stern, unlit.

The boat was pushed out. Doria Luce lay absolutely still, eyes closed, face pale among the flowers. The boat headed for the mist.

Nellis said, quietly: "Spooky, isn't it?"

Gallagher did not reply. He had the Nikon out and was triggering off motorized sequences. As he moved round the pool taking shots of the slowly drifting boat, a strange feeling came over him. The pool had suddenly become a place of primeval force. The sensation was so strong, he was barely able to continue taking pictures. When he'd finished the reel, the boat had entered the mist and was stopped at the far end. He had taken several shots of it actually entering the suspended curtain.

He found he was shaking.

He began reloading inside his anorak. Jameson had surfaced and was pushing the boat back to its launch point. Doria lay unmoving. By the time Jameson had got the boat back and had disappeared once more, Gallagher was ready for the second part of the session.

Again, the boat was pushed out and he took

more photographs of its slow, funereal drifting. Then all at once it rose briefly out of the water before capsizing, throwing Doria and her bed of flowers into the pool. She sank like a proverbial stone, while the flowers marked her passing like brightly colored beacons bobbing in the wash of the disturbed waters. Then out of the dark green depths a gleaming black figure erupted, with Doria limp in its arms. The figure continued to rise. Water cascaded, then fell back, displacing great gouts of spray that rose in response to its plunge. The water settled, becoming still. The rain continued to pound.

Gallagher felt the trigger stop. He had shot the whole of the second roll. He realized that he was holding his breath. Where were they?

The water remained still.

Then there was a second eruption, and Jameson was coming toward the shore with her, supporting her on the surface with outstretched arms. When the pool became too shallow for him to swim she stood up and got out. Nellis handed her the cloak. She wrapped it about her, began to walk back to the lay-by. Her slippers were still on her feet. Jameson went back for the boat.

Gallagher went after Doria Luce.

"For one horrific moment," he said, when he'd caught up with her, "I actually thought you were dead."

There was a flash of green in the darkness of her eyes as she looked at him. "Perhaps I was."

They walked on to the lay-by in silence.

Just before they reached the Mercedes, she said: "I remembered to keep my mouth closed."

"Good."

She smiled at him just as Tramm slid the door open. The rain continued to hammer down.

2

The building looked no different from the others that bordered the sleepy square in the heart of London. The rain that was trying to drown Surrey had shifted away from the capital, after half-heartedly blessing it with a few passing showers. As a result, the square was damp and devoid of human life.

Sir John Winterbourne stared down from a third-floor window, at the wooden bench he could see from where he stood. A pigeon pecked hopefully at the ground near it. The empty bench, gray in the gloom of what had initially promised to be a bright June day, seemed to mesmerize him.

Someone entered his office. Winterbourne turned. It was Fowler, his second-in-command. There was no love lost between them.

"I asked for you ten minutes ago, Fowler," he began immediately, with barely controlled annoyance.

Fowler, tall and slim to Winterbourne's shortened roundness, appeared quite undisturbed by the testiness in his superior's voice. He knew the Department and its workings inside out and was never perturbed by Winterbourne. This was something that rankled, Fowler knew, and he took a small pleasure in it. Winterbourne, having been sent to take over the post of the former Head of Department, now deceased, still felt very much the new boy and tended to react accordingly.

In a just world, Fowler would have been given the job. There was no one better qualified. But that had not happened. As was so often the case with government bureaucracies, the appointment had been made with a minimum of tact, and little appreciation of the Department's working structure. Winterbourne was ex-Navy in a Department staffed in the upper echelons by ex-Air Force personnel. Fowler had long since stopped believing in just or even reasonable worlds, and there was very little in life that could spring surprises on him. Winterbourne's appointment was not one of those. His own appointment . . . now that would have been a surprise.

Fowler said, calmly: "An urgent intercept has come from an outstation in Turkey. I was waiting for the decoding. It is of interest to us. I thought you'd like to know."

Knowing he could not win a psychological game with Fowler, and hating it, Winterbourne said: "Of interest? In what way?"

"Naja is on the move."

Winterbourne's eyes showed a definite interest. "On the move," he repeated. "Where from?"

"We are not as yet certain. The intercept was a car phone conversation."

"Where?"

"Bulgaria."

"Car phones in Bulgaria?" Winterbourne was skeptical.

Fowler did not close his eyes to show the exasperation he felt. Winterbourne sometimes had the habit of thinking that anywhere east of the channel had barely made it out of the Dark Ages.

Fowler said: "Someone passing through."

"Then why speak in Bulgarian? He must have known there would be an intercept. Everyone's after him."

"Precisely."

Winterbourne stared at Fowler. "What exactly are you getting at?"

"He wants us to know," Fowler said in his mild way.

"Why?"

Good God, Fowler thought. *It's so bloody obvious.*

He said: "Naja likes warning the world when he's about to carry out a mission. Vanity. But that's not all. It also confuses. By now, any organization that has made its own intercept will be tingling with anticipation and frustration. If Naja apparently betrays his presence somewhere, that is not where he is. He likes his little games. We once thought he was in Tokyo. On the day he was supposed to be there we lost two good men in Turkey. He let us know, some time later, that he was responsible."

"I know nothing of this."

"Before your time, Sir John." Fowler poisoned his arrow with a brief smile.

Winterbourne was not going to let that pass. "And are we quivering with anticipation and confusion, Fowler?"

Fowler took his time. "No, Sir John. We are not. I leave such displays to other intelligence agencies."

"Complacent, are we?"

"I am never complacent." Fowler's eyes were steely behind glasses that gave him the air of a benign academic. Many people had been fooled by that exterior; to their eventual cost.

"He may be heading this way." Winterbourne was reluctant to lose points.

"He may already be here," Fowler said unhelpfully. "Even after all this time, no one knows what he looks like. It would be very easy for him."

"Then we are unlikely to know where he is, until he has struck."

"Just like a cobra." Fowler gave another brief smile.

"I do not consider this a signal for amusement, Fowler. I do not want this . . . Naja creating his mayhem here." Winterbourne went on almost to himself: "I do wish people would not insist on exporting their terrorism to this country. They should play in their own backyards, dammit."

"We don't know who is paying him this time. It could be a private job. He has been known to work for individuals."

"Nevertheless, we should be on the alert."

"We are."

The face of a petulant cherub stared up at Fowler. The faintest of flushes stained Winterbourne's cheeks.

"I'm not sure I like your attitude, Fowler," he said pompously, "but we'll let that go for the moment. I have something of greater importance to discuss with you." He reached forward to pick up a sheet of paper from his large inlaid desk, straightened, and stood there frowning at it.

Fowler waited patiently. Winterbourne was going through the waiting room act. It always served to amuse Fowler when those who could not carry it off tried this out on him. The longer they chose to make him wait, the greater was the effect of his own imperturbability upon them.

He continued to divert himself by casually looking about the office he knew so well. Part of a suite designated for the use of the Head of Department, it was large enough and had sufficiently well-upholstered furnishings to do justice to the inner sanctum of an exclusive private club. Which, he reflected, was exactly what it was.

But he had never liked its huge windows. The expanse of so much glass tended to make him feel naked. Had he been appointed Head, he would have done something about that. He much preferred his own office, almost tiny by comparison, with its single window well away from where he sat. It was not that he expected someone to take potshots at him from across the rooftops—though one never knew with such things in the business. But only two months ago, an innocent bystander had been hit by a spent bullet that had come in through an office window. The shooting had occurred nearly 300 yards away, in a different direction. The bullet had ricocheted. That the person had not been badly hurt was luck. Imagine being topped by a ricochet.

Fowler had long decided that if he were to go, it would not be by accident. He found no contradiction in the fact that he walked and drove through the streets, traveled about the country and abroad, quite openly. His well-cultivated façade of the benign academic worked so completely, he actually looked the part. Fowler was the classic faceless wonder.

"This report," Winterbourne was saying, looking up at last, "came to me direct from the Minister. Couple of divers missing somewhere in the Midlands. Place called Vicar's Pool. One of them . . . let me see . . . yes, Jack Donlan, worked on the North

Sea rigs. Didn't turn up for work. He was apparently very conscientious and a top-class diver. The firm he worked for got in touch with his family. *They* thought he was already at work. He had a diving partner, weekend recreation only: a Tom Millar. He's missing too. The police were contacted. Now this thing has found its way to my desk. I want to know why. I would have thought it more of a police affair. We are not a missing persons bureau. Any ideas, Fowler?"

"At this moment, I am as mystified as you are, Sir John. I shall look into it."

"Can't see what it has to do with us," Winterbourne muttered querulously.

Winterbourne, Fowler knew, would never go so far as to dare criticize the Minister's judgment. Not like Kingston-Wyatt, the former incumbent and a good friend with whom he had seen active RAF service, and who had been the scourge of Ministers. Winterbourne saw greater things for himself, including an eventual peerage, so would not rock the boat. Kingston-Wyatt had not given a damn; which was why he had been so good. But some time ago, Kingston-Wyatt had killed himself. The casualties in the business came in all sorts of ways.

"I'll look into it," Fowler repeated neutrally. He had no intention of holding Winterbourne's hand. "Can I have the report?"

"What? Oh, yes. Yes." Winterbourne handed it over.

Fowler turned to go.

"You'll need a diver," Winterbourne began with calculated pettiness. "The Navy has very good divers."

Fowler paused. "Do I have control of this, Sir John?"

"Yes," Winterbourne replied after a while, with some reluctance. "Yes, Fowler. You have."

"Thank you, Sir John." Fowler deliberately said nothing about the divers from the Navy. He walked across the thick pile of the deep red carpet, paused again at the door. "I believe Naja to be already in this country. A Turkey intercept. The very place where he took out two of our personnel. I think that was a message from Naja . . . to us."

Fowler let himself out, returned to his office. He sat at his desk, read the report carefully, several times over. He did not like the looks of what Donlan and Millar might have blundered into.

The party was already in full swing when Gallagher arrived at Nellis's neo-colonial mansion on the banks of the Thames, a mile or so outside Henley. Advertising paid well. It was a black-tie affair, and Gallagher had been forced to persuade his reluctant body into a dinner suit. Since his resignation, he had avoided such functions but always kept a suit in readiness. His present job required it even more frequently; which was ironic.

Doria Luce came up to him, dressed for the twentieth century in a black, shimmering dress that was as daring as it was daunting.

"Mmm!" she said to him. "I like what I see!"

He smiled at her, trying to disguise a glance at her cleavage, which seemed in imminent danger of overspill. Free from the wig that had earlier hidden it, her tawny blonde hair was close-cut and decorated with dark streaks. She reminded Gallagher of a ti-gress.

She said: "It's all right. You can look. Every male in here *and* a few females have had a good goggle." Her smile was devoid of any coyness. "I don't mind if you like what you see."

"No one could ever accuse you of being. . . ."

"Shy? Who wants to be shy? If you like someone, it's stupid to waste the time. I can't stand all those martyrs who suffer in silence when what they'd really like is to jump into bed with the person they fancy. Oh, the *agony* some people put themselves through!"

"That's a very refreshing policy."

The black eyes surveyed him appraisingly. "Are you teasing me? That would not be very nice." She pouted.

"As if I would be so cruel. You're a very different person this evening," he added.

"Ah!" She opened her eyes theatrically, then squinted at him. "You're missing your princess of the lake. Is that it?" She struck a regal pose. "I'm an actress, darling. I can be whoever I choose." She dropped the pose, added quite seriously: "I *was* a different person on that lake." She leaned sideways to look behind him. "What's that you're hiding behind your back?"

"The reason I'm late. The pictures."

"Already?" she cried eagerly. "Charles said you'd be quick. Jerry didn't believe him."

"He wouldn't. Talking of bad smells, where's the Brain of Britain?" Gallagher glanced about him, collected a few grins and knowing winks. "Everybody else seems to be here."

"Careful," she warned jokingly, "you're talking about the man who's going to make me into a movie legend."

A girl in black fishnet tights and the shortest of black skirts that was pinched at the waist by a postage stamp white apron came up to them with a tray of drinks. Doria exchanged her empty glass for another. Gallagher picked up the first and only one he intended to have, thanked the girl. She gave him a big smile and went in search of other thirsty guests.

Doria watched her legs with seemingly detached appraisal. "Not as good as mine," she remarked as she took a sip of her drink.

"I agree," Gallagher said.

"How gallant you are."

"Nothing to be gallant about. I spoke the truth."

A ghost of a smile came and went on her face. There was a sudden blare of music that died abruptly.

"They've got a disco in one of the rooms," she said. "Do you dance?"

"I like to, now and then. I can just about keep one foot out of the way of the other."

"I don't believe you. I'll bet you dance very well."

"As long as you don't say I've got natural rhythm."

"I wasn't going to. Why did you say that?"

"It really isn't important."

The eyes were still thoughtful. "All right. Well?"

"Well, what?"

"Are you going to hang on to the pictures or will I get to see them?"

Gallagher hesitated. "I thought perhaps Charles should see them first. After all, he's paying for the assignment. His job is to make a selection of the best shots. We wouldn't want to upset your exalted manager, would we?"

"Oh, come on," she said, daring him. "Charles won't mind. Besides, I'm sure you've done a good job."

"After your ducking today, I bloody well hope so. By the way, how did the video session go?"

She made a face. "All right, I suppose. But by then I was fed up of getting soaked."

"Well, you didn't catch a cold. Tramm will have to find someone else to sue now."

She grinned at him. "You two really hit it off."

"Oh, yes. Bosom pals, we are."

She took his hand. "Let's go and find a room. I want to see those pictures."

"If you insist," he said, giving in.

The house was two-storied, with a central staircase up to a square balcony with rooms leading off it. The first two rooms they tried were occupied by squirming, fully clothed bodies. It was third time lucky. They found themselves in a wide bedroom with large french windows. Outside was the room's own balcony, which overlooked the Thames. The curtains were open.

Doria sat on the floor, legs together and tucked close. She leaned against the foot of the bed. The dress strained tightly against her body, riding high up her thighs. Gallagher felt a jump in his pulse rate, took a sip of his drink to divert him, then sat down opposite her. Placing his glass down out of harm's way, he withdrew the photographs from their large brown envelope and spread them in a display for her inspection.

She put her glass down slowly, stared at them for long moments. It was some time before she spoke. Gallagher had brought eight color photographs with him. She picked each up in turn, studied it closely.

When she had looked at all eight, she said, softly: "Fantastic. Absolutely fantastic. I could almost believe they were taken several centuries ago;

as if you'd gone into a time machine to take them. You make me look very dead."

Gallagher shook his head. "I only took the picture. You did the rest. You, the weather and Chris."

"Jerry won't believe this," she said, still looking at the photographs on the floor. "He didn't have much faith in you, you know."

"Tell me about it," he said dryly.

She gave him a quick smile, turned back to the photographs. "It's eerie. I don't look like me at all. No. No. That's not what I meant to say. I *do* look like me, but. . . ."

"Like somebody else. You can be whoever you choose. Your own words."

"Yes. Yes." She spoke almost absently now. Abruptly, she stood up, went to the french windows, opened them. The sounds of the disco, previously registering only the insistent percussive throb of bass and drums, came at them in full chorus. Doria went out on the balcony. After a moment, Gallagher followed.

"Are you all right?" he queried.

"Oh, yes." She was leaning against the stone railing, staring out at the dark sheen of the river. She took a long inhalation of the night air. Though the rain had stopped, the overcast sky had brought darkness early. "I like the smell of the earth after heavy rain."

Gallagher took a cautious sniff. "At least it's better than by those pools."

"God, yes! I had three very hot baths before I felt I had got all that stuff off me."

Behind them in the room, someone said: "Yes, indeed. Good work. Very good work, Gordon. Spot on."

Nellis greeted them with a knowing smile as they turned and reentered the room.

"Not interrupting anything, am I?" He gave them a sideways glance before squatting on his heels to study the photographs.

There were two other people with Nellis: Jameson and a young woman Gallagher did not know. She was about five feet seven or eight, he judged, and was quite pretty. Her brown hair, with lighter tinges, was wavy and hung just above her shoulders, clipped back on each side of her face so that her ears were bared. They were, Gallagher noted, very nice ears, a little rounded and in perfect proportion to her features. Her face was saved from over-roundness by the slight prominence of her cheekbones, and her mouth from being unremarkable by the suffused redness of full lips. There was the barest hint of a point to her chin, and her nose just missed being too small and too finely pointed. It was as though Nature's sculptor had wanted to push the whole design to its limits, but had stopped just in time. The result was very pleasing.

Her body was fuller than Doria Luce's, with less exaggerated curves; but curves there were, complemented by her simple pink frock. Her well-shaped legs were bare; she was lightly tanned and seemed full of a barely contained energy. She did not have Doria Luce's devastating mix of elegance and sensuality; but there was something magnetic about her. Gallagher wondered who she was.

"No, Charles," Doria was saying, "you have not interrupted anything. We were just admiring your view."

Nellis looked up. "You should see it in the early hours of the morning. Now there's something to take your breath away." He picked up four of the photographs, handed them to Jameson. "There you are, Chris. You are the rising monster of the deep, claiming the princess as your own. Or are you saving her?" Nellis paused. "It's an angle we could work on. I'll have to think about that. In the meantime, I'll remember my manners while Chris is admiring himself and introduce this young lady to you, Gordon. Doria's already met her. Rhiannon, meet Gordon Gallagher. Rhiannon is Chris's sister."

Gallagher surprised himself by feeling suddenly glad. She offered a hand which he shook, found her grip much stronger than he'd anticipated. She gave him a warm smile and her astonishingly pale brown eyes sparkled.

"I've heard a lot about you from Charles," she said. Even her voice was warm and lively.

"All lies."

"We shall see."

Jameson saved Gallagher by saying: "I look pretty good, even if I say so myself."

"Oh, the ego of the man," Nellis said. He was clearly pleased with the way the session at the pool had turned out. He looked at Doria Luce. "Well, Doria? What do you think? Will Jerry be satisfied?" Jameson handed the photographs back to him.

She gave a fleeting smile. "He'll hate to admit it, but yes . . . he'll be satisfied."

Nellis said to Gallagher: "Are the others like these?"

"Some are better."

"Wonderful. We've got a campaign that should please even our very own humorless Jerry Tramm." He stooped to pick up the remaining pictures, returning the lot to the envelope as he straightened. "Now, children. That's the end of shop for tonight. The merrymaking awaits. Go and enjoy yourselves.

Gordon, take Rhiannon for a whirl in the disco. She hasn't had a dance yet, poor thing."

Doria Luce took Gallagher's hand firmly. "Gordon promised me a dance. Didn't you, darling?" She smiled sweetly at him, towed him out before anyone realized what was happening.

As they left, Gallagher had a vivid impression of Rhiannon Jameson's pale brown eyes following their progress interestedly.

Doria Luce didn't speak again until they were on the stairs. At the bottom, a gaggle of dinner suits looked up at her admiringly.

"That sorted out little Miss Bright Eyes. Well . . . not so little," she added with a gentle barb. " 'We shall see,' " she went on, mimicking Rhiannon. She continued to tow Gallagher down the stairs.

"Doria . . . what's this all about?"

"As if you don't know. Your eyes were out on stalks. A woman can get quite upset when the man in her company takes a fancy to a pudding like that."

Gallagher wanted to laugh. "I don't believe it. You're not jealous of Rhiannon Jameson. Every man in this place would grovel at your feet if you just gave the command. Look at that lot down there."

The dark eyes flashed green. "Every man? Including you? No. Don't answer that. I already know the answer. That's my point, you see. What interest is there in a man who would grovel? So when I find the only man who intrigues me in this group of soft-bellied drips, I don't like being upstaged by a . . . a. . . ." Her voice had dropped to a fierce whisper.

"Pudding?" Gallagher supplied.

Another glance, this time accompanied by a quick smile. "Exactly."

They had reached the bottom and immediately the group of admirers surrounded them. Doria smiled ravishingly at the men she had just recently maligned. She wriggled her way out of a few aspiring hands, dragged Gallagher away.

"See what I mean?" she said out of the corner of her mouth.

"What did you want me to do? Beat them up? They are your adoring public, after all."

"Lecherous public, you mean."

He refrained from pointing out that her dress didn't help. He allowed himself to be hauled into the disco. A body-popping song blasted out of four massive speakers placed at each corner of a large room, which Gallagher recognized as the main dining room, now wisely devoid of Nellis's pricey furniture and carpets. At the far end, on a low platform, the black disc jockey body-popped with unbelievable athleticism to a small, awestruck audience. A fair number of people had taken to the floor, some young and supple enough to emulate the disc jockey's energetic exertions and making a passable go of it, others less agile who should have known better. But they seemed to be enjoying themselves. Multicolored lights on gantries had turned the place into a disco that would have graced any club.

"This must have cost a packet," Gallagher shouted in Doria's ear.

"It's in the budget!" she shouted back. "Come on, let's dance!" And she pulled him on to the floor.

Doria Luce then proceeded to give body-popping a new meaning as Gallagher waited for her dress, glowing with a spectral many-hued fire lent to it by the lights, to abandon the unequal struggle. So did many others. In no time at all, she had deprived the disc jockey of his audience. People allowed her room and soon Gallagher found they were two islands on a polished, flashing sea. Then she began to drift away

from him, completely taken by the music. The disc
jockey was urging her on with a rapping commen-
tary on his microphone punctuated neatly into the
beat.

Doria's flaming, writhing dress continued to
keep her clothed, against all odds. Hoping she would
not notice, Gallagher edged off the floor, toward the
anonymity of the watching crowd. He liked dancing,
but this was one occasion when he preferred to be a
spectator. Doria danced on. The disc jockey had
smoothly put on a new record, altering the music so
subtly that she did not notice.

Someone said in Gallagher's ear: "Too much for
you?"

Gallagher looked around. Rhiannon Jameson's
face was inches from his. The lights appeared to
cause her features to change constantly; but her eyes
held his steadily. There was a fresh scent to her that
came pleasantly to his nostrils just beneath the trace
of her perfume. The press of the onlookers had
brought her against him and her body heat filtered
itself through his clothes. It charged him.

"Look at those men," she said. "They're all hoping her dress will fall off."

He didn't look. Rhiannon had moved her head
once more so that she was facing him. Her lips were
very close. Someone behind her pushed to get a better view of Doria Luce. The action made their faces
touch.

So Gallagher kissed her gently. Her lips were
warm and very soft.

"Hmm," she said.

Then the music stopped. There was a burst of
spontaneous clapping.

"That's it!" the disc jockey was saying. "Give the
gorgeous lady a big hand!"

People, mainly men, began to surge toward Doria as the music started up again in the midst of the applause. The men were all hoping she'd dance with them.

"Shall we sit this one out?" Gallagher said to Rhiannon.

"Gladly."

As they left the room, he thought he saw Doria staring at them from the throng of her admirers.

He spotted one of the apron-clad girls with a tray of filled glasses. "Can I get you a drink?" he asked Rhiannon.

She shook her head. "No, thanks, but you have one if you'd like."

"I've had my quota for tonight."

"Well," she said, pale brown eyes surveying him with humor, "what shall we do?"

"The rain's been stopped for some time. Why don't we go down to the river? Charles has a cruiser moored by his boathouse: at least, it usually is. Let's go and sit on the deck and listen to the Thames."

"Why not?" she said.

The extensive garden sloped down to the river bank a hundred yards away. The grass was not as wet as Gallagher had feared.

"Are your shoes all right?" he asked her.

"Yes. The ground's not too soft. What if there are people already on the boat?"

"We've got a whole garden."

"Hmm," she said.

"And what's that supposed to mean?"

"Just 'hmm.' " He knew she was smiling. "Charles thinks very highly of you. He said you've got an interesting history."

"Does he?" Gallagher wondered just what.

There were parts of his personal history he was quite certain Nellis knew nothing about.

"He said your father was an Irish don at Oxford and that your mother was half-Jamaican and half-Scottish."

"He said correctly. She was a Gordon. They're both dead."

"Yes. I know. He told me. I'm sorry."

Gallagher shrugged in the twilight of the glow from the house. The body-popping music of the disco assaulted the night. "It happens to all of us."

But he didn't tell her about how his father had died, blown up in his car at Oxford. How his past had brought such a terrible death to a man living in a world where such things were not supposed to happen, one of the innocent bystanders. He did not tell her how Lauren had been murdered, and how he had taken his revenge on the killers. He did not tell her, because such things were a part of the history that only a few people knew.

She said: "We lost our parents too, Chris and I. I was very young. Chris practically brought me up." She gave a warm chuckle of affection for her brother. "Well, he tried. We have a fairly large retinue of relatives, so an aunt did her duty; but we're very close, even though his work used to take him away. He used to be an officer in the Navy. His diving still takes him away, of course, but not as often and not for as long."

Well, I was wrong about the Army, Gallagher thought, *but not about the service background.*

"Has he been out long?"

"About eighteen months."

They had reached the mooring. The river bank had been shored up by a close-packed barrier of stripped and proofed logs that had been driven perpendicularly into the river bed, to protect the Nellis garden from possible flooding. Two iron rings set in concrete behind the barrier held the cruiser, secured by its moorning lines fore and aft. Even in the gloom, now that they were well out of the direct lighting from the house, Gallagher could see the familiar shape for what it was.

The craft was an expensively converted RAF air-sea rescue launch, with two powerful Volvo turbo diesels.

To their right, the large boathouse straddled the slipway that sloped into the unseen, deep approach channel. Nellis, Gallagher knew, seldom brought the boat in.

"Watch where you put your feet. I don't want you falling in."

"I can swim."

"I've no doubt, but that's not the point."

"Yes, sir." She was pleased by his solicitude for her safety. The Thames murmured at them.

"There doesn't seem to be anyone around," he said. "Shall we go aboard?"

"Aye, aye, Cap'n." She laughed softly.

"Are you taking the mickey, Miss Jameson?"

"Oh, absolutely, Mr. Gallagher. Absolutely."

She stopped, and they stood there by the boat, looking at each other. Incongruously, the soft noise of the river made the night seem strangely quiet. Even the sounds of the disco and the voices from the house seemed to have receded to the faintest of background whispers upon the gloom.

He reached out to take her hand. It closed warmly about his. He drew her slowly toward him, and her body pressed itself against him, its softness and warmth sending a slight tremor through him.

He released her hand, took her face in his hands

gently and began kissing her. She placed her arms about his waist, held on to him tightly. It was, he thought, a quite wonderful feeling.

They paused to look at each other. She did not take her arms from about him. He lowered his hands from her face, locked them behind her. They stood thus, seemingly joined to each other.

At last, she said: "We were a bit quick off the mark. One hour since meeting. That must be a record of some kind."

"Compared with some people up at the house, we'd be well down on the list." Nevertheless, he too was surprised, despite knowing he had wanted to kiss her again.

"For me it is. In fact so rare, it has never happened before." She was quite serious.

"I. . . ."

"Hello the boat!" someone called with levity. Jameson.

"Oh, oh," Gallagher said. "Here comes big brother to chop off my head."

They released each other reluctantly, moved slightly apart.

Jameson came up, looked at each in turn. "Having fun, you two?" He appeared to be smiling.

Gallagher said: "We thought it would be nicer by the river. Less crowded. We needed a bit of air."

Jameson was definitely grinning. "Don't sound so sheepish, Gordon. Rhiannon's a big girl now and is quite capable of looking after herself. More to the point, can you?"

"What do you mean?"

Rhiannon gave a little laugh. "I think he's talking about Doria Luce." She began walking back to the house. "The ladies' room calls. Don't go away. I won't be long."

Gallagher watched her go, enjoying the way the light from the house silhouetted her. She walked beautifully and the shape of her legs, even part of her thighs, was etched by the light through her dress.

Jameson said: "She'll only be gone a few minutes."

"You don't mind?" Gallagher continued to look at Rhiannon's receding form.

"Rhiannon and I get on well because we have a deal. We don't interfere."

Gallagher knew that was not strictly true. Jameson would seek to protect his sister fiercely if anyone chose to do her harm; but he understood what the other was telling him, and felt a warm regard for the man.

"However," Jameson was saying, "Doria Luce is furious."

"Why should she be?" Gallagher said, genuinely astonished. "She flirts with everybody. I knew she was not serious. She's bloody amazing, but I'm not crazy. Besides, I think Tramm believes she's his personal property, and I don't need that kind of bother."

"Yes. I wondered whether you'd thought about that side of it. Still, that's not the point. One does not choose Doria Luce. She chooses; and when she has chosen, one does not walk away. *She* does the walking."

"For God's sake. I only met her today."

"You met Rhiannon tonight. Imagine it. The ravishingly sexy Doria Luce publicly passed over for. . . . Even allowing for my own bias as a brother, Rhiannon's quite dishy; but to Doria Luce, she's a nobody. That's not going to sit well on her. In front of all those people, too."

"You're having me on. In that disco she was virtually surrounded by panting males."

"I know. I saw that crazy dance of hers. I was drooling too. I shamefully admit it. But I didn't come out here to talk about the sensuality ratings of either my sister or Dorian Luce. I came to talk to you about something else entirely. How much do you know about diving?"

The way Jameson asked the question made Gallagher's spine tingle.

3

"Diving?" Gallagher said. "I know a bit about it; enough to put on a pinhead with room to spare for a football pitch."

Jameson made a noise that sounded like a snort. "That's more than most people who aren't themselves divers. But I think your knowledge is not as sketchy as you would have me believe."

"Oh, yes? And what makes you say that?"

For answer, Jameson said: "Let's walk." Seeing Gallagher look toward the house, he added: "We'll keep an eye out for her and make it back to the boat in time."

"All right."

As he walked with Jameson, Gallagher felt alarm bells begin to sound within him, yet could not understand why.

Jameson said: "I'd like you to go on a little adventure with me."

"A little adventure? You sound like someone from the nineteenth century—you know . . . *Journey to the Center of the Earth,* and all that. Jules Verne."

Jameson stopped abruptly, stared at Gallagher, who had continued for a few steps before coming to a halt. Gallagher turned, puzzled.

"Why did you make that remark?" Jameson queried. "Do you know something about it?"

"About what? For Christ's sake, I don't know what you're going on about."

Jameson seemed to be making up his mind about something. Appearing to have come to his decision, he approached Gallagher.

"Let's walk," he said again. As they sauntered along the edge of the flood barrier, he continued: "About six weeks ago, a diver called Jack Donlan and his partner Tom Millar disappeared in underground water near Mansfield. Donlan was a North Sea diver. Before that, he was Navy. Millar did not work in the North Sea but he had plenty of experience around the coasts and in subterranean dives. Donlan always took him as partner for those. He would not have lasted half a second with Donlan unless he'd been bloody good.

"A tiny mention appeared in a local paper; then nothing. Total blackout. There was no mention of the incident either in the national press or on the radio or television news."

"A lot of things do get left out," Gallagher commented.

"Granted. But let me continue. You'll soon understand. Donlan was an excellent diver. I should know—I've worked with him, both in and out of the Navy."

Jameson paused. Gallagher said nothing. He didn't want Jameson to go on. He didn't want to know. He didn't like the way all his instincts were beginning to tell him that the allegedly mysterious disappearance of the two divers was going to impinge upon his life. When things he didn't like came into his life, the Department was invariably not far behind.

Was Jameson with the Department? And had the little episode with Rhiannon been a put-up job? Gallagher sensed a rising feeling of embarrassment. Had she been making a fool of him, after all? A slight anger was welling in him at the possibility. If that were the case, he'd better not make a bigger fool of himself but leave her to it. Get out now, before he was reeled in closer. . . .

Yet he couldn't believe it of her. She was so lively, so spontaneous. He didn't want to believe that she could be so devious.

He realized with a sense of shock that, despite the turmoil now in his mind, he would stay put and continue to listen to what Jameson had to say. He did not want to walk out on Rhiannon. She had already got to him. He was nicely hooked.

Jameson was saying: "Jack Donlan and I were good friends. His mother rang me when she found out he hadn't gone back to the rig after his weekend dive. They live in Hornsea on the northeast coast, just up from Hull."

Gallagher knew the area well. He'd seen it often enough from the air, barreling in with his Phantom, low from over the gray waters of the North Sea during practice attacks, hoping to catch the Binbrook boys, in their Lightnings, with their pants down. He did not interrupt Jameson, keeping his thoughts to himself.

Jameson went on: "Jack would sometimes go straight up to Scotland after one of his weekend jaunts, to catch the chopper for the flight out to his rig. On those occasions, he would leave the gear with Millar. But of course that didn't happen, because Millar went missing as well. The whole thing smells. Someone's sitting on what really happened. I want to find out. Jack and I had some good times together. I want to know what they've done to him."

"They?"

"There has to be a 'they.' Donlan was too bloody good to have been caught out by anything natural. He was an ace."

"I don't know anything about cave diving or whatever it was he was doing, but surely there must be earth movements, rock falls, sudden flooding. . . . You wouldn't get me going down one of those places. Christ, it would be bad enough just pot-holing; but *diving*. If that isn't hairy, I don't know what is." Gallagher shook his head at the thought of anyone wanting to do that for fun.

"Jack was one of the best. He never took risks. I've watched him work often enough for me to make a statement like that. There are ten people I consider are the very best divers in the world, including a couple of Russians."

The alarm bells jangled. *Russians?* Jameson knew Russian divers well enough to include them in his top ten? Gallagher maintained his silence, knowing that the more Jameson spoke, the less he was bound to like what it would mean.

"Among that bunch," Jameson continued, "I'd place Donlan in the first five. That's how good he was."

They walked in silence. The music from the house beat upon the night. The Thames murmured to itself. Behind them, the boat creaked and sighed at its moorings.

At last Gallagher said: "What do you want of me?"

"Come with me. Let's go and find out what happened up there. You'll need an underwater camera and a good flash unit. There's no natural light where we're going. I want to bring back some evidence. If you haven't got an underwater kit, I can get one."

"I have an underwater camera," Gallagher said, "a Nikonos, and a good flash unit. . . ."

"Fine. . . ."

"But I'm not going down that pisshole with you, whatever it is."

Jameson stopped, forcing Gallagher to come to a halt for the second time. They stood facing each other.

"Why not?" Jameson asked.

"Because, in the first instance, I haven't got the diving skill to handle something like that."

"I could teach you. . . ."

"And in the second, even if I did have, I still wouldn't go."

"Why not? Worried about the risks? About being stuck down there?"

"For a start, yes. You could say that." Gallagher stared through the gloom at him. "I have a healthy regard for my own continuing survival. If Donlan was as good as you say, whatever got him would find me easy meat; and he was in his element. If you won't accept that, let's just say I have a thing about deep dark holes full of water."

"This is strange coming from a man who, among other things, used to spend his days throwing several tons of metal about the sky, with enough high-octane fuel wrapped up in it to turn him into toast several times over."

The background noises appeared to die suddenly and briefly. It was as if the night had blinked. Gallagher felt a gradual metamorphosis coming over him. All his instincts and the tenets of his past training began to combine, allying themselves, concentrating their forces into a single purpose: the protection and survival of the organism. The part of him that he tried so hard to suppress had gone on the alert and, in that condition of readiness, had become extremely dangerous to an adversary. The transformation had taken fleeting seconds. Gallagher had not moved.

He said, softly: "Who the fuck are you, Jameson?"

Even as he spoke, Gallagher continued to assess the odds. Until he knew exactly what Jameson was up to, he would consider the other man potentially hostile. His body tuned itself; senses became antennae that monitored his surroundings, listening, scanning.

They were in a part of the garden that had no cover and which had been made less dark by the glow from the house. The house itself was now well over a hundred yards away. But beyond the edges of the glow was plenty of darkness, plenty of cover. Were there others with Jameson? And if so, did they now have a target? What had been Rhiannon's role in all this?

Gallagher assessed Jameson. The other seemed as tall as his own six-foot-one, and broader too. More weight; but that could be used to advantage if Jameson were caught out in the right way. Gallagher's own body had retained its fitness, a legacy of the rigorous training it had previously received as well as its inherent physiognomy. He was confident he could deal with Jameson, if need be. He would take his chances with any others, anyone from the party in the house who might have gone to cover in the dark. Time for that later. The first priority was Jameson.

Now that he had primed himself, he thought of Rhiannon with some chagrin and a mounting anger.

How could he have been so stupid? She had conveniently gone back into the house just after Jameson had arrived. It now seemed so blatant, so obvious. Gallagher found space in his anger to smile inwardly. Oh, male vanity! Because Doria Luce had made such an open play for him, he had allowed that to cloud his judgment. He had made himself believe Rhiannon responded to his own attraction to her. All the time, she had been playing her brother's tune.

Despite what was going on in his mind, Gallagher still had not moved. He was sharply alert and waiting.

Jameson said: "I am not what you think."

"And what might that be?"

"I imagine that, right now, you're all set to take me, should I make the wrong move. Haven't forgotten anything, have you?" Dryly.

"No time for riddles, Jameson. Make yourself clear."

"All right, I will. O'Keefe."

O'Keefe.

Gallagher's mind went into reverse through the years. O'Keefe: Warrant Officer, RAF. His mentor in training and staunch companion on missions. O'Keefe had died on one such mission when Gallagher's gun had jammed. In Africa. O'Keefe's death still haunted him. He had been too slow. O'Keefe had been one of the reasons he had left the Department. The incident had only served to increase his growing disenchantment with what he had been doing, supposedly for Queen and country. Sometimes, under certain conditions of stress, he believed he could hear O'Keefe's voice. It had saved his life on more than one occasion. He never ignored it.

Gallagher said, quietly: "Who is O'Keefe?"

"You're denying it?"

"You're wasting time, Jameson." Were there other people out there in the dark? Gallagher felt his white dress shirt had become a marker beacon.

"You're angry, I suspect, with Rhiannon. With yourself too. A man like you would be. You feel you've let your guard down and she slipped in to make a fool of you. Well, whether you want to believe it or not, you and Rhian went for each other with no prompting from me. Astonishing. I have known my sister for twenty-three years and she took even me by surprise. Not like her at all. She used to be a bit of a tomboy; no shrinking violet. But what happened tonight was unusual, even for her."

"You expect me to believe that?"

"In time, you will. She knows nothing about this."

"Tell me about O'Keefe." Gallagher did not intend to let any discussions about Rhiannon distract him.

"A stopover in Gibraltar a few years ago," Jameson said. "I knew O'Keefe. Did a joint dive with an RAF team up in the Shetlands; looking for wrecks . . . ostensibly."

"Ostensibly?"

"That's what you'll get from me."

"I'm not trying to get anything out of you. You're the one who's telling me."

"Then let's say I know O'Keefe did sensitive work. I saw the two of you together in Gib. I never forget a face."

"And so you've put two and two together and have come up with seven."

Jameson ignored the sarcasm. "I couldn't believe it when I saw you, working as a photographer, of all things. At first I thought it was a cover and that you were after somebody. Now, I'm not so sure. I shouldn't be surprised, after all. I spend most of my time giving sub-aqua lessons and lectures. At other times, I work for people like Charles Nellis. Pays well." Jameson appeared to be grinning. "Better than HM's Navy. I suppose you're doing all right for yourself too, judging by that car of yours."

In his mind, Gallagher swore. It was inevitable. Anyone who'd been through the Service stood the risk of being recognized years later. There would always be someone who had seen you somewhere. It was the same with any relatively closed world; school, university . . . so why not the Service too? Even so.

A brief stopover in Gib. He remembered the occasion well. He would never forget it. It had been the jumping-off point for O'Keefe's last mission. Who would have thought that a man O'Keefe had dived with in the Shetlands would be there on that very day? And here he was, all that length of time later, in a darkened expensive garden on an equally expensive bank of the Thames, talking about the disappearance of a friend.

Gallagher wanted to sigh with frustration. There was no such thing as total security. He wondered why the world's intelligence services bothered. Habit, he suspected. They were so caught up in their labyrinthine plottings, they were no longer able to stop, even if they wanted to. Intelligence services produced intelligence to stay in business. They were reproducing themselves. Palingenesis gone mad.

Jameson was saying: "I thought you might be able to help. If something really is wrong up there . . . and I don't see how there could not be . . . someone like you is what I need."

"Why me? You must have your own connections."

"I was only on the fringes. The odd job, now and then; diving. Ninety-nine percent of the time, I was a seaman officer; frigates and destroyers."

"Christopher! Gordon!" Rhiannon on her way back. "Where have you two got to?"

"Over here!" Jameson called, turning to look. "Over here, Rhian!"

Gallagher could see her, silhouetted against the house lights as she paused uncertainly, trying to trace the direction of the voice.

"Here!" Jameson called again and, when she had located him, turned back to speak rapidly to Gallagher. "She really knows nothing about this. I have not told her. She knows of Jack Donlan's death, naturally; but not about what I intend to do. And as for whatever it is between the two of you, I can only repeat that it has nothing to do with me. It never entered my head that when I brought her here tonight you would. . . ." Jameson made a brief chuckling noise. "It was indecently quick. Small wonder Doria Luce's nose was put out of joint. I really thought you'd be fully occupied with Doria."

Jameson paused. Rhiannon was not far away now.

He went on, lowering his voice: "Will you do something for me? Tonight? I don't think you'll mind." Another hint of a chuckle?

"What is it?"

"Would you mind driving Rhian home?"

"But. . . ."

"There. Knew you'd jump at the chance. I've got to see some people before morning and it would be a great help if you could. Otherwise, I shall have to leave her here to spend the night. I don't think you'd like that . . . not with all those randy males around."

"I thought you said she could look after herself."

"Oh, she can, but no one's perfect. Think of how you'd hate yourself. Anyone would think you didn't want to."

"Oh, I want," Gallagher said before he could stop himself.

"Thought you did."

"Want what?" Rhiannon had arrived. She peered from one to the other. "What have the pair of you been up to?"

"Gordon's taking you home," Jameson told her. "He's helping me out of a spot. I've got to see some people and I've got a lot of driving to do. It would be a help, sister mine."

"I'm a spot, am I?"

Jameson said to Gallagher: "That's code for yes, she'd be happy to go with you."

"He's a mind reader too," Rhiannon said.

Jameson kissed her on the cheek, said to Gallagher: "Have fun." And walked quickly away toward the house.

Rhiannon said, as they watched him depart: "Did he say where he was going?"

"No," Gallagher answered; but he wondered about it himself.

They watched in silence until Jameson had entered the house, then she turned toward him.

"Well. I seem to have been dumped on you."

"I think I'll survive the experience." He could feel the scrutiny of her eyes.

"Doria Luce is gone," she said. "Flounced out with some man slavering at her heels. Do you wish it was you?"

"No," he told her truthfully.

"You don't have to take me home. Charles Nellis says there's plenty of room."

There certainly was. He said: "I'll take you. I want to."

"It's a long drive," she warned. "We have a small cottage that we use at weekends. It belonged to our parents. Sometimes we go there together, but usually we take alternate weekends. It's my turn this week. Christopher was going to drive me down after the party."

"Where is it?"

"Owermoigne."

"Where the hell's that?"

"Dorset."

Gallagher said nothing. *Thank you, Jameson.*

She said: "I told you it was quite a drive."

"There's no one at the cottage?"

"No." She was standing close and the feel of her body heat came strongly. The scent of her teased him.

From the house, peals of laughter and the throb of the disco continued to float on the night. It was the kind of party that would go on and on.

"I don't really want to sleep here," she said.

"Neither do I. Let's say our goodbyes to Charles, if we can find him, and leave. Besides, the car would like a long drive."

"All right."

He reached for her hand, felt its warmth as it closed about his, the way it had done before. They began walking back to the house, bodies touching now and then as they moved.

Gallagher again wondered where Jameson had gone, and whom he had gone to see. He had a feeling it had to do with Jack Donlan.

London.

The telephone rang in one of the rooms of a

small Bayswater hotel. The man picked it up after three rings.

"Yes?"

"Mr. Ryszynskow?" the voice on the phone said. "Mr. Andrej Ryszynskow?"

"Yes. This is Andrej Ryszynskow," came the reply in a heavy Polish accent.

"I was told to contact you to ask about progress."

"Progress is continuing. It is necessarily slow as this is a very delicate matter and great care must be taken."

"Nothing must go wrong."

"Things can always go wrong."

"But I was advised that you said. . . ."

"I said I would succeed, my friend, in my *own* way." A steely hardness had come into Ryszynskow's voice. "I did not say nothing would go wrong. Only incompetents and fools give such undertakings. They make no allowances for the unexpected. That is why they fail."

"Yes. Yes, of course." Quickly said, as if to apologize. "I . . . have every faith in you. *We* have faith in you."

"You are very kind," Ryszynskow said dryly. "Do you have more to say to me?"

"Well. . . ."

"Thank you for your call," Ryszynskow cut in pointedly. "I do not need to be checked up upon. Do not try to reach me at this number again. I will call when I need to. Goodbye." He hung up, smiled with satisfaction.

If anyone had wanted to check, it would have been found that his accent belonged to the region near Jaroslaw in the southeastern border area with the Soviet Union. A native Pole would have been fooled by it, so thorough was the man known as Naja.

The room was like the hundreds of others throughout the city, in the small hotels that were specially geared to a fast turnover in clientele: tidily boxlike, with a dreary sameness; but it suited Naja's purposes perfectly. It was time to leave.

He got up from the bed upon which he had perched himself during the phone call, let himself out of the room, locked the door behind him. He had left on the bed the briefcase he had brought with him.

He went out of the hotel, the key to the room still in his hand. He walked on to the Bayswater Road, turned right toward Notting Hill. He dropped the key into the first bin he found, attached to a lamppost. Throughout, he had worn lightweight gloves. He now removed them, put them into a jacket pocket. He walked on.

At the traffic lights, he turned left, heading for Kensington. He walked all the way to Kensington High Street, where he took a taxi to the Strand. He left the taxi, walked to Covent Garden where he had parked his car, just off the piazza.

It was 1 A.M.

A watcher would have thought him a late-night reveler who had been to the theater. He looked the part.

He entered the car, shut the door firmly before reaching into the glove compartment for a small radio transmitter, no bigger than a pocket calculator. It was very powerful, with a range greater than its size indicated. He pressed an unobtrusive black button at its center.

In the hotel room he had left, the briefcase on the bed erupted in blinding flame and a thunderous roar that was heard within a radius of five miles. The room, and the ones above and beneath it, simply disappeared, leaving a gaping wound in the three-story building. Two people who were sleeping in the lower room died instantly when the ceiling and walls collapsed upon them. No one had occupied the one above. There were no other casualties. It had been a neatly localized blast.

As he started the car and drove off, "Ryszyns-kow" smiled to himself. It was always good to let people know what you could do. He could hear sirens clamoring through the empty streets as he pointed his car east, away from all the excitement.

The *quattro* hurtled through the night. Rhiannon sat strapped into the passenger seat with eyes closed, a faint smile on her lips. She had reclined it a little so that her head was slightly lower than, and behind, Gallagher's. Every now and then she would open her eyes to look at him.

He had removed his jacket and bow tie and had dropped them into the back. She watched the way his black-gloved hands held the wheel of the power-ful car lightly, almost caressingly, yet knew that he was in total control of the speeding machine. The back glow from the lights danced upon the planes of his face.

She watched as his hand dropped swiftly to the stubby gear lever to change down. The car slowed perceptibly before accelerating hard round a tight bend. The forward surge pinned her to the seat while the way the *quattro* hugged the corner held her fast, sideways against the belt. Then the corner straight-ened out and he was changing gear upward once more. Despite its speed, the car continued to leap forward.

She closed her eyes once more, feeling secure, sensing the powerful throb of the engine pulsing through her, as she was borne swiftly through the night.

Some time later, she opened her eyes again. He seemed as alert as ever, at one with the car. It was almost, she thought, as if he were alone with it. He seemed to be part of it, guiding it fast along the deserted road with an ease which told her that man and machine knew precisely what was expected of one another. The darkened ribbon seemed to flow toward her with unbelievable rapidity.

She studied Gallagher. She had liked what she had seen at the very instant of their first meeting, and knew he had felt the same. The eyes had caught her first: hazel eyes in a bronze-colored face that had a honeyed texture to it. She had seen many things in those eyes. Gentleness; but most of all she had seen great pain. And something else. Lurking behind all the things she had seen had been an element of the untamed, something wild and dangerous. But it did not frighten her. She found it exciting.

He had been blessed, she felt, by his mixed heritage. He had a fine face, good-looking in an understated way. A good forehead rose above a sharp nose with nostrils that flared slightly—a legacy, she guessed, from his mother—and his mouth managed to look firm and gentle at the same time. The loose, soft brown curls of his close-cut hair grew richly down the back of his neck, making her want to play with them. She resisted the temptation.

She savored the hurtling progress of the car.

"A magic carpet," she said, almost to herself.

Gallagher heard her, and smiled as he powered the car round a tight curve on the A354 out of Salisbury. A magic carpet. The *quattro* was all of that. They had been on the road for just under an hour now, since leaving Henley. The car had eaten up the miles with an ease that left him feeling as relaxed as when he had begun the journey.

He said: "Awake, are you?"

"My eyes may have been closed," she said, "but I haven't been asleep. I've been looking to see if you've been following the route I gave you."

"Ah ha. Checking up on my driving now. And how have I been doing?"

"Not bad."

"Why, thank you, ma'am."

"You're welcome," she said in a mock-American accent.

They laughed.

He felt good. Jameson's preoccupation with the disappearance of Jack Donlan receded from Gallagher's mind, leaving him free to enjoy the presence of the woman beside him. He glanced at her, catching her eyes full upon him. In the back glow of the lights, they seemed golden. She had removed the slides from her hair, which now fell like wings down either side of her face. He felt a sudden dryness on his lips, and a pleasant tremor shivered its way through him. Had he really met her only a few hours ago?

They had not been able to take their leave of Nellis personally. He had been nowhere to be seen. Gallagher had left a message with one of the video people, thanking Nellis for the party and saying he'd be in touch on Monday. The video man had seemed ready to collapse from a surfeit of drink. Gallagher strongly doubted that Nellis would get the message.

He slowed briefly for Coombe Bissett before unleashing the *quattro* once more. It didn't really matter whether Nellis got the message or not. The job was almost over. There were others waiting, for other clients. Nellis was favored, however; not because he paid well, but because he was good to work with and for. He wouldn't like Nellis to think he had walked out because he had not enjoyed himself. Some people tended to get a bit upset if they thought you'd hated their party.

As if she knew what he was thinking, Rhiannon said: "You didn't like the party much, did you?"

"Yes, I did."

"Not true."

"Very true." He had begun to enjoy it as soon as he'd met her. "When I saw you," he added.

The hum of the car folded itself about them. The lights cut into the darkness. The speedometer blinked to itself, settled at 115 mph. He was aware she was looking at him. He kept his eyes on the road. She gave his arm a brief, gentle stroke; a butterfly settling for the tiniest of moments. It said everything to him.

"How did you get the name Rhiannon?" he asked.

She did not answer right away; then she said: "Do you know where it comes from?"

"I know it's Welsh, from Celtic legends. The *Mabinogion.*"

"You know about that?" She sounded very surprised.

"You're forgetting. I had a father who was as Celt as you could find, and an academic to boot. He fed me a lot of folk tales when I was a boy, most of which I've forgotten. But I always remembered the name Rhiannon; not the story, though."

"Why did you remember the name?"

He shrugged. "Who knows? I must have liked it, I suppose. A name like that, to the mind of a boy, is full of wonderful mystery. I imagined all sorts of fantastic things."

"You even say it properly. Not many people can."

He smiled. "That's about the only Welsh you'll hear me speak."

They fell silent and the miles continued to speed beneath the wheels of the car.

"She was punished for something she didn't do," Rhiannon said after a while, speaking almost to herself. "They accused her of killing her baby. She had come to the man she was to marry, riding a white horse."

" 'Behold a pale horse,' " Gallagher quoted, " 'and the name of him that sat upon him. . . .' "

" '. . . was Death. . . .' " she finished. "I used to think about that sometimes. But, of course, that's not about Rhiannon. Besides, she was innocent. My mother loved the name, so she gave it to me. She was Welsh . . . from the North, near Bala. Father was a man of Wessex to his roots."

"How did they meet?"

"The corniest of all ways. She was a Wren . . . his secretary."

He chuckled. "I don't believe it."

"You'd better. I'm here to prove it. So's Christopher. She was a very pretty Wren."

"That I do believe."

"I'll assume that's a compliment." The golden eyes appeared to be smiling.

"You look like a witch," he said, "a witch from a Welsh legend."

"A handsome one, I hope."

"A veritable goddess."

"In that case, I won't put an evil spell on you . . . only a very pleasant one."

The golden eyes were staring at him. The spell had already been cast.

They made good time on the stretch from Salisbury to Blandford Forum, and the twenty-one miles were covered in just over twelve minutes.

As Gallagher slowed right down for the passage through the town, Rhiannon said: "Who is Lauren?"

The unexpected question jolted him. He concentrated on his driving as he sought a way to answer her.

Judging accurately what was going on in his mind, she continued: "You thought I had fallen asleep. You took the car round a very tight bend quite fast, and you were talking to it."

He had not even been aware of doing it. He'd have to watch that in the future.

"Why do you talk to your car?" Rhiannon asked into his silence.

"It's a long story."

"And Lauren?"

"She's been dead for some time."

The tone of his voice precluded further conversation. An uncomfortable silence now descended upon them and it lasted the eleven miles to Puddletown.

"Take the road to Tincleton," Rhiannon said. "There . . . on the left."

Gallagher followed her directions.

"I'm sorry I asked about her," she went on, "but I think you should let go a little. It's unhealthy to hang on to something like that. I mean. . . ." She paused, as if sensing she'd gone too far.

He made no comment.

She tried again. "Look. I know it must have been bad for you. I saw. . . ."

"You do, do you?" he interrupted, more harshly than he'd intended. "And what do you think you know about it?"

He glanced at her and was appalled to see her flinch away from him. The new silence this brought with it was punctuated only by her brief, half-apologetic directions as she guided him toward their destination.

The road had bypassed Tincleton, now it curved into the village of Pallington, where it split itself into a fork. Rhiannon directed Gallagher to take the right fork. It joined the B3390 for the last stretch.

"Not far to go now," she said. "We'll turn left just after Moreton station, then it's straight down into Owermoigne."

He said: "I didn't mean to sound. . . ."

She touched him gently. "I know."

"Why did you shy away from me like that?"

"There was something in your eyes," she answered, staring at the blaze of the lights as it danced through the woods of Moigne Combe. "Normally, you hide it well. But just then . . . it came out for a little while. Even in here, I could see it. For a moment, I was frightened."

He thought about that as they came out of the wood. The road took them over a tributary of the River Frome, curved gently to the right. The car took it at eighty.

"You don't have to be frightened of me," he said at last.

"I'm not frightened of you."

"Then what. . . ."

"I'm frightened *for* you. I'm frightened that what's inside could destroy you. I wouldn't like that."

"I'll live to be eighty, ninety, a hundred," he said jokingly.

"There are other ways of being destroyed. You don't necessarily have to die."

Unexpectedly, she placed her hand upon his thigh. There was no hint of suggestiveness about her action. It was as if she somehow wanted to retain physical contact with him. The hand rested lightly, its warmth coming to him through the material of his dress trousers.

"Do you mind?" she asked. He sensed the golden eyes upon him.

"No," he answered. He found the touch of her hand strangely comforting.

She turned away to stare once more at the night. The hand remained where it was for the rest of the journey to Owermoigne.

On the dashboard, the green readout of the digital timer said 03.00.

4

Fowler lay on the camp bed in the small room
adjacent to his office, stared at the ceiling and
thought of the report Haslam had brought in. It was
just after three A.M. and Haslam had already gone
home: nearing sixty, he needed his sleep. Fowler was
not much younger, but sleep was not for him tonight.

Haslam was one of the Department's best liaison officers, very accomplished when dealing with
the police. He always managed to get everything he
wanted out of them, without giving anything in return. Some liaison men tended to pull rank; but not
Haslam. Not for the first time, Fowler decided it was
Haslam's avuncular manner that did the trick. Few
people knew that in his youth Haslam had been one
of the Department's most cold-bloodedly efficient
agents in the field. His official service job had been
as an RAF catering officer and, in keeping with the
role, he had actually become a fully qualified chef.

But Fowler did not have Haslam's cooking abili-
ties on his mind. Fowler was thinking of someone
who, pitted against the younger Haslam, would still
have to come out on top.

Fowler was thinking about Gallagher.

He sighed, removed his glasses with studied care, rubbed the bridge of his nose wearily before putting them back on. Haslam's report had been as detailed as could be expected in the circumstances, and Fowler's own instincts told him that the bomb at the Bayswater hotel had been planted by Naja.

The police had discovered that someone called Andrej Ryszynskow had booked for three days, paying in advance; and that Ryszynskow's room had been the source of the blast. Having established this, they had gone on to assume that the man was either the victim of an attack—for reasons as yet unknown—or the unwitting casualty of his own bomb. They had not found a body, and they had not managed to come up with a reason for Ryszynskow's presence in the hotel, with a bomb.

They never would, Fowler thought pityingly. The man they were dealing with could have them for breakfast and not notice it. Naja had killed that innocent couple and had blasted the hotel not in a gesture of bravado, but simply to let Fowler know he was around, and to demonstrate his ruthlessness. Whatever he had come to do would be done, at whatever cost to those who would dare try to stop him.

Fowler had to accept the challenge. There was nothing else he could do.

The phone warbled. It was one of the three new extensions from the outer office; the blue one, the scrambler. Winterbourne's idea of efficiency was more phones. He stared at it, shifted his gaze to his desk which he could see from where he lay. The blue main phone was also warbling. He picked up the extension. The call was from Turkey. Anyone trying to eavesdrop would hear only a continuous, high-pitched tone.

"Fowler," he said.

"We've traced the owner of the car," the English voice said, sounding hollow in transmission. "A man called Selim Antak, well-known businessman from Istanbul. The car was apparently stolen over a month ago. The story's genuine." The voice chuckled. "He's complaining about having to pay the phone bill."

"Anything more on him?"

"Antak's got a solid commercial background. Nothing suspicious."

There wouldn't be, Fowler thought bitterly. "Is that absolute?" he said.

"Yes. The authorities vouch for him."

"Where is he now?"

"Eskesehir."

"Eskesehir? What's he doing there?" Fowler knew Eskesehir well. Twenty years ago, he had flown Canberras from Luqa in Malta to both Eskesehir and Larissa in Greece, on NATO dispersal exercises. There was nothing at Eskesehir to interest a businessman of Selim Antak's apparent caliber. The place, as Fowler remembered it, was not big enough, a town of nine to ten thousand souls. Hardly a high-catch area for the Selim Antaks of the world.

The voice at the other end gave the reason: "Family."

Too bloody neat. Fowler said: "Do *you* know he's there?"

"I've been told. . . ."

"Being told and *knowing* are not the same things," Fowler said mildly.

There was a pause at the other end. "Would you like me to verify?"

"It would help." Fowler kept the sarcasm out of his voice. Rubbing it in would not gain him anything. It was not his way when dealing with field people, who were invariably under stress. He had no such compunctions when engaged in his constant battles with Winterbourne. This affair would bring plenty of those.

The voice, slightly chastened, said quietly: "I'll be in touch." The connection went dead.

Fowler hung up thoughtfully. Naja was either Selim Antak or someone working very close with him. Naja was not a one-man band, but an individual with a watertight organization, arranged in fully autonomous cells, ignorant of each other's identities; ignorant, also, of their leader's true identity. The system had worked for years; too successfully for those on the hunt, whose mounting casualty rate marked their persistent failure.

Even after twenty years, Eskesehir would not have changed all that much; at least, not for business purposes. There would be, however, plenty to interest someone like Naja. Turkey was still a NATO partner, and Naja was the ultimate personification of nonalignment. He would work for, and sell to, anyone. He had even been known to change clients in the middle of a job. Naja was everyone's friend and everyone's enemy. He would sell his own grandmother if there was a profit in it. He would kill her too.

Fowler lifted his glasses for a brief moment while he rubbed the bridge of his nose reflectively. He settled back on the camp bed and waited for events to take their course. He shut his eyes. He did not fall asleep immediately.

The "small" cottage, Gallagher found, turned out to be a four-bedroomed thatched job in spacious grounds surrounded by a rough stone wall about six feet high. Although it was still well over an hour to sunrise, the sky was pale enough for him to see much of his surroundings when they arrived.

He had pulled up before a high, wrought-iron gate which Rhiannon had climbed out of the *quattro* to unlock. She had opened the double gate for Gallagher to drive through and had shut it again, but without bothering to lock it.

Now he looked about him while Rhiannon disappeared into the kitchen to make coffee. Oak beams everywhere, pricey antique furniture, good prints on the walls. The place was tidy and looked cared for.

The smell of the strong dark roast soon came to him. He was peering at a Whistler miniature when Rhiannon entered with two red mugs full of hot black coffee. She handed him one.

He said, as he took it: "We shouldn't really be drinking this. Not if we want to sleep."

"Are you tired?"

"No." It was the truth. A feeling of excitement pulsed quietly through him.

The golden eyes held his levelly. "Good. I was not thinking of sleep." Then a tiny smile teased her lips. "Shocked?"

He stared at her. "A little off balance, but pleased."

She nodded as if to herself, took a swallow of her coffee.

"I'm shocked," she said, not looking at him. "Not me at all." A quick smile. "But there's always a first time for everything." She turned to look at the Whistler, reached out to touch the tiny frame briefly. "Do you like it?"

"Yes."

"What about the others?"

He glanced around the room. "Good stuff. Who chose them?"

"I did. Well, most of them. That's what I do for a living. I work in an art gallery."

"Where?"

"Somewhere in Knightsbridge," she answered.

"Doesn't everybody?"

"I don't like the way you said that," she remarked, partly serious. "It wasn't kind."

He leaned forward to kiss her briefly. "Teasing."

"Anyway, it's interesting, and I do get good commissions." She sounded defensive. "This place takes some looking after, you know."

"You don't have to justify anything to me."

Her eyes held his. "I seem to want your approval."

"I'd approve of you if you waited on tables, swept the streets. . . ."

"I did, once." She was quite serious now. "Spain. No money to get back home." She shrugged. "So. . . . I had to do it. Worked in some horrible club, full of the type of people you'd run a mile from on holiday. I got pestered a lot, but I sorted them out." The golden eyes blazed.

"Couldn't you have called your parents?"

She took a swallow of coffee, shook her head firmly. "I got myself into it. Running to them for help was not my way."

He liked her more and more. "What happened? How did you get stranded in the first place?"

"A Spanish friend at university invited a group of us down to spend the summer on the family estate . . . miles and miles of vineyard. I had a sort of lightweight affair going on with a bloke called Neil— so lightweight, it was practically nonexistent. . . ." A smile of vague amusement as she remembered. "We went down in his car with another friend and her man of the moment. What I didn't know was that

Alfonso Jesus Garcia y Santiago y Torréon had taken a rather strong shine to me. It had all been nicely arranged with Neil, the Wringing Wimp. His job was to persuade me. I went for a nice easygoing summer, quaffing private plonk. What I found was a raving Alfonso panting for my body. I wouldn't have minded, except that I didn't fancy him.

"Like an idiot," she went on, "I hadn't taken reasonable funds with me. That is to say, I hadn't asked my father for any. I was the normally broke student. Even though I had no money with which to get home, and precious little to spend on hotels, I left panting Alfonso's lovely estate and hitched into the nearest holiday town. He was scandalized. His pride was shattered. He couldn't believe I'd do it." She gave another shrug. "That was his problem. So that's how I eventually became a waitress. I spent the whole summer out there, keeping mainly to myself and hanging on to my virtue. Looking back, I sometimes marvel at the close shaves I had during that time. I must have been crazy. But that's the kind of thing you do when you're nineteen." The golden eyes held his, with no hint of guile. "Perhaps not only when you're nineteen. I'm doing something crazy tonight."

She took his hand. "Come with me. There's a Matisse upstairs I think you'd like. Leave your jacket and my bag down here. We'll sort it out in the morning."

She turned off the lights as Gallagher allowed himself to be led up the oak-banistered flight of stairs.

"Do you have a thing about lights when climbing stairs?" he queried.

"I know where I'm going."

"That's a relief."

"And besides, I can see in the dark."

"That's another relief."

She stopped as they came to a small landing and turned to face him. He imagined he could see the golden glow of her eyes.

She said: "It's because I'm a witch and tonight I have bewitched you." She moved on, still holding his hand, along a short corridor.

"I'm not complaining."

The hand squeezed briefly. "You'll remember tonight." There was a hint of suppressed excitement in her voice now. It was as if the darkness had given her leave to allow her anticipation to show itself.

"So will you," Gallagher promised.

The hand gave another squeeze; sharp and tight. "Hmm," she said.

By the time they reached the door to her room, Gallagher's own eyes had become perfectly attuned to the darkness in the house. He could see Rhiannon's shape quite clearly.

She released his hand to push the door open.

"No need for the lights," he said. "I can look at the Matisse later."

"All right." She seemed pleased.

They entered. The night had grown appreciably paler, the beginning day's grayish luminosity flooding the low-ceilinged room through the single, deeply recessed window and giving everything a steely sheen. The triple-paned window, much wider than it was tall, began halfway up the wall. A long narrow cushion lay along the seat, with smaller cushions piled upon it at one end. Leading up to the window were wide, low steps which seemed to be carpeted. A low brass bed was pushed against an adjacent wall, with a bedside table on either side of it. The tables were draped with cloth that gleamed whitely in the subdued light and on each was a small brass lamp. On both sides of the window recess, deep wardrobes had been built. The room's walls were flecked with a motif that the available light prevented Gallagher from identifying. A single armchair was placed near the window steps. Above the bed was a framed picture which he assumed was the Matisse that Rhiannon had spoken of; it was still too dark to make out which work it was.

"Well," she said, standing close to him.

"Well, yourself."

Her arms came up slowly, locked themselves behind his neck and he felt the heat of her body plastered to his, the fullness of her breasts flattening against him. Then his own arms were about her waist and he was kissing her as he had wanted to all night, with a passion that left them pausing momentarily, almost startled, for breath.

Soon their hands were busy with each other's clothing. Even as Gallagher was trying to remove her dress without ripping it, she kicked off her shoes and attacked his shirt feverishly. Amidst the mutual undressing they continued to kiss one another: on the lips, cheeks, neck, shoulders. . . .

As Gallagher's lips found a firm, generous breast Rhiannon gave a sharp gasp, pushed herself against him. Cloth rustled, slithering down heated skin. Gallagher thought he heard the spiteful crack of static electricity; but it could have been his imagination.

Anchoring herself to his mouth with her lips, Rhiannon pulled urgently at his trousers, dragging him down to the floor with her. He felt the smooth warmth of her nakedness as she stretched herself beneath him. There was a brief pause as Gallagher sought to complete the job she had begun, hauling off the rest of his own clothing with ill-concealed haste. Then their bodies were at last free. Rhiannon opened to welcome him and he entered gently, but with a continuing power that caused her body to raise itself in response.

She was strong, and all the energy he had sensed when he'd first seen her now seemed to burst about him. She held him tightly as she moved, kissing him repeatedly, frantically. "Oh, God, oh, God!" she kept saying with rising fervor.

Gallagher's own enjoyment was creating a strange music in his head. Once, twice, he thought he saw her eyes glowing up at him. His mind drew images that built upon the excitement already within him: Rhiannon's body glistening in the gray light; strong legs rising, shifting, clasping; torso arching, limbs outflung like a great St. Andrew's cross. . . . And all the time she moaned and twisted, sometimes rolling on top of him.

Then she was shuddering beneath him, lifting as her body pressed upward to mold with his, and making soft whimpering sounds that gradually increased in volume and pitch. Suddenly a series of explosions began from deep within him, rushed boilingly to the surface.

They strained against each other, an arch of tautened flesh in the dim light of the coming day. At last, with a great combined sigh, their bodies relaxed, collapsed to the floor.

After a while, she said softly: "My God! Who seduced whom?"

Gallagher, feeling more relaxed than he'd done for a long time, said: "Let's chalk it up as a draw."

She was lying on her back, arms and legs spread wide. She giggled at his reply. He leaned over her, kissed her at first gently, then insistently. She remained spreadeagled, but her body had slowly begun to shift against him once more.

"What's this?" she murmured in a voice that had become thick with incipient arousal. "Aren't you tired?"

"We've only just begun," he said, moving his attentions to her throat.

"Oh, goody!" she said in a slow whisper.

It was seven o'clock by the time they finally fell asleep. They had made it to the bed by then; but neither was sure when, or how.

On his camp bed, Fowler opened his eyes and yawned once. He glanced at his watch: 07.30. He wondered where Gallagher was. He picked up one of the phones, punched out a seven-digit number. It rang twice, then a recorded message cut in. Fowler listened until the message had run its course, then hung up.

He stared at the phone. Perhaps it was just as well Gallagher was out. Talking to him would not help, nor change anything. The game was already running.

Fowler yawned a second time, grimaced at the thought that he'd be having Department coffee for breakfast.

It was nearly midday when Gallagher came awake, feeling pleased with himself. Seconds later he was tensed, alert, an animal in the wrong territory. Rhiannon was not in bed with him. From where he lay, he could see the spot where they had discarded their clothes in their haste to get at each other. The clothes were gone.

Then two things made him smile sheepishly: he could smell cooking, and snatches of humming came

through the closed door of the bedroom. He thought
ruefully that the old life would never leave him.
Even here, in this delightful country cottage with
someone like Rhiannon, the organism had gone
screaming into condition red because she had not
been there when he awoke.

The light coming in through the high window
told Gallagher the day was well advanced, but overcast. Out of habit, his eyes studied the room, noting
that, like what he'd so far seen of the rest of the
house, it was well kept. He wondered who looked
after it when Jameson and Rhiannon were away.

But these thoughts came to him only idly. He lay
on the bed, relaxed now, enjoying the memories of
the past night. He craned his neck to look up at the
Matisse that was hung above the bed, turned over so
as to see it better.

Nu assis, bras relevés. The naked female figure
seemed to be looking quizzically back at him.

"Well?" he said to it. "Did you approve?"

"I don't know about her," Rhiannon's voice said.
"I certainly did."

She was standing in the doorway, in a long thin
nightdress that revealed more than it concealed, and
carrying a heavily laden breakfast tray. Gallagher
climbed naked out of bed to help her.

"Careful," she warned, looking at him pointedly. "The coffee's very hot. I'd hate you to have an
accident. It's all right. I can manage." She entered,
leaned against the door to shut it. She smiled, sniffed
exaggeratedly as she approached. "Anyone coming
in would certainly know what we've been up to."

"And is anyone going to come in?"

"Not unless they want to get murdered, they
won't," she said with a sudden grin. "Of course,
there's always Mrs. Price." She paused by the bed,

looked him up and down. "As you're out of bed, we might as well eat Japanese-style."

She placed the tray on the floor, sat down cross-legged, tucking them beneath the loose skirt of the nightgown. "Croissants, jam, toast, orange juice, coffee. Come and eat. You'll be needing your strength." She smiled mischievously.

Gallagher sat down next to her. "Mrs. Price?"

"The lady from the village who's looked after the place for us for the past six years. She even stocks up for the weekends. Which is why you're able to have all this for breakfast. She keeps the place tidy when we're not here. Sees to the garden too. A treasure."

He watched as Rhiannon poured the coffee, then leaned over to kiss her briefly on her neck.

She gave a quick smile of pleasure. "Drink your orange juice like a good boy, then you can have the rest of the goodies."

"Which ones?"

"Why don't you wait and see?" she suggested with meaning.

After breakfast they made love on the floor, taking their time about it.

It was one o'clock when Rhiannon said, languorously: "I suppose we'd better do something about a bath." They were lying some distance from the bed now, where their exertions had taken them. She lay on top of Gallagher, head on his chest. Now she raised it, to look at him. "Hey. Wake up. Didn't you hear me?"

Gallagher's eyes were closed. "I heard. Have mine for me."

She tickled the tip of his nose with a playful finger. "Worn you out, have I?"

He opened one eye, briefly. "You and whose army?" he teased.

The phone rang. The sound was so unexpected, both their bodies jerked in unison to its summons.

"Don't do that!" she murmured, kissing him. "You'll set me off."

"Shouldn't you answer that phone?"

She sighed. "I suppose I'd better."

She rolled off him, stood up, went to the phone. The instrument was on the floor, on her side of the bed. She reached down, picked it up. "0305 . . . *Chris.*" She widened her eyes at Gallagher. "Where are you? I thought. . . ." She stopped to listen, now and then nodding her head. "I see . . . Yes. All right. Oh, we're getting on quite well. . . ." She was trying hard not to giggle. "How can you say that! You're supposed to be my brother." A flush appeared on her cheeks. "Some brother you are. . . . I'm sure we will. 'Bye."

She hung up, came back grinning. "You should have heard what he said. You must be in favor. He seemed more worried about you than he was about me. Normally he watches any man who comes near me like a hawk. He never interferes, of course; but he keeps a close watch."

"I think he cares very much for you."

"I know," she said seriously. "Which is why I think he trusts you. He seems quite glad that we met."

Gallagher thought he knew why. He said nothing about it.

Instead, he asked: "What was that all about . . . leaving the bluer parts out, of course."

"How do you know he said anything. . . ."

"I can read blushes."

"You two are as bad as each other. It seems

Charles Nellis wants him to take the cruiser down to Cornwall. Padstow. Charles has a cottage at Trebetherick."

"Yes. I know. I've been there once or twice. We did a photo session on Brae Hill. That's on the Camel estuary. Ever been there?"

She shook her head. "No. Chris has, of course."

Gallagher nodded. He wondered why Nellis wanted the boat at Padstow. Another photo session, this time on the cruiser? But if Nellis had wanted him, Jameson would have relayed the message. He decided to forget about it. He was obviously not going to be involved.

Rhiannon said, the mischievous smile back on her lips: "Chris said to enjoy ourselves. Do you think we should take him seriously?"

"I think we certainly should."

They made it to the bathroom by two o'clock.

In Jameson's room, Gallagher searched for something to wear. Rhiannon had decided to take him on a little tour of the Dorset coast and had suggested he tried her brother's wardrobes for something more suitable than the previous evening's dress clothes. This was the second of the two wardrobes in the room. The first had yielded nothing he wanted to put on. This one, however, was full of Chris Jameson's old service clothes, plus a few of Jameson senior's.

It was a large wardrobe and part of it had been reserved for the uniforms of a naval captain. The other contained Jameson's. The two thick gold rings with the thinner one in the middle, on the sleeves and shoulders of the various kits, proclaimed that Jameson had been a two-and-a-half-striper: a lieutenant commander.

Rhiannon had said that her father had served at

Hal Far on Malta, in the days before the George Cross island had become a republic, in 1974, and that he had been there right up to the end, and she with him. Then both parents had died. She had not said how. Her brother, some years older, had been at naval college at the time.

Gallagher found what he was looking for: a long-sleeved faded khaki drill shirt and an olive-green pair of trousers with pouched hip and back pockets. They looked more like commando working dress, but there were no telltale holes in the shoulder flaps to betray previous markings of rank. Perhaps Jameson had bought them at a surplus store.

Gallagher removed the dressing gown Rhiannon had found for him—her father's—saying she hoped he was not superstitious about wearing a dead man's clothes. Unlike the museum piece of the deceased Captain's uniforms, the old dressing gown didn't seem to matter.

He found a pair of black fabric ankle boots that seemed a bit the worse for wear but were serviceable. They fitted him perfectly. The shirt, however, while fitting at the shoulders, was a little baggy about the waist, as were the trousers. He had to adjust the side straps to their tightest limits. Satisfied, he picked up the dressing gown and went back to the room he had shared with Rhiannon.

She was not there, but he could hear her moving about in another room. He laid the gown on the chair, sat down on the newly made bed to wait.

Thinking about Rhiannon, he felt the familiar sense of disquiet that plagued him whenever a woman seemed in danger of getting too close to him. Each one who had managed to do so had somehow wound up being lost to him. First Karin, who had eventually decided that a fledgling Pilot Officer could not support her in the style to which she had hoped to become accustomed and who had subsequently married someone in the City. Gallagher's colleagues on the squadron had at the time expressed the hope that she would marry someone rich but totally boring, whom she would eventually cuckold. Gallagher smiled ironically at the memory, for after Karin, the next woman to have got close had been Celia.

He still felt that the shock of Karin had been a major factor in his succumbing to Kingston-Wyatt's blandishments to volunteer for special duties. Kingston-Wyatt, now dead by his own hand, had been the CO of the next squadron to which Gallagher had been posted. Kingston-Wyatt had eventually become head of the Department. In the meantime, as well as rising in rank and becoming rather better at his special job than even Kingston-Wyatt had hoped, Gallagher had met Celia, whom he'd married. All she had known about his service work was that he was a Phantom pilot. She'd come to dread his flying, after having sat through a night comforting a friend whose husband had flown into a mountain on a bad winter's evening.

The growing disillusionment with the Department, accelerated by O'Keefe's death, had led Gallagher to resign. Celia had been relieved, attributing his resignation to her fear of his flying duties. Then he had come home one day to find her in bed with someone else.

After that, he had met Lauren, only to lose her to an assassin's bullet on a ski slope. Then had come Lucinda MacAusland, alias Major Irina Alieva, deep-cover GRU. She had turned out to have been on the side of the angels—assuming there was anyone around naïve enough to believe in angels—and had bled to death on Skye, from a bullet hole the size of a fist in her side.

And now there was Rhiannon, who had managed to dig herself into him faster than anyone. Approaching the end of his thirty-fourth year, he was getting softer with age, he decided sourly. He ought to leave now. It had been an interlude he would remember for a long time; but he would ruin the memory of it if he let it continue. The wise thing would be to get out of his borrowed clothes, put on his own and head back to town. Then Rhiannon came in, and the decision was stillborn.

She was dressed in white. A high-necked, close-fitting smock with a row of buttons down the front hugged her body and reached only halfway down her thighs. Her legs were bare and she wore white track shoes and ankle socks. She was aglow with that same barely contained energy he had seen in her when they had first met. He looked appreciatively at her legs and memory of the past night came flooding back.

"It's a good thing I'm the only one who can see your face," she said as she entered.

"And what's wrong with my face?"

"You can put your tongue back in, for a start."

"My tongue wasn't hanging out. What you mistake for lust was aesthetic appraisal. You look like a nurse," Gallagher went on, "albeit a very pleasing one."

She stopped before him. "Navy nurse, forties style, updated for the eighties; but functional. Tara," she sang, and with two swift movements, she had sprung the fastenings open to reveal the bra and pants underneath. "Not real buttons. Functional, as I've said."

"Show-off," he said as she took a quick step back.

She smiled teasingly at him and began to do up the dress. "If we start anything now we won't get out."

"Who's worrying?"

"I want to show you Dorset. Come on, lazybones." She went out laughing, still working at the fastenings.

He followed her out with a silly smile on his face. Whatever disquiet he felt, there was no denying he was enjoying himself.

As they went downstairs, he said: "Do you mind if I call my machine at home?"

"Of course you can. But there's a house rule: no work at the weekend."

"I promise to obey it. But I always like to check, so as to know what I've got to prepare for."

She seemed to look deep into him. "I'll never forgive you if you decide to cut the weekend short." She was quite serious. A worried, uncertain look had appeared in her eyes now.

"I promise not to," he said.

She gave him a quick smile. The worried look had disappeared and with it the uncertainty. "In that case, make your call, workaholic. I'll be waiting outside."

"Won't be long," he called after her.

"Better not be," came her disembodied voice. "I want a ride in the magic car."

"Ah ha. So it's my car you're after. And here I am thinking it's my body."

A rude noise answered him.

There was a phone mounted on a wall in the kitchen. He went there to make the call. When the machine had answered, he placed his pleeper against the mouthpiece, activated the machine's replay. A few jobs had come in, but none that required his getting in touch with anyone before Monday. There were also a couple of social invitations. Then came a call but no recorded message, because whoever had made it had not wanted to speak to the machine. Gallagher shrugged. Many people hated answering machines. Another job offer. Another invitation. Next, a click. Someone else who hated speaking to a machine.

Then: "I called earlier, but got this wretched machine." Doria Luce. "Charles gave me your number. He said you wouldn't mind. This is my second call and since you have still not answered, I assume you're still with that plump medieval princess." Gallagher could almost hear claws being sharpened. "So that's how you like them. Sweet, scrubbed faces." A pause. "Rhiannon. The stuff of myth and legend. How in keeping. So droll. But be careful, darling, of clean-limbed medieval princesses. They can sometimes be bad for your health." A throaty laugh. "Charles has my number if you want to get in touch. *Ciao!*"

There were no more messages. She must have made the call even while he and Rhiannon were enjoying their latest tumble on the bedroom floor. He gave a fleeting smile. Doria Luce could not stand being upstaged. He replaced the receiver, wondered briefly who had made the second, mute call. Well, whoever it had been could always try again on Monday. Meanwhile, the weekend stretched ahead, to be enjoyed to the full. He thought of Rhiannon, and the prospect became very pleasing.

Outside, she was standing next to the *quattro*. Although there was an empty two-car garage, Gallagher had parked by the front door. Neither of them had felt like going to the bother of putting the car under cover.

Rhiannon was looking at him as if for the first time. "Christopher's clothes seem to fit you."

"Judicious tucking," he said. "Well, madam? What have you in mind for the day?"

"Let me into the car, sir, and I shall tell you."

"Your wish is my command."

"Hmm," she said.

He unlocked the *quattro* and they climbed in. As always, the car seemed to mold itself about him, absorbing him. He clipped on his seat belt, aware that Rhiannon was looking in his direction.

He inserted the ignition key. "What's wrong?" he asked her as he started the motor and the Treser horses roared deeply into life.

She said: "Nothing's wrong. I was just watching the way you seem to caress the wheel before you start up. She doesn't mind, does she?"

"Who doesn't mind?"

"Lauren. Do you think she'll mind that I'm here?"

Gallagher didn't know whether she meant the car or Lauren herself. He realized with a start that, for the first time in many months, Lauren was not at the forefront of his mind. At long last, it seemed he was beginning to let go. Was the potency of Rhiannon's presence so strong? Or would it have happened by itself in any case?

"No," he answered. "She won't mind." He was thinking of both Lauren and the car.

Rhiannon seemed to understand. She reached across to kiss his cheek lightly. "I'm glad. We're going to Portland," she went on as she settled in her seat.

A sad little smile came and went. "I like going there. It reminds me of something." She would not say more.

Gallagher drove through the village, paused at a junction. A little church sat drowsily to his left.

Rhiannon said: "Go right." Adding: "A friend of mine got married in that church. It was a lovely, bright day." She peered at the overcast sky. "Brighter than this, but it should get better." She looked at him, placed her hand on his thigh. "Can I leave it there?"

"Yes."

She smiled. "When we get to the main road, turn right toward Dorchester, then go left at the first roundabout, for Weymouth."

He nodded. At the main road, he did as she had instructed. The road soon widened into a fast dual carriageway. He put his foot down and the *quattro* reared upward slightly, launched itself forward. The digital speedometer went berserk. At 100, Gallagher eased back. It would soon be time to slow down for the roundabout.

Rhiannon gave a sigh of pleasure and said: "Mmm. Magic."

They drove slowly through Weymouth, inching their way through the traffic. There were also quite a few pedestrians.

"This is nothing," Rhiannon said, glancing at clusters of them milling about with seemingly little purpose. "The season hasn't really started, so it's still good to drive around."

"Don't you like holidaymakers?"

"Even holidaymakers don't like holidaymakers."

They drove up the hill from the town, heading for the Isle of Portland. A sharp right took them through Wyke Regis and then they were on the narrow strip that connected Portland to the mainland. Out to sea on his left, Gallagher saw the three massive breakwaters that enclosed Portland Harbour. Close in was the lean, dark gray hull of a berthed destroyer. To his right, a great mound of shingle disappeared into the western distance.

Rhiannon noted his glance. "The beginnings of Chesil Beach. It goes on and on for miles . . . ten to Abbotsbury and another eight or so to Bridport, although it's got different names up there. I'll show you after we've been up to the Bill."

Gallagher knew she meant the tip of the peninsula. He took the *quattro* up the steep incline toward Easton, where the road leveled out and began to hug the south-facing cliffs.

Presently she said: "Here. Stop here."

He pulled off the road, parked the car on pale, bare ground. For a moment, Rhiannon stayed where she was, looking thoughtful, then she gave a quiet sigh and climbed out. Bemused, Gallagher followed suit.

He had parked about thirty feet or so from the edge of the cliff, and he watched her walk over the lumpy ground toward it as he locked the car. He went slowly after her, enjoying the way the muscles moved in the backs of her legs as she walked.

When he had reached the cliff edge, she stopped, staring out to sea. A slight breeze teased at her hair, now and then baring the back of her neck. For one crazy moment, Gallagher thought she was going to throw herself over.

As if realizing what he was thinking, she turned at that instant. "It's all right. You don't have to look so worried," she said as he came up to her. "I'm not going to throw myself off." She turned again to stare at the sea, the little sad smile back on her lips.

Far out, a tiny speck of a motor launch was heading in toward Weymouth. It wasn't Charles Nel-

lis's cruiser. Even at forty knots, there was no way
it could have made it this far. It was probably still
negotiating its way down the Thames. Besides, the
silhouette was all wrong.

Gallagher turned from his scrutiny of the distant launch to idly survey the land about him. To his
right, colonies of bramble had successfully established themselves on low mounds among the sparse
tufts of parched grass that hung grimly on to the
poor soil. Here and there, the bleached earth pock-
marked the area, reminding him of someone who
had had a rough time at the hairdresser's. It was as
if a gigantic pair of shears had been wielded willy-
nilly with lunatic abandon. Great chunks had been
hacked out of the cliff during a period of quarrying.
Now, the discarded slabs of its disuse lay in forlorn
piles, looking like the marker stones of ancient
burial sites. At the far end of the old quarry was a
fortlike structure carved out of the cliff. It was a
huge mound that had been cut in half, it seemed. Its
windows faced the sea and grass covered its roof.
From landward, it would look like just another
mound.

Gallagher peered down the drop at his feet. A
good fifty meters, he judged. The whole place reminded him a little of Malta.

Rhiannon said: "Have you ever been to Malta?"

"No," he lied, with instant caution. He had not
served with the air force there; but he'd been. Another jumping-off point, for another job for the Department. There was no need for her to know about
that.

She said: "This reminds me of Malta. Dingli
cliffs. Of course, we're not looking out at the Med; but
it reminds me all the same. Dingli is much higher
too."

Gallagher knew the Dingli cliffs. They were the southern ramparts of the island. In places, the drop was over eight hundred feet.

Rhiannon said: "My parents died on Dingli."

From half a mile away, the man focused the telescopic sight. The cross hairs settled squarely between Gallagher's shoulder blades. The sight moved to the right, framing Rhiannon's profile as she turned to say something to Gallagher. The watching man could see her lips move.

He moved the scope away from his eye, squinted at the distant figures. The sun had broken through and its rays beat through the car windscreen, making him hot. He looked casually about him. This was not a good place to try for a hit. Though he had picked his position well, it was still too vulnerable to the sudden appearance of wandering holidaymakers. Killing one of them would be untidy.

He replaced the scope in the attaché case which contained the other sections of the rifle. He shut the case, picked up a small, slab-sided two-way comm unit, spoke briefly into it. Finished, he put the radio down on the passenger seat. He kept his attention on the black *quattro*. When it moved, he would move.

There was still plenty of time to do the job.

5

Rhiannon said, her face turned out to sea: "Funny thing about this place." She smiled at Gallagher. "Let's go."

"What's so funny about it?" he queried as they walked back to the car.

She linked an arm through his. "Portlanders never say the word rabbit. According to an old legend, terrible things are supposed to happen to them if they do."

They had reached the car. She freed his arm and went round to the passenger side.

Gallagher said: "You've just said it." He unlocked the *quattro* and they climbed in.

"Ah, but I'm not a Portlander," she said as she clicked her seat belt home.

He smiled at her. "Then we're all right." He started the engine. The powerful motor roared into life, sending its pulses through the car. "Where to?"

"Abbotsbury. I'm taking you to Chesil Beach."

Gallagher drove the *quattro* slowly back the way they had come. They descended steeply into Fortuneswell, then they were on the two-kilometer stretch of the harbor road to Wyke Regis. He gave the accelerator a gentle pressure. The car surged forward.

A glance in the mirror showed him an indistinguishable dark saloon that grew abruptly smaller. He smiled briefly, then lost interest in it.

The car was still a speck, but it began to grow again as Gallagher slowed down for the approaching T-junction. The road came in from the right from Weymouth. They would be turning left on to it, toward Abbotsbury and Bridport.

Gallagher glanced in the mirror as he brought the *quattro* to a halt. The saloon seemed in no hurry to catch up.

He slid a cassette into the stereo. Pachelbel's Canon oozed out of the four speakers.

A green Range Rover, from the direction of Weymouth, rushed past on high, fat wheels. The two men in it wore pouched jackets and flat caps. They looked like gentleman farmers. Neither of them glanced at the gleaming Audi, but looked straight ahead, faces like stone.

"People usually stare at her," Gallagher said as he turned on to the road.

"At whom?"

"This." Gallagher patted the wheel briefly. "The car."

"Not everybody's having a love affair with a *quattro*," Rhiannon remarked, tilting her head at him.

He glanced at her. "Jealous?"

She shook her head. "I can do things no car can."

"You can say that again," he remarked with feeling, remembering the past hours. They grinned at each other.

He gave the accelerator a firm continuous pressure and the car's speed built up swiftly.

"Mmm!" Rhiannon said with appreciation.

They soon caught up with the Range Rover, which appeared to have slowed down. A mile later, the road skirted past Chickerell. Gallagher stayed behind the Range Rover, waiting for an opportunity to pass it.

"Fancy wheels," he commented. "Almost like a bloody tractor's."

"They need them," Rhiannon said. "The ground can get very soggy around here, on the farms."

The little convoy came to a circle in the road masquerading as a roundabout. A sign pointed left, to somewhere called Fleet.

"I must take you there. To Fleet," she said as the *quattro* followed the Range Rover.

The road curved right from the circle and began to climb gently. The Range Rover accelerated away. Gallagher smiled to himself: it didn't have a hope.

"What's so special about Fleet?" he asked. A vague memory stirred.

She made no immediate reply.

The big four-wheel-drive Range Rover had breasted the rise and was beginning to descend. Gallagher eased the power on. The *quattro* arrived at the crest soon after, and he saw the long empty road stretching ahead. It swept downward in a long straight, before curving gently left as it rose again to breast a hill in the far distance, a mile and a half or so away. A smattering of houses bordered its trough, giving way to neatly cultivated fields on the slope of the far hill. Save for the Range Rover, there was no other traffic. A fine haze crested the distant skyline.

Gallagher gave the *quattro* its head. It lunged forward, speed building in a continuous, thrusting urge. The digital speedometer went crazy once more. The twin exhaust roared deeply.

"Oh, no!" Rhiannon uttered softly. The golden eyes seemed to come alight as she glanced at Gallagher; then she turned up the volume on the stereo, settled herself back in her seat and closed her eyes.

The seventeenth-century sounds filled the car.

They passed the Range Rover at 110 just before the curve, then the *quattro* was charging up the rise. The road was still empty beyond the hill, as the car rushed along, its turbo humming and sighing loudly with each change of gear.

The Range Rover appeared to have vanished, still hidden by the brow of the hill.

The road was climbing another hill, this one steeper, and large letters spanning the lane warned him to slow down. Planted into the verge, a road sign with two red-bordered triangles sandwiching the words BLIND SUMMIT added an edge to the caution. Gallagher obeyed, decelerating rapidly enough to lock the seat belts.

He saw why the summit was blind. A side road poked its way out at the very apex. Then the *quattro* was over and the road stretched emptily once more. Down went his foot and up surged the speed. He was enjoying himself.

"This is almost like being in a big jet," Rhiannon said with excitement, her eyes still closed.

She opened them as he again began to slow down, approaching another village. Portesham, the sign said. On the stereo, Pachelbel came to the end of his Canon. The Gigue began.

Rhiannon said: "The other Thomas Hardy lived here." She turned down the volume to make herself heard. "After all, this is Navy country."

"I think I could just about persuade myself to like the Navy," he said. *But not Winterbourne,* he thought sourly, wishing the name had not suddenly sprung into his mind.

"Could you?" A curve full of mischief came to her lips as she stroked his thigh with slow suggestiveness.

"Hey," he said, "I'm driving."

"Excuses, excuses."

They entered the village and eventually came to a T-junction. The road turned sharply left past a large double-roofed house, continuing toward Abbotsbury, two miles further. Branching off to the right was the road to Dorchester.

"We can get to Abbotsbury that way too," she said.

He checked in the mirror as he began to follow her directions. "Look who's here."

The Range Rover was just coming up behind them.

Gallagher turned on to the Dorchester road and drove slowly. The Range Rover went left.

"He's had enough," Gallagher said.

Rhiannon commented: "Perhaps you've upset him, passing him like that."

They continued through the village. The road once more began to climb.

Just before the outskirts, Rhiannon said: "Stop! It's Alicia."

He pulled the *quattro* into the side of the road. A tall woman, bareheaded and in casual riding gear, was leading a fine chestnut mare. She had a rich tangle of blonde hair that fell well past her shoulders, and a strong face colored by the cumulative tans of many hot summers. She walked with sturdy, purposeful strides.

"Christopher used to fancy her like mad," Rhiannon said in a hushed voice, though the woman was still too far away to have heard anything over the low rumble of the idling machine. "He thinks older women are far more interesting. And don't you dare agree with him."

"All right. I surrender."

She bared her teeth briefly at him in a mock snarl. "Lucky for you. Christopher calls her Devonport," she added.

"Devonport? Not very flattering. I can think of all sorts of lewd sailors' connotations; and I'm not a sailor."

She pinched him painfully on the thigh.

"Ow!"

"That will teach you," she said with a sweet smile. "Her name's Alicia Davenport. Devonport was Christopher's nickname for her."

Alicia Davenport had been staring puzzledly at the *quattro* as she approached. Now she crouched a little to speak to Rhiannon. Gallagher turned off the stereo.

"For a moment," she began, "I thought you were driving. The wheel's on the wrong side." Her accents were those of expensive schooling, with all regional traces effectively wiped out.

"Spoken like a Davenport," Rhiannon said. "We are at the center of the universe. Left-hand-drive cars are out of step."

Alicia gave a wide smile. She was clearly accustomed to Rhiannon's ways. "Where are your manners, Rhiannon? Aren't you going to introduce me to the owner of this fabulous machine?"

"Hands off. Alicia, Gordon Gallagher. Shake hands, but don't make a meal of it."

"Trusting, isn't she?" Alicia said, reaching into the car to shake Gallagher's hand.

Gallagher found her grip to be quite strong. It

was a hand that was accustomed to work. Her face was boldly structured and there were laughter lines about the corners of her pale blue eyes. This close, he saw that she was much younger than he had at first thought; early thirties or thereabouts. Hers was an independent face, a face of the outdoors. Rather bigger than Rhiannon, she radiated a more powerful version of the same storehouse of energy. Perhaps they bred them like that in Dorset. In her own way Alicia was quite attractive. There was a suppressed sensuality about her.

Her eyes settled on the shirt he was wearing. "Looks like one of Christopher's."

"It is," Rhiannon put in. She took Alicia's hand and firmly disengaged it from Gallagher's. "I didn't say you could hang on to him."

Alicia grinned, showing rows of gleaming teeth. "As I said . . . trusting." She leaned on the window jamb. "What's the story, Rhian?"

The mare was growing restless and stamped a hind leg. Gallagher hoped it would not display too much impatience. He did not fancy a pattern of hoof dents in the *quattro*'s bodywork.

Alicia read Gallagher's expression accurately. "Don't worry. She's very well-behaved." She gave him an amused smile before turning back to Rhiannon. "Well? Let's have the story."

The mare raised its tail and dropped fresh fertilizer on to the ground. The lumps seemed to fall in slow motion. Gallagher was glad the equine rear was pointing the other way.

Rhiannon said: "There's not much to tell. Christopher took me to a party given by one of those ad people he sometimes works for, and Gordon was there. Christopher had a change of plans and couldn't drive me down, so Gordon kindly agreed to help."

Alicia's eyes spoke volumes. "Just like that. I suppose," she went on dryly, "it would be hard to resist a car like this. And, for his kindness, you're showing him around . . . in Christopher's shirt."

"Alicia! We stopped to say hello, not to have you embarrass me."

"Isn't she lovely when she blushes?" Alicia said to Gallagher unrepentantly. "Tell you what . . . why don't you drop by for tea when you've done your sightseeing?" She patted Rhiannon on the shoulder. "Then you can really tell me all about it." She winked at Gallagher, straightened, and led the mare away. "Have fun, children!" she called back at them.

The horse punctuated the road with a neat line of droppings as it clopped past.

"She's right," he said, craning round to watch the departing Alicia. The faded jodhpurs clung to her behind. He would well understand Christopher Jameson's lustful desires.

"About what?"

Gallagher turned round once more and settled in his seat. "You do look lovely when you blush."

"Get that thing moving." She sounded pleased.

"Yes, ma'am."

Neither of them had noticed the innocuous dark saloon that had pulled up further down the road.

The *quattro* rushed up the steep hill out of the village.

Rhiannon said: "She'll never change."

"Alicia? Very capable-looking lady."

She gave him a sideways glance. " 'Capable-looking.' You can do better than that. Christopher has a more forceful way of putting it."

"I'll bet he has."

"Watch it. There's lechery in your voice."

He grinned. "Not guilty. There's lechery in my mind . . . but for a different target."

"Hmm."

The ground leveled out and they came to a crossroad.

"Turn here," Rhiannon said. "On the left."

The road turned sharply. Gallagher took the *quattro* round with a burst of acceleration. The car hugged the narrow road as if glued to it. He was glad for the continuing, but surprising, scarcity of traffic. He reveled in the emptiness of the road and hoped it would remain so. There was barely enough room for another car to pass.

He enjoyed the landscape. To the right was a great depression about two hundred meters deep, arranged like a vast amphitheater. There was a cluster of farm buildings in the far hollow.

"The Valley of Stones," Rhiannon said. "This area is full of ancient ruins. This is a region of ghosts. Alicia's farm is near here."

"Was that it?"

"No. It's another one, but on the edge of the valley. There's a track that leads off this road, to the right. The farm's surrounded by ruins. She calls them Alicia's ghosts."

"I like her sense of humor."

"Some of the farm workers will swear to you they've heard and seen things."

"And Alicia?"

"Oh, she believes them." Rhiannon turned her golden eyes upon him. "This is a ghostly county, as she'll tell you."

"How did she get the farm?" Gallagher asked, steering the conversation to more earthly matters.

"An inheritance. It's been in her family for generations. Funny how things sometimes turn out. Alicia once thought she was going to be an Italian countess and never imagined she would end up running the farm."

"What happened?"

They passed a track going off to the right. "There, that's the one," Rhiannon said. "She should be back by the time we return."

A tight left-hand bend approached. Gallagher powered the car into it. The road began to descend.

"What happened," Rhiannon said, "was that, some years ago, Christopher fell madly in love with her. He met her in London and didn't even know she came from around here. To cut a long story short, he took her aboard his ship to a wardroom party. Some Nato officers were guests, one of whom was an Italian count. He went bananas over her Junoesque body. Swept her off her feet. Poor old Christopher was quite shattered. How could a solid sub-lieutenant compete with a dashing young commander who looked like a film star? Alicia spent a lot of time in Italy after that."

The road dropped steeply into a 1-in-5 corner.

"You'd better slow down. We're coming into Abbotsbury," Rhiannon warned.

"Yes, ma'am."

"Hmm."

"Let's hear the rest, then."

"It all went really badly for her. The commander was a passenger in a VIP plane that crashed into the sea off Sicily or Sardinia—I can't remember which—and that was that. Alicia became a widow before she'd had time to get married. Christopher was very supportive and they've remained good friends; but they've gone their separate ways. Alicia never married. In a way, I think both she and Christopher still have a very strong love for each other. I have the feeling that if she ever did decide to get married it would be to Christopher."

"She certainly recognizes his shirts."

Rhiannon dug him in the ribs. "Behave yourself. When the farm came up," she went on, "Alicia virtually plunged herself into the task of running it. It's been like that ever since. She enjoys it. We always try to visit her whenever either of us is down. And here we are. Abbotsbury."

The ancient village that had seen the reign of King Cnut greeted them with its long rows of neat thatched cottages bordering each side of the B3157, its main thoroughfare. In direct contrast to the empty roads they had taken here, on this street a line of parked cars, seeming to run the whole length of the village, met their eyes. The souvenir shops were packed with customers.

"Abbotsbury saw hot times during the Civil War," Rhiannon said. "There are still bullet holes in the parish church. Would you like to stop for a while?"

Gallagher shook his head, not interested in doing the tourist rounds.

"No. Take me to the beach. I'd rather see that."

"All right. Go through the village. Where the main road bends to the right, there's another going to the left. Take that one. It's the way to the beach."

He cruised the *quattro* through.

At the end of the village, he saw to his left a squat, churchlike building perched on a hill.

"What was that over there?"

"St. Catherine's Chapel for seamen; fifteenth-century. Great views of the beach from Chapel Hill. We could go there after we've been to the beach."

"Might be an idea. I've got my camera kit in the

boot. The chapel looks interesting. Might be able to use it for some shots. Let's see how the time goes. Mustn't forget our tea date with Alicia."

"Watch it," she said, "or I'll begin to wonder if it's just her tea you're after."

An archway of tall ilex trees covered the road for about 900 meters; then it was into the open for another 400 meters, sloping gently toward the beach. The tarmac narrowed, turned sharply right.

Rhiannon said: "Turn off here, to the left."

Gallagher turned on to the gravel and drove slowly, the fat tires making a crunching noise. Countless billions of pebbles stretched in a rising bank in either direction as far as the eye could see.

"Quite amazing," he said softly. "Really quite amazing."

"Thought you'd like it," she said. "Wait till you see the rest."

They drove along the gravelly track that skirted the huge bank of shingle, until they could go no further. Gallagher parked the *quattro* with its nose pointing up the slope. Despite the number of cars they'd seen in Abbotsbury, few drivers had come to the beach. They had passed only two other parked cars, and those were now some distance further back.

Gallagher turned off the engine. Through the Audi's lowered windows the continuous, sharp hiss of the sea and the tangy smell of the eighteen-mile mound came strongly.

"Shall we go?" Rhiannon suggested.

"We shall."

He turned the ignition on briefly to enable him to raise the windows before climbing out of the car. He clicked the boot open, went to get his Nikon from the equipment case. The camera was fitted with a motor drive. He also took out a special, lightweight zoom lens that gave him a range of 50–500 mm, and fitted it to the Nikon. He shut the boot. Rhiannon was waiting for him when he went back to lock the car.

"Always prepared, are you?" she queried, pointing to the camera, which now hung from his neck.

"Never know what I might find." His eyes looked her up and down.

She arched an eyebrow. "Want me to pose for you?"

"I have other ideas."

"Come on, you," she said with mock severity, and began crunching up the slope.

Gallagher followed her, enjoying the rhythm of her body as she walked on the shifting pebbles. The noise they made made him think of a marching troop of soldiers. It seemed an awful lot of noise for just two pairs of feet.

The structure fascinated him. The pebbles, most no more than three-quarters of an inch in length, had been worn uniformly smooth by the battering they had taken from the sea over the centuries. They varied richly in color when inspected individually, but seen *en masse* they looked like a great, yellowish-brown speckled carpet. Rhiannon stooped to grab a handful.

She reached the crest, stopped and turned to wait for him, shaking the pebbles together in her cupped hands.

"If you drove a pole down to sea level from this spot," she began as he reached her, "it would have to be twenty feet long to clear the top. Perhaps even thirty." She opened her hands. "Look," she went on, "aren't they pretty? Flints, limestone, black chert, quartz. . . ."

Gallagher looked. "Quite the seaside geologist."

She threw the pebbles in a wide arc toward the sea. "Our parents used to bring us here quite often when we were children. My father would spend a lot of time telling us about it and how it came into being. I know this place like the back of my hand."

She fell silent, staring out to sea the way she had done on Portland.

Gallagher left her to her silence and looked about him. To his right, the pebbles stretched out toward Bridport, seemingly to infinity, flattening the mound the further they went. To his left, the pebbles disappeared into an equal distance, except that here, the mound grew progressively higher. About a hundred yards away, a shattered concrete structure poked drunkenly out of the seaward slope. Beyond it, a row of blocks, made small by the distance, curved over the top from inland and down toward the sea, ending just beyond the crest. Trapped between the bank and the land was a large body of water that began by the concrete blocks and stretched uninterruptedly toward Portland.

He turned to look at the blue-gray sea, bare to the horizon, hissing incessantly at the pebbles. It made a sound that was uncannily like a loud, human sigh.

There were only four other people about. Three were almost pinpricks, away toward Bridport. Closer in, but still a good 400 meters off, a man was sitting in a canvas chair, fishing. Gallagher idly wondered if he'd had any luck.

Rhiannon turned from her contemplation of the sea. "The storms can be quite nasty around here. Sometimes the sea comes right over, or penetrates the pebbles to flood the ground behind us. This used to be a wreckers' paradise. Ships were always being blown along the whole bank. Once, in the last century, one was even blown over into the Fleet. That's the inland water."

"*Moonfleet,*" Gallagher said suddenly. "I knew I was reminded of something when you first mentioned it. The book and the movie. I saw the movie on the box years ago. My father gave me the book when I was nine."

She smiled at him. "Childhood memories. Fleet itself was flooded completely in a great storm. Sometimes the wrecks would litter the bank with hundreds of bodies from Portland to Bridport. This place has seen its fair share of tragedy; but I find it beautiful." She reached for his hand. "Come on. Let's walk to the Fleet."

They began stomping along the crest, picking up their feet exaggeratedly in order to make progress.

"I'd hate to have to run in this," he remarked. "It would take all day to run a few yards."

The dark saloon entered Abbotsbury slowly, cruising through the village until it came to a blind left-hand corner that led to the Swannery and the parish church. It turned into the corner gingerly, continued along the narrow street.

It drove past the church, climbing the incline toward the Swannery; but it was not going as far. Instead, it took a right fork along an unpaved track.

It was going to St. Catherine's Chapel.

Gallagher and Rhiannon passed a sign planted midway down the seaward slope of the bank. It was hazardous to bathe, it cautioned.

She noted his look. "It is very dangerous," she said. "The shelf stops suddenly and the pebbles would give you no purchase. Imagine how it would feel with both the waves and the pebbles clawing at you. Then there are the currents."

"You sound as if you're speaking from experience."

She shook her head. "Not me; but when we were children, Christopher went too close to the edge. He began to sink into the pebbles, further and further into the water. My mother and I began to scream. Poor Christopher was yelling his head off and squirming, making things even worse. My father ran to drag him out and was almost caught himself. He too began to sink; but he was very cool about it. He was like that. By the time he had managed to pull Christopher away, people had gathered around, some forming a chain to help him. I asked him afterwards if he had been frightened. He said yes. You never would have believed it to have seen him."

Gallagher put an arm about her shoulders. "You still miss him a lot," he said gently.

She nodded. "Not always, but certain things remind me more strongly than others. You'd think the cottage, and his old uniforms, would; but they don't. I've learned to live with them. Yet this beach. . . ."

"Well, it's hardly an event you could forget."

"Poor Christopher. Always getting himself into deep water. Though he always manages to get out, somehow."

"And he took care of you."

"Yes. He did." She smiled. "And, as you know, he still worries about me."

"There'll be two of us now to do the worrying." Gallagher surprised himself with his involuntary statement.

The golden eyes were looking at him. "You mean that, don't you?"

"Yes," he heard himself say.

"Hmm."

They came upon the gaping concrete structure, which to Gallagher looked like a ruined pillbox.

"Wartime defenses," Rhiannon said, confirming his suspicions. She pointed to the other blocks, which he now saw were in parallel rows. "More of the same. I think it was a slipway, though I'm not too sure. I seem to remember my father saying it was, but that was years ago. I could be wrong. See anything you want to take a picture of?"

"Wait till we get to the blocks. You can pose there for me."

"You're joking. I don't know how to pose." She was looking a little unsure of herself.

"Oh, yes, you do. And don't say you're not Doria Luce."

"I'm not. . . ." She grinned and squirmed away from him with a sudden twist of her body. She moved ahead, stomping across the shingle.

Gallagher followed, and soon found how right he was about trying to run on such a surface; but he continued to chase after her, refusing to give up. He caught up with her just before she reached the blocks.

She gave a shriek like a delighted child as he grabbed her about the waist to turn her toward him. Her face was glowing.

"You're . . . you're out of condition," she said. "You're breathing hard."

"Look who's talking." He stared at her chest. "*You're* breathing hard, unless my eyes deceive me."

"Avert your eyes, sir, and unhand me."

"But first, a forfeit," he said, and kissed her.

She squirmed away once more and made for the blocks, where she started going through a series of mock poses. Shifting the lens sleeve through different focal lengths, he triggered off some shots of her, before going up to the concrete barrier himself.

A weathered sign of big red letters on a white background was fixed to one of the blocks. NO ACCESS, it warned. It was a nature reserve sign. Beneath the red lettering was a large handwritten note stating that birds were nesting on the beach, particularly the Little Tern which was legally protected from disturbance.

"We'd better be careful," he said, pointing to the sign. "We wouldn't like to be taken to court by a bird, would we?"

"Don't be silly," she said, going into another pose.

For answer, he took a portrait shot of her.

"Besides," she went on, "if we don't go beyond here, it will be all right."

Gallagher saw that, inland, the twin rows of blocks went all the way to the shore of the Fleet. In the space between the rows, the ubiquitous pebbles had formed themselves into a pathway, tufted here and there by hardy marine plants that had long ago migrated from the sea.

It didn't seem like a slipway to him; but who was he to judge? On either side of the blocks, stakes had been driven into the shingle at roughly three-meter intervals, linked by lengths of twine to form a second-line barrier. They went from the edge of the Fleet, over the crest and down again toward the sea. The barrier was more psychological than anything.

Rhiannon patted one of the blocks. "There are lumps of these scattered along the beach. This was an important place during the war. There were a lot of Americans, according to my father." She looked out at the Fleet. "The RAF practiced here too; with the bouncing bomb."

"That must have given the fish nightmares. What's in there, anyway?"

"Mainly eels and bass."

"And swans."

He had the camera up to his eye and had drawn the lens up to its greatest focal length. The swans were clustered in a small bay beyond a headland 500 meters away.

"That's the swannery."

"Want to look?"

She nodded.

He handed the camera to her, draping the strap about her neck. "Watch out for the lens. Hold it underneath, elbow against your body. There. Is that all right?"

"Yes." She looked into the viewfinder. "Hey. This is great. I can see everything clearly. There are two swans. . . . Oh, ho!" she chortled.

"Give them their privacy. Look somewhere else, voyeur."

"I was only joking."

"That's what they all say."

She bumped her bottom against him and continued to look at the swans.

Gallagher stared down the Fleet, looked round at the Dorset hills until his eyes settled on the distant shape of St. Catherine's Chapel. For no reason that he could fathom, he suddenly felt uneasy.

In the warmth of the sun, he felt cold.

The man in the dark saloon switched off the engine. He had, with some difficulty, managed to turn it round within the space available and had now parked tucked into the verge, pointing the way he had come. Though the track was deserted for the moment, it mattered little to him if someone noticed the car. It had been hired under a false name, and he had not done the hiring. The number plates, like the hair on his head and his moustache, were also false. Further, before the plates had been changed, the car had been legitimately licensed in the North-East. They would be replaced before the car was returned.

The man picked up his radio and spoke softly into it. He then placed it in the pocket of his lightweight jacket, picked up the briefcase and climbed out of the car. He calmly locked the door.

Then he started walking up the hill toward the chapel.

7

Gallagher had taken the camera back from Rhiannon and was sighting along the crest of the bank in the direction of Portland. There was a lulling effect to the brightness of the day, with the still waters of the Fleet on one side and the soporific hissing of the sea on the other. Rhiannon was sitting on a block close to where he was standing. Her knees were drawn up and were clasped by linked hands. Her eyes were closed, her face tilted upward to the sun, her back turned to the green of the hills.

Gallagher paused to look at her. "Heliotrope," he accused.

"I'm not purple," she said, keeping her eyes closed.

"But you love the sun and . . . you're fragrant." He kissed the back of her neck lightly.

She smiled. "Bet you say that to all the girls."

He put the camera to his eye once more and turned toward the Bridport end of the bank. The fisherman came up in fine detail: a full head shot. A man well into his fifties. Weatherbeaten. A man who had fished for years.

The lens moved on, searching along the beach.

The three distant specks changed into a couple with a young child.

Suddenly, there was a loud, echoing bang. Gallagher felt his stomach muscles tighten even as his mind identified the sound.

Shotgun. Well out of range. Not hostile.

Rhiannon had not even flinched. He wondered if he had.

"Some poor rabbit's just caught a packet," she said. Her eyes remained closed.

"That's twice you've said 'rabbit.' "

"Ah, but we're not on Portland."

Gallagher turned the camera on the hills. The shotgun had made him jumpy. Would he spot the rabbit hunter?

A faint noise impinged upon his senses, growing louder, a noise in the sky. He pointed the camera, caught an old *Wessex* helicopter flying low along the beach and a little out to sea. The winchman was clearly visible. Rescue patrol.

"I wonder if they can see me." Rhiannon was waving at the aircraft.

"Flirt," Gallagher said.

"Jealous?"

"As if I would be."

"Why not? Say you are."

He smiled. "All right. I'm jealous."

"That's better." She closed her eyes again, hands once more clasped to her knees.

Something was wrong. He knew it.

He panned the camera along the hills slowly from right to left, the lens at its maximum focal length. He paused when the squat chapel came into view. Its image filled the lens, its details picked out clearly. He continued panning left, toward a copse close by.

Suddenly a shiver streaked all the way down his spine. He had seen something. He had seen a man shift quickly across a short space between two trees. The man had been carrying what looked like a briefcase, and a rifle.

A rifle?

Perhaps it wasn't a rifle. Perhaps it was the shotgun he had heard. . . . But Gallagher was already rejecting the idea. A man in a suit and carrying a briefcase did not go with a shotgun. Perhaps there were people who shot rabbits while clutching briefcases; but somehow he didn't think the unknown man was likely to be one of them.

Even as these thoughts were racing through Gallagher's mind, instinct had taken over. He was panning across the entire wood, triggering a fast series of shots.

Almost simultaneously, he said to Rhiannon: "Get down off that block."

He could be wrong about the whole thing. Even the unusual fact of a man with a rifle hiding in a wood near the chapel did not necessarily mean either of them was the target. He would in all probability look very foolish.

Even so, better a live fool. . . .

"Get down!" he repeated.

Rhiannon turned to look at him, a smile upon her face. "Hmm. I like that masterful voice."

Jesus. She thinks I'm playing.

"Make me," she said. She didn't move.

Oh, God.

The man was out there, lining up, going to shoot. Gallagher knew it. *He knew it.*

Why was he moving so slowly? He had to reach her in time.

Then his hands were grabbing at her, pulling

her unceremoniously down off her perch. He cushioned her fall on to the pebbles with his own body while he mentally prayed the Nikon would be all right. He held her tightly to him.

"Hey," she said, slightly winded. "I know I drive you to the wildest of distractions, but isn't this a little public?"

But Gallagher was not listening to her; for, as they had fallen to the ground, he had seen what she had not. Something waspish had ploughed a sudden furrow into the block she had been sitting on, scattering tiny slivers of concrete, before ricocheting invisibly on its way toward the sea. The expected sharp report came loudly and echoingly soon after.

Rhiannon said: "The rabbits are catching it today."

"Don't move!"

Her golden eyes widened with puzzlement. "Gordon? What is this? You're not playing, are you?"

"Correction. *He's* not playing."

"He? What are you talking about?"

"I wish I bloody knew."

"Gordon. . . ."

"Don't *move!* Listen to me, Rhiannon," he went on quickly, but in calm tones so as not to panic her into doing something fatally stupid. "That was no shotgun. That was the sound of a high-powered rifle. No, no. Don't ask questions now. Just do as I say. All right? *All right?*"

He still held on to her tightly.

"Y . . . yes." She was beginning to look frightened.

"Listen. Don't freeze up on me now. Take it easy and just do as I say. *Exactly* as I say."

She swallowed, and nodded.

"Good. Now I'm going to let you go. Just remain perfectly still. I'll put the camera about your neck. When I say go, I want you to go on your hands and toes as fast as you can . . . *keeping low* . . . until you reach the seaward slope. Go as near as you dare to the sea, then lie flat on the pebbles. You'll be out of sight there. Remain in that spot until I come for you. I'll bring the car."

"The . . . the car? It can't travel on this."

"Oh, yes, it can. Now don't worry. Stay between the blocks and keep low. You'll be quite safe. I'll distract him."

"Gordon . . ." she began in a now quite terrified voice.

"Shhh! No more. Get ready."

Gallagher carefully removed the Nikon and passed it to her. Time enough later to check it for damage; if they got out alive. If they didn't, it would hardly matter.

"All right," he told her. "Now turn around slowly."

He tried not to think of the very visible beacon her white dress would make. When they had started the day, the possibility of being a hunter's target had not been remotely upon their minds. It now appeared that the attire he had earlier viewed with such admiration could well spell her death.

He stared at her as she crouched, almost like a runner waiting for the off. Her entire body was stiff with fear.

"Relax," he said soothingly. "It's a very short distance. You can make it."

"Gordon, you may be wrong. Perhaps there's no one. . . ."

"A bullet hit just where you were sitting," he interrupted with more brutality than he'd intended;

but he had to give her some motivation for making the run. "There may be a madman out there who thinks this is great fun. I don't know . . . and we're not hanging around to find out. Right. Are you ready?"

The back of her head dipped once. She seemed to have relaxed a little.

He allowed a few seconds to tune himself, making use of his natural instincts, as he'd been taught years before. By moving off together, they'd be splitting the gunman's concentration. Rhiannon's white dress, flitting between the blocks, would be the attention getter; but Gallagher would be the more truly visible target . . . and the more difficult. He had no intention of running predictably. He could only hope the man with the rifle chose to go after him, instead of Rhiannon. Her route was predictable. All the man had to do was aim between one of the spaces and wait for her to appear.

Gallagher put the thought savagely out of his mind. No point crouching here thinking the unthinkable. He had to get moving.

"All right! *Go!*"

Even as he suddenly leapt out into the open between two of the blocks he was gratified to note that she had not hesitated. *Good girl,* his mind said as he began his sprint; then he concentrated on his objective, putting Rhiannon completely out of his calculations. There was nothing he could do for her now. He was already offering himself as target. The rest was up to her.

The twine between the stakes!

He nearly tripped over it, but managed to clear the potentially lethal obstacle in time.

Run. Zigzag. Never in one direction for more than a few heartbeats, or the heart will stop beating

forever; and never the same beats. One here, four
there, drop, roll, up again, two there, three, five
... *this is the worst, but do it! He's got to try and keep
up with you. Drop, roll, two beats, up, go. Change
direction. Don't think about the noise of a shot. If you
hear it, he's missed. If you're still running and you
haven't heard it, he hasn't shot, or he's got someone
else. Keep running, dropping, rolling. It's not as far
as you think. Don't think about Rhiannon! Heartbeat, heartbeat, heartbeat. . . . Still there. No shot.
Christ, the pebbles make it difficult to run. . . . Don't
think about it. Run!*

At the bottom of the slope, stretching from the
Fleet almost to where he'd left the car, was a field of
tall plumed, reedlike grass. That was his cover. The
tops of their plumes were about six feet above the
ground and thickly concentrated; more than enough
to screen him from the man on the hill. All he had
to do was get to them.

Then, suddenly, he was there. A narrow path
entered the reeds. He flung himself upon it and lay
still. No shot. She had made it. He had made it. His
reason told him only seconds had passed, though it
had seemed like a thousand years.

But it was not yet over. He had to get a move on.

Cautiously, he raised himself and began crawling along the path. He came to a junction where
another path came from the direction of the Fleet,
continued left to where the car was. He paused,
checked both to his right and to his left. *What if there
were others waiting among the reeds?* It was not a
thought to give him peace of mind. Still, he had to get
on. No point hanging about. The man on the hill
might already have worked out what he was intending to do. Gallagher tried not to think of the scope

cruising slowly across the reeds, watching for the suspicious waving of a plume.

He turned left along the path, running at a crouch, careful not to touch the tall stems. At times, he was forced to crawl beneath small arches where in places the reeds had almost overgrown the path. Soon he could see the *quattro,* about fifty meters away. Cover had become sparse; but there was still enough for him to use . . . except for the last ten meters or so.

Ten meters of open country across the sights of a rifleman lying in wait might as well be ten miles.

Gallagher checked his surroundings. From his position, he could not see the hill, but he thought it possible that, even without the screen of grasses, he was now out of rifle sight from someone waiting up there.

Think. *Think.*

Two hills. The furthest, the one on the right, was Chapel Hill. That was where the gunman was. The next hill, the one on the left. . . . He paused. From this low down, Chapel Hill should now be hidden from view. He inched forward to take a sighting between two clumps of coarse bushes that had now taken over from the reed field.

And it was so.

All that greeted his cautious eyes were the ancient Anglo-Saxon terraces on the massive flank of the hill, and a few peacefully munching cattle.

Gallagher did not waste time on relief. The gunman might or might not have accomplices. It was not prudent to find out the hard way. He reached into his pocket and fished out the remote, which had two other functions besides triggering off his answering machine. Pointing it at the *quattro,* he activated one of those. The car's headlamps flashed briefly. The doors were now unlocked. He had no intention of being nailed while trying to insert the key.

He put the remote away, took out the ignition key.

"Here goes," he muttered and left his hiding place at a run.

No shots were fired. He grabbed at the left-hand door, opened it, climbed in and shut it again almost without pause. *Start the bloody engine. Come on, girl. Let's have you.* Ignition. Engine growling into immediate life. Lock the center and rear diffs for extra traction. Pray the surface is not too loose to take the weight of the car. Second gear in to avoid hopeless wheelspin on all four. Power on, gradually but firmly. Brief spin of wheels, diff-lock lights coming on. *Movement.* Warning note pinging away, nagging him to fasten the seat belt, which he did one-handedly.

The *quattro* urged itself steadily, surefootedly up the slope, speed building as it climbed.

"Oh, you beautiful, beautiful lady!" Gallagher said softly.

Out of the corner of his eye, to the right, he caught a moving flash of green and could not believe it.

The Range Rover with the big wheels was racing along the track to where he had previously been parked. So much for farmers needing big wheels for soggy ground.

What the hell was going on? Why were these people and the gunman on the hill after him?

Perhaps they weren't after him. Perhaps. . . .

Rhiannon? He shook his head. He couldn't see how she could be involved in anything. Yet any number of people, even the most inoffensive-looking, could be involved in all manner of things. It merely depended upon how far their affairs encroached upon your own life.

He glanced in the mirrors. The Range Rover was following him up the slope.

He took the *quattro* over the crest diagonally and risked a little more power. The car slid briefly, but the wheels bit nicely and it kept going. Pebbles flung by the wheels hammered at the underside. Gallagher tried not to wince or think of the floorpan and the running gear being flayed.

As he roared down, he caught movement away to his right. The fisherman had leapt to his feet to stare disbelievingly.

"Hope I didn't scare any fish," Gallagher said; but the set of his mouth was grim.

There were tidal ridges on the seaward slope and he took them with circumspection. The last thing he needed was to bottom on one of them with all wheels hanging uselessly in the air. The Range Rover had an advantage, with its balloon wheels and high ground clearance; but the *quattro* had advantages too. It was lighter, for a start.

He looked for Rhiannon but could not see the white beacon of her dress anywhere.

Where was she? Why hadn't she done what he'd asked her to?

Then he saw a peep of white. The pillbox. She had taken refuge there. Better than feeling naked out in the open. A good idea, provided the gunman didn't know she was in there and did not send a stream of bullets through its gaping holes. Ricochets in such a confined space would not be fun. The pillbox would be visible from the hill. She would have been safer where he'd sent her; but he decided not to criticize her decision, understanding her need for some kind of shelter.

He slowed down as he reached her, but kept the car moving at a crawl. He didn't want to lose momentum.

"Get in!" he yelled at her.

She ran out from the ruined pillbox, keeping low, down toward the car. He prayed the gunman was not still on his hill. She would only be in his sights for a very brief moment before the rise of the bank took her from view; but just such an instant was all a professional would need. The men in the Range Rover were beaters, flushing them out. It had gone slightly wrong, because Gallagher had made it to the car first.

Rhiannon made it safely, ran round the car and grabbed at the moving door. She glanced round and what she saw made her eyes widen. She momentarily lost balance as she trotted to keep up with the slow-moving *quattro,* staggered, sorted herself out and was tumbling in. Gallagher did not need a backward glance to tell him what she had seen. It was there in the mirrors.

"Gordon . . . !" she began as she shut the door.

"Put on your belt!" he cut in, gradually increasing pressure on the accelerator. "Yes. I know they're behind us."

She was staring at him wide-eyed even as she put on her belt. The Nikon was hanging from her neck, apparently none the worse for wear. She removed it gingerly and put it on the back seat. Then she turned to the front again, after a nervous look at the pursuing Range Rover.

Gallagher continued to let the power build. Pebbles sprayed from the roaring wheels, drumming against the underside of the car. He held it steadily midway up the seaward slope, keeping clear of tidal ridges. The more the speed built, the less was the likelihood of being bogged down. The pebbles seemed to be sufficiently hard-packed beneath the surface cover to support the weight of the *quattro*.

He turned off the diff locks. After a brief pause, the indicator lights winked out. Now that he'd achieved momentum, there was no further need for the locks.

In the mirrors he saw that they appeared to be gaining on the Range Rover.

"Where are we going?" Rhiannon asked.

"Portland."

She stared out at the bank that disappeared into the distance. "On *this*? It's eight miles. The car won't be able to do it. The pebbles turn into four-inch stones at that end."

"We haven't a choice," he said, jerking a thumb briefly toward the back. "Besides, the rally cars have to deal with far worse than these conditions."

"This is not a rally car."

"True, but. . . ." He patted the wheel. "She won't let us down. Are you all right?"

She nodded. "There's a rifle range at Charlestown. That's about two miles before Portland."

"We'll just have to hope no one's at the butts today."

The wheels roared over the pebbles. The speedometer read 60. Gallagher let the speed creep upward, his senses alert for any sudden movement by the car. A quick glance in the mirrors showed the Range Rover some distance behind. Why weren't they trying harder? With their big wheels, they should have been making better progress. What were they planning? Was the man with the rifle even now trying to get to Portland? Perhaps they were trying for a sandwich, with the Range Rover pushing the quarry into the waiting sights.

"We'll be disturbing the terns today," Rhiannon said incongruously.

Gallagher knew she was trying to remain calm. Thinking about the nesting terns helped to blot out the reality of the pursuing vehicle.

"Let's hope they'll forgive us."

She seemed to be studying him. "I don't really know you, do I?"

"What do you mean?"

"Oh, I've heard about you from Christopher . . . but that's not the point I want to make."

He concentrated on holding the car steady.

"Last night," she said, "I told you I saw something frightening in your eyes. It's there now. Those people have brought it back. Who are they, Gordon? What do they want with us?"

"It's as much a mystery to me as it is to you."

He wasn't telling her the whole truth. He was feeling more and more certain it had to do with what Jameson had said to him in Nellis's Thameside garden. Had someone seen them together? Someone who had been watching Jameson and lurking out there in the dark?

Gallagher thought it unlikely. His senses had been fully attuned to the night. He had not sensed any hostile presence.

He did not like where the train of thought was leading him. If someone wanted to influence Jameson in no uncertain manner, what better way than a hit on the sister for whom he cared so much?

Gallagher felt cold. The target really was Rhiannon. It had to be.

And I've walked bang into the middle, he thought with dry resignation.

But had he? It was beginning to look as if Jameson, having failed to persuade Gallagher to go diving with him, had opted for a second tack. Perhaps fearing for Rhiannon's safety, he had contrived to place Gallagher close to her and had not, after all, been using Rhiannon to soften him up.

"It's the way you seemed to know what you were doing," she was saying into his thoughts. "You knew it was not a shotgun, and you knew exactly how to cope. Did Christopher send you to look after me?"

No one could accuse her of being slow on the uptake.

"I'm only just beginning to work that out myself. I am as much the unknowing player in this as you are."

"Those people are really trying to kill *me?*" Her voice shook. "But why? Is Christopher in some kind of trouble?"

In deep trouble, Gallagher didn't say. Deep enough to have brought the killers out.

"I don't know," he answered. Jameson might not have expected the swift attraction between himself and Rhiannon; but her presence at Nellis's party had certainly been premeditated.

"You two were talking for a long time in that garden. . . ."

"He made no mention whatsoever to me about taking care of you," Gallagher said truthfully. "All he asked was that I should drive you home. You were there. He seemed amused at the time, if you remember. I thought it was because he's seen us . . . er . . . getting on so well. It's obvious he had another reason too."

She nodded slowly. Some of the healthy color had gone from her cheeks.

"Do you think they've . . . they've got him?"

"I wouldn't jump to conclusions like that," Gallagher said firmly. "After all, you did talk to him today."

"I think he rang to check that I was all right and that you were still at the cottage with me."

"Perhaps," Gallagher conceded.

He was also now reasonably certain that Jameson had not taken Nellis's boat to Cornwall. That had been a story to explain his absence to Rhiannon. Gallagher had the awful feeling that Jameson had either decided to do the dive alone or had managed to persuade someone to go with him.

Gallagher looked in his mirrors to check on the Range Rover.

It was gone. But where?

His alarm bells began to jangle. The bank, he noted, was getting progressively higher. Although he had kept the car roughly in the middle of the slope, the distance from the sea, as well as from the crest, had certainly increased. If the Range Rover was not on their side of the massive spine of shingle, it could only have gone across to the opposite slope. Gallagher thought he knew why.

"Brace yourself," he said to Rhiannon sharply.

She gazed at him questioningly but said nothing. Her face was still pale from fear and confusion and from anxiety for her brother's safety. Out of the corner of his eye, Gallagher saw her take a firm hold of the grab-handle in the door, for additional support.

He angled the *quattro* up the bank. It took the ridges like a speedboat traversing a low swell, now and then giving a little twitch as the pebbles shifted beneath its churning wheels; but it climbed powerfully, heading for the top.

He had made his move none too soon.

The bulbous front wheels of the Range Rover

leapt suddenly over the crest, seeming to rear skyward for long seconds before slamming downward
once more with such force, the shingle scattered
from them like arcing lines of tracer. The Range
Rover pointed its nose at the *quattro* and charged
like an angry rhino.

Rhiannon screamed. *"Gordon!"* She appeared to
shrink against the high back of her seat, bracing
herself for what she clearly thought was the inevitable.

But Gallagher had already begun to take avoiding action. He jinked briefly to the right and, as soon
as the Range Rover began swinging to its left to
counter, he went left again and booted the car up the
crest. As it surged upward, he prayed there wasn't a
lump of hidden wartime concrete waiting to tear at
the suspension and turn it into useless chunks of
twisted metal.

The Range Rover had misjudged the turn and
went into a wide, skidding curve; but it was coming
back.

Gallagher thought he knew their game. They
weren't going to wait to squeeze the sandwich. They
intended to get their quarry well before Portland.
The gunman was most likely putting as much distance as possible between himself and the scene, the
job having now been left to the two "farmers."

They weren't shooting, and Gallagher momentarily wondered why. The reason became clear as
soon as the *quattro* went over the top. On this section
of the bank, the landward slope was far steeper. Its
ridges leveled out in places into ledges and tiny pla-
teaux which at times ended in precipitous drops to
the waters of the Fleet below. These drops were not
particularly long, sometimes no more than perhaps
fifteen to twenty feet; but a car going off at the speed

they were doing on this type of surface would probably tumble quite nastily as it flung itself into the water.

The men in the Range Rover, he decided, didn't want to shoot because after the failure of the first attempt they wanted no telltale bullets in the bodies. It was one thing to carry out a killing from a distance, with no one around to notice you. One shot should have been enough, but in being forced to complete the job this way, they had come out into the open. Anyone watching from the other side of the Fleet would think that a pair of lunatics were playing chicken on the bank. Too bad if one of them went into the water. They should have known better.

Gallagher was not too happy with that line of reasoning. The simplest fact could be the true one. They didn't have guns.

Cold comfort, he thought, as the *quattro* seemed to nosedive toward a fragile-looking ledge that seemed barely wide enough to accommodate it. On the periphery of his vision, he saw Rhiannon nibble at her lower lip; she was clearly thinking they were heading straight for the water.

The ledge crumbled as the car reached it.

The *quattro* slid abruptly broadside-on and downward for about six feet before the permanent four-wheel-drive did its stuff and forward momentum was almost instantly regained.

Rhiannon made a little squeaking sound. She gave Gallagher a quick, trusting smile, then resumed staring through the windscreen. The rushing shingle seemed to mesmerize her.

The Range Rover had come over the top again, some distance behind; but if the man driving knew what he was about, he could catch up again. The big wheels and high ground clearance would give him an edge.

There was only one way to end this contest. Attack. One of the combatants was definitely going into the water. Gallagher was determined that it wouldn't be the *quattro*.

He went back up to the top and over, turning toward Abbotsbury.

Rhiannon was looking at him in surprise. "Aren't we . . . ?"

"No, we're not going to Portland."

"We're *not*?"

"No," he repeated, "and neither are they. They're not going anywhere."

The Audi's powerful engine seemed to roar with a new purpose as he swung the car to the right, heading back for the crest. As they went over once more the Range Rover, further along, paused in the act of crossing to the seaward slope. It tightened its turn, rushed along the top before seeming to tilt over as it came down a steep incline, heading directly toward them.

Gallagher noted its approach, kept the speed up, racing for a ledge that ended in one of the perpendicular drops to the water. He selected both center and rear differentials, watched as the indicator lights came on. He was locking the transmission solid, turning the *quattro* into the approximation of a rally car. He fervently hoped he was not going to do some expensive damage to the gear train. The jokers in the Range Rover could afford to wreck their transport: it probably didn't even belong to them. He needed his. Besides, it would be his wallet that would feel the blow.

Assuming I'm still around to worry about a wal-

let, he thought. *And if I don't survive, Rhiannon won't.*

Her eyes seemed fixed upon him. She was still biting at her lip and hanging on to the grab handle.

The Range Rover missed them, came tightly round on their tail. Gallagher towed it toward the trap he hoped would work. Their pursuers would be caught unawares and would not expect the crazy stunt he was about to throw at them. It would have to work first go. They'd not fall for it twice.

As he approached the drop, Gallagher took his foot momentarily off the accelerator. The pebbles building up at the wheels slowed the car suddenly and dramatically. Gallagher swung the wheel to the right. The *quattro* began to turn. He floored the accelerator.

All four wheels spun with the massive and sudden injection of power from the turbocharged engine. The car flung itself sideways up the slope, describing an arc through ninety degrees as it did so. Gallagher stopped the slide when the nose began pointing directly at the Range Rover. The wheels bit. The car hurled itself downward.

Things began to happen very quickly after that.

When the *quattro* had slowed down, there had been no telltale warning from the rear lights. The Range Rover had been taken unawares and its driver had reacted suddenly, stamping on the brakes and putting the vehicle in an unstable condition. It was also very close to the edge. With the black car now bearing down upon him, he again reacted instinctively; this time in panic and the need for survival. He turned the wheel sharply left to avoid what he thought was certain collision.

First one front wheel, then the other, cleared the lip of the ledge, which had begun to crumble. The man sawed ineffectually at the steering wheel, his panic causing him to brake and hit the accelerator alternately in desperation. The Range Rover propelled itself over, did a half-flip. The descending nose smashed into the bank, bouncing the stricken vehicle outward. It seemed to fly for brief seconds before rolling twice to hit the water upside-down, in a cascade that rose like a fountain which then collapsed upon its underbelly, folding about it in liquid embrace.

Gallagher had seen only fleeting images of what had happened. He had been too busy with disengaging the diff locks, swinging the car away from the doomed Range Rover and praying there would be no slide to take them over the crumbling edge in the wake of their erstwhile pursuers.

The *quattro* turned its tail to the water and fled back up the slope. It had missed the edge by two feet.

He stopped the car on the crest, its nose pointing toward Portland, engine running at idle. It sounded pleased with itself.

He looked down at the water. The Fleet was about a kilometer wide at that point. There was no sign of either the Range Rover or the two men.

"It must be deep around here," Gallagher said. "I heard screaming," he went on. "Was that you or me?"

After a while, Rhiannon said: "I was screaming." She was looking at him with a new understanding and wariness. "You killed those men."

"They killed themselves," he said evenly. "They were going to kill us. If they'd had their way," he glanced again at the water, "we'd be down there, in their place. Someone else tried to kill you with a rifle. Remember that. *He's* still alive."

He put the car into gear, moved off slowly down the seaward slope, turned back toward Abbotsbury. They drove along the edge of the blue-gray sea in a silence that lasted until they reached their point of entry. The fisherman was still there. He watched their passage as they crunched past him on their way to the top of the bank.

"He'll remember us," Gallagher said, "when someone finds those two."

"There's a coast guard post on the hill at Fleet," Rhiannon said. "If it was manned, they'll have seen everything. We'll find the police waiting for us."

"Better than that man with the rifle."

"You sound so calm about it. I'm just about managing to hold back a fit of hysteria."

"In the circumstances, I think you're doing very well."

"You've killed before, haven't you?" she asked suddenly.

Gallagher sighed. There it was. The past was always there, waiting to ambush you.

He said: "A few years ago, I worked for the nation. Let's just leave it at that."

More silence, then: "How did Lauren die?"

"Someone shot her."

"I see," Rhiannon said after another long pause.

Gallagher pushed thoughts of Lauren Tanner out of his mind. It was no good dwelling on the past. Rhiannon was here, and alive. He had to make sure she remained so.

No one was waiting for them in Abbotsbury.

Gallagher said: "It looks as if the post wasn't manned, after all. No police. But we're not going to hang around, just in case."

"Are we still calling on Alicia?" Rhiannon asked.

"It's imperative that we do. We've got to put you out of circulation until I find out what the hell is going on. The man with the rifle could be anywhere. How well do you trust her?"

"Alicia? With my. . . . I was going to say with my life."

"Let's hope she never has to prove it."

They climbed out of Abbotsbury in silence.

After a while, Rhiannon said: "I'm sorry."

"For what?"

"The way I behaved."

"You didn't. . . ."

"Yes, I did. You know it. I was shocked to find out what you could do, when in fact I should have been thankful that you saved my life. I would have died out there on the beach if . . . if you hadn't been with me. No . . . wait. I've been thinking about this. If I hadn't met you at the party, I might have been down here alone, at the cottage. Christopher might have brought me down, but he would probably have gone back up to do whatever it is he's involved in; and I would have stayed in bed for a while, if you weren't here. I like a long lie-in on Saturdays. And that man . . . would have come into the cottage . . . and, and. . . ." She stopped, gave a slight shiver before regaining control of herself. "What a day this has turned out to be. It could have been the day of my death." She nibbled at her lip. "I'll be all right in a minute."

Gallagher said nothing, letting her get it out of her system. He drove at a leisurely pace, keeping a sharp eye on the mirrors. There was nothing in them to worry him.

"It shouldn't have come as such a shock, I suppose," she went on. "After all, I am a Navy brat. One is sometimes aware of certain things with a father in the armed forces. My father never spoke of some aspects of his work, even to my mother. I expect he met people like you at . . . at times. Then there's Christopher. . . ." She sighed. "As long as it never comes near you, it's all right. You feel detached. It's there, but not there. Like . . . like nuclear war. Everyone knows what would happen if things fell apart; but that knowledge would not lessen the shock if it *did* happen. Am I making sense? I'm just rambling. I'm sorry."

"I understand perfectly what you're saying," he told her gently.

Just before they turned off the road to take the track to Alicia Davenport's farm, she laid her hand lightly on his thigh.

"I'm glad you're here," she said softly. "For today, and for last night."

Her words made him feel good. He smiled at her, before glancing into his mirrors.

No one was following them.

7

Valley Farm was a six-bedroomed seventeenth-century main house with several scattered outbuildings, set in a hundred acres of land given to arable and stock. A long, winding paved drive led to the two-storied stone building. Alicia Davenport was waiting for them, looking very different from the last time they had seen her.

She was wearing a simple, elegant white dress that gave her a regal air, and upon her feet were white-soled sandals with thin golden cross-straps. Her hair was done up with a looseness that accentuated the regal impression. The attire went well with the strength of her features.

Gallagher said: "Looks as if Alicia decided to dress for tea."

"That's just to impress you," Rhiannon said. She gave a weak smile. Some color had returned to her cheeks.

"The old Rhiannon's coming back. Good. How are you feeling?"

"Despite the odd maniac with a rifle and two other homicidal loonies in a Range Rover, I'm not doing too badly. I think."

"You're doing fine. Now let's see how Alicia takes our news."

He brought the *quattro* to a halt, turned off the engine. Alicia came up as they climbed out.

"We'll have tea in the garden," she began; then her welcoming smile died as she looked hard at the expression on Rhiannon's face. Her eyes shifted twice from one to the other, trying to work it out. "Rhian? Have you two had a row?"

Rhiannon looked at Gallagher, as if waiting for his permission to speak. Alicia's puzzled eyes now turned back to him.

"Let's go into the garden," he said. "You'll need to sit down."

He reached into the back for the Nikon, then locked the car.

Looking even more puzzled, Alicia said: "All right."

She led them along the front of the house before turning right, through a long archway of vines and clematis. Several different species of roses bordered the grassy path, filling the air with the sweetness of their scent. The archway felt like a cocoon, a safe haven from high-powered rifles; an illusion, he well knew, it would be dangerous to dwell upon.

They came out on to a wide, stepped terrace that overlooked a large, well-kept garden. Tall, mature trees formed natural barriers on either side, stretching from the house to the far end, which was open, and looked out upon part of the farmland. Beyond that was a magnificent view of Abbotsbury and the beach, 600 feet lower down. The distant bank of shingle, Gallagher judged, was perhaps a good two miles away.

From where he stood, he could see several clumps of rich woodland scattered about the farm;

plus low shelter belts, planted in geometric patterns to protect young crops. Though Rhiannon had said that the property was at the end of the valley, the house and its immediate surrounds were on a small flat-topped hill, with an extensive view of the Davenport spread. The garden sloped gently toward Abbotsbury, finishing in a dip beyond its border of trees. The vegetation was a deeper hue of green, betraying the presence of water down there. The ground rose again from that point. The entire farm was a series of swooping, gentle curves. On some of the slopes, cattle stood around or munched with complacent indifference. Part of one paddock could just be seen behind an outbuilding and, except for the occasional lowing from the small herd in the distance, the place was peaceful.

"This is a pretty farm," Gallagher said to Alicia, "if you'll pardon the description. It's just that it looks so much like a painting. I hope you don't mind."

"I don't mind. I've got the best of both worlds. A pretty farm that's also efficient." Her smile widened. "And all run by a mere woman."

"No one in his right mind would call you a 'mere woman,' Alicia."

"He says such nice things," she said to Rhiannon. The smile faded when she saw Rhiannon's own smile was somewhat strained. "Oh, Rhian, I'm sorry."

Rhiannon said: "It's not what you think."

"Then you two haven't fallen out?"

"No."

Alicia brightened. "Oh, good. So?" she went on. "What is it?"

They had gone off the terrace and on to a long veranda that was thickly entwined with vines at each end. A table set for three was waiting, gleaming

whitely in the late afternoon sun. A few feet away
was a smaller table of white-enameled wrought iron.
Further along the veranda, a three-seat sofa of white
cane with white cushions sat in solitary splendor.

Gallagher said: "Someone with a rifle shot at
Rhiannon while we were on the beach." His words
sounded harsh in the peace of the garden.

Alicia Davenport's eyes widened with shock.
"What? You've got to be joking!"

"No joke," Gallagher said, and proceeded to tell
her the rest. Rhiannon joined in from time to time
when he made light of the part he had played in
their escape.

Alicia paled beneath her healthy outdoor tan as
she listened. Slowly, she took a chair and sat down.

"My God!" she said softly. "A man with a rifle
. . . and those two in the Range Rover. . . ." She shook
her head, bewilderment joining the horror already
marked upon her face. "But for what reason? Rhian,
who could possibly want to do such a terrible thing
to you?"

"Gordon thinks he has an idea."

Alicia's eyes turned to him.

"I'm still guessing," he said, "but there are some
people I may be able to talk to."

It was not something he looked forward to with
any pleasure; but the danger had to be deflected
away from Rhiannon.

Alicia was looking at him with a new understanding. "You know people who. . . . But of course
you would, if what Rhian's said is anything to go by.
She's only alive because of what you were able to do.
So who or what are you, Gordon Gallagher? And how
is it you're very conveniently around when someone
takes a shot at her?"

"I'll only tell you what I told Rhiannon. Once, I was on Her Majesty's payroll."

"That's all?"

"Yes."

" 'Her Majesty's payroll.' That can cover a multitude of sins—from policeman to postman. But you're not talking about those, are you?"

Gallagher smiled but said nothing further on the subject.

"I expected as much. . . . You remind me of someone I used to know." Briefly, Alicia's eyes looked into a personal distance. She stood up, said to Rhiannon: "You can come and help me with the tea."

"I don't think I could eat anything. . . ."

"Why don't you wait and see?" Alicia cut in briskly. "Come on."

French windows led into the house. She entered without waiting for Rhiannon.

Rhiannon glanced at Gallagher.

"She wants you to relax," he said. "Go in. Busy yourself. It will help. Have a chat with her. Tell her as much as you want to. I'll wait out here."

She hestitated. "I've seen you looking at the woods up on that hill. You . . . you don't think he's somewhere up there, do you?"

Gallagher shook his head. "No. I was just wondering how safe you would be here. I'm going straight up to London after I've had some tea."

"I don't want anything," she said. "I couldn't keep it down."

"Yes, you could. Now's the time you really need to. Have a little snack. You'll be surprised at how much of an appetite you'll suddenly have."

"Do you always feel hungry after something like this has happened?"

"It varies," he answered.

"Rhian!"

She gave a quick little smile. "The dulcet tones of Devonport, I believe. I suppose I'd better go before she comes back to drag me in by the hair."

He looked at her concernedly. "Are you all right?"

"Yes. Yes, I am."

And, when he continued to look worriedly at her, she added: "Really."

He kissed her gently on the lips.

"Hmm," she said.

"Nothing's going to happen to you," he promised. "I'll make sure of that."

The golden eyes looked steadily into his. "I believe you." Then she went into the house.

Gallagher turned to look down the garden. It was an intruder's paradise. There was so much cover. He surveyed the slopes beyond; the trees, the hollows. From a defense point of view, it was depressing. True, there was plenty of open ground; but a skilled attacker could come right up to the house without being detected. The house was itself quite solid, but he didn't like the french windows.

He smiled ruefully. This was a farm where people worked and lived in peace with as much contentment as they could manage; not a bloody fort.

Was he wrong in deciding to leave Rhiannon here? Going back to her own cottage was out of the question; so was taking her up to London with him. He wanted a free hand. Worrying about her safety in London would slow him down.

Yet. . . . He paused. He was being observed. The silent presence was palpable; and close. He felt a prickling along the surface of his skin. Whoever it was, was to his left.

For seconds that seemed like years, he remained quite still. It was odd, but the presence did not feel overtly hostile. It did not feel friendly either. He was being assessed.

With infinite slowness, Gallagher turned his head.

He found himself looking into the baleful eyes of the biggest Afghan hound he had ever seen. Its coat gleamed with health; but it was no pretty, pampered dog. This one was a hunter, with all the instincts of its illustrious ancestors clearly visible in its stance. Gallagher sensed it would be at him if he made the slightest of sudden movements, and it seemed prepared to bide its time till doomsday for him to do just that.

Man and hound stared at each other neutrally, each waiting for the first hostile move.

Gallagher was not certain for how long he had stood there keeping his eyes locked upon the dog's when Alicia Davenport's voice came from behind him.

"Trebi!" she scolded. "Behave yourself. Gordon's a friend."

The dog gave a little whine, but did not relax its stance.

"*Trebi!*" Alicia repeated, more forcefully. "Don't be silly."

Another whine, but the dog stayed.

"Oh, ignore him," Alicia said to Gallagher. "He's a decrepit old fool. He'll come round in his own time." She placed a tray laden with sandwiches and cream cakes on the table. She began unloading it.

Gallagher noted with dry amusement that Alicia Davenport always tended to give her pets sterling character references. Trouble was, the animals themselves appeared to have other ideas. The Afghan showed all the capabilities of being a thoroughly nasty bit of work if one were unfortunate enough to get on its wrong side. As for being old and decrepit, it looked in indecently good shape and could probably bring down a running man with the barest need to breathe faster.

Perhaps, with a beautiful monster like that around, Rhiannon would be safe here, after all.

He moved cautiously round to a chair and sat down facing the dog. It kept its eyes upon him.

Rhiannon came out, carrying the tea and milk. She saw the Afghan, smiled at it and said: "Hello, Trebi."

The dog looked briefly at her, gave two wags of its tail, whined for a third time, before fastening its baleful eyes upon Gallagher again.

"He seems to like you," Rhiannon said, transferring the tea and milk from her tray to the table.

"Really," Gallagher said, unconvinced. "Pity I can't see his smile."

"He's harmless," Alicia said to Gallagher as she took her seat. "He'll come to you and give you a great big lick. You'll see."

"As long as it won't be a tasting session."

"Oh, Gordon," Rhiannon said with mock reproach, "he's not going to eat you." But the strain of what had happened was still in her eyes.

Gallagher studied the shape of her mouth closely until she was forced to smile at him.

"That's better," he said. "And as for not being eaten, tell that to my baleful friend over there."

Alicia said: "Don't tell me you're afraid of dogs."

Not afraid of them. Some dogs he positively hated; especially if they were a pair of Ridgebacks coming at you through the bush, in a country where you had no right to be in the first place. O'Keefe had killed them both, with a knife, and had proceeded to do the same to their handlers, who had been following not far behind.

That's how to do it, sir. Nice and quiet. We don't want to warn their mates, do we now? Don't worry, sir. You'll get the hang of it soon enough. You're a natural.

A natural. Accolade indeed from the hard-boiled Warrant Officer.

O'Keefe. Gallagher wondered how his dead mentor would have handled this situation. He smiled at the dog, putting friendliness into his eyes.

The Afghan wagged its tail, lowered its head and came forward slowly, the wags growing in frequency as it drew closer. It reached Gallagher, placed its head upon his lap and gave a barely audible whine. He patted the head. The dog licked his hand briefly, then, satisfied, disappeared into the house.

Alicia was pouring the tea. "There. I told you. He just wasn't sure that you liked him. Harmless, as I said."

Gallagher wouldn't bet on it. "Why Trebi?" he asked. "Unusual name."

"Short for Trebizond."

"Very Byzantine."

"There's a little story behind it." Alicia seemed unsure about whether to go on. Her eyes had again become distant, as if remembering something, or someone. "Trebi is a gift. I got him as a puppy from Lino. Lino is, I mean *was* . . . umm, Rhian told you about him."

Gallagher glanced to his right at Rhiannon, not certain about how to react.

"It's all right," Alicia said. "We had a general talk about what happened today and Lino cropped up in the conversation. One day, he mentioned he'd been to Turkey; to Trebizond. The name, he said, had always fascinated him and he preferred it to its other name, Trabzon. When he got me the puppy, we decided to give it that name. Hence Trebi. Lino crashed that same year." She paused, the memory of that horror showing clearly in her eyes, then she brightened. "And that's enough of the past. Your tea will get cold. Try the ham. Genuine Valley Farm."

He began to eat. The ham was excellent. "Marvelous," he said appreciatively. Rhiannon, he was relieved to see, had rediscovered the need to eat and was tucking in without restraint.

He thought of Lino, the Italian Commander, going to Trebizond. On the northeastern flank of Turkey, the small Black Sea port stared out across a body of water nearly twice the area of the whole of Britain; and on the opposite shore was the Soviet Union. That same body of water was famous for something else: it was home for one of the most powerful naval fleets around.

The Russian Black Sea Fleet.

Unfortunately, there was only one exit to the open sea and that was through the 27-kilometer-long Bosporus, a choke point that gave every captain in that fleet nightmares. Gallagher wondered whether Lino had been a submariner, one who had played footsies with Russian ships in those dangerous waters. Choke points could work against intruders too.

Another train of thought claimed his attention: Lino the possible submariner, and Jameson the diver; Rhiannon and Alicia. All four were linked somehow, while hovering in the background was Turkey.

He shook his head. Too tenuous. He was constructing links where there weren't any. The real link was the simplest and most natural: a sibling link between Jameson and Rhiannon, and an emotional one between Alicia, Jameson and the dead Lino. True confessions stuff.

Except that someone had tried to put a bullet between Rhiannon's shoulder blades; and two men were lying dead in the Fleet.

Alicia was looking at him. "Sorted it all out?" she queried.

He was still deep in thought. "What? Oh, sorry. I've been rude. I didn't mean to be."

"You're working something out."

"Trying to, would be more like it. How many people do you have here on the farm?"

"There's a family in the biggest cottage; the Leggatts. Three generations of them have lived there. Tom Leggatt's the manager. He's got a wife and two sons. They're all part of the farm staff. Then there's Betty, who lives here with me and helps me look after this place. She's been like an older sister and an aunt at the same time. She's fifty-two, and I've known her all my life."

"Is she here?"

"No. She's holidaying in France. She's got a cousin in the Dordogne."

"What about casual help?"

"We get them when there's a need, but there's no one at the moment. Generally, between the six of us and the farm machinery, we manage quite well. Now I shall answer the question you really want to ask. It would be quite mad," Alicia went on before Gallagher could say anything, "to let Rhian go back to the cottage. So the answer is yes, we can look after her at Valley Farm. If you're worried about our being unprotected, I've got six shotguns and my father's hunting rifle in the house. I can use all of them, and I'm fairly certain Rhian knows how to point and shoot one. The Leggatts have got another three between them."

"I want no one else involved, and no guns going off, if you can possibly help it," Gallagher said. He didn't tell her of his quiet nightmare. If anyone got close enough, the shotguns would be virtually redundant. A massacre at Valley Farm was not something he wanted to think about.

"Then there's Trebi."

"I thought you said he was old and decrepit."

Alicia smiled. "He can be quite a guard dog when he wants to be. I'd strongly advise anyone against trying to sneak in here when he's in an aggressive mood."

"Somehow I didn't think he was a shy dog," Gallagher said.

Rhiannon said: "Now that the two of you have finished discussing my future, do I get a choice?"

"No," Gallagher said.

"Masterful, isn't he?" Alicia said to Rhiannon.

"And what's more," he continued, "you're staying in Dorset until this whole thing's sorted out."

Rhiannon stared at him. "But my work! I've got to be at the gallery on Monday."

"Sorry. You've got flu, yellow fever, cholera or anything else I can think of. I'll call them on Monday. You must have no contact, particularly not from here."

"You expect them to go to the *gallery?*" The consternation in her voice was matched by a flicker of fear in her golden eyes.

Gallagher said: "They knew how to find you down here. You can be certain they know where you work. By now, whoever these people are, they'll know their attempt has failed. They'll want to try again. That's why I want you out of the way."

Alicia was studiously smearing cream on half a tea cake. "While we were inside, Rhiannon said you believe this all has to do with Christopher." The blue eyes looked up at Gallagher as she bit into the cake.

"I think someone's trying to get to him through Rhiannon."

"But you don't know why."

"No."

"You don't know or you won't say."

"I don't know."

"Fair enough." It was clear she was reserving judgment on that. "Well. Don't worry about Rhian. She'll be quite safe here."

Rhiannon was still eating heartily. Gallagher knew it was a reaction to what had happened on the beach. With some people, it was drink; others smoked. Sensing his eyes upon her, she gave him a sheepish smile.

"I'm making a pig of myself," she said.

"Nonsense. You used up a lot of nervous energy down there. It's only right that you should replace it. I'd definitely be worried if you had not eaten at all, as you'd previously threatened. This means you're perfectly all right."

"Hmm," she said, and attacked a cream cake.

"I'll need your phone number," he said to Alicia.

"Of course."

"And a bolt hole."

"A what?"

"Somewhere else; a second line of defense in case it gets too hot around here."

Both Alicia and Rhiannon stopped eating, to look at him.

Rhiannon said: "What do you mean by 'too hot'?"

"It is just conceivable," Gallagher began to explain, "that they really have done their homework. They may know of the connection between Christopher and yourself," he went on to Alicia. To Rhiannon, he continued: "We've got to assume they know."

"So you believe they may come here, after all."

"I'm not saying that. I'm merely suggesting it's a possibility to be considered. Therefore, we need another place . . . just in case."

Alicia said: "I know some people. . . ."

"We shouldn't involve them."

"They've got holiday cottages. I could always say I wanted a few days on my own."

"Where are they?"

"A few here in Dorset; but, if you prefer, I can get access to others in Devon, or Cornwall. There's always mine, of course, although you might not like that idea. It's in Fleet."

"Fleet?" Gallagher turned to Rhiannon. "Is that the same place you promised to take me to? The half-drowned old village?"

She nodded. "Yes." She read the expression dawning on his features. "You're not suggesting. . . ."

"It's perfect. If you want to hide, do it in plain sight . . . in a manner of speaking. Few searchers think of looking. They expect you to put a lot of distance between yourself and the place you were last seen. There have been cases of deserters living quite openly in their hometowns, while their units scour the world for them. The same thing happens in wartime. The safest place to be is sometimes right inside the enemy's camp."

"What if the enemy has the same idea?"

Gallagher smiled tightly. "Good question."

Rhiannon suppressed a shiver. "Alicia's cottage

is close to the water's edge; almost directly opposite where those men went in."

"We may not have to use it; but if we do, there'll be a lot of activity around when the Range Rover is hauled up. Activity means plenty of police in the area. I don't think our man with the rifle would be too happy about that."

"As you've said nothing about going to the police yourself," Alicia began, "I assume you don't want them to know about this."

He shook his head slowly. "I know people who can handle it better."

Alicia stood up, a knowing smile on her tanned face. "Of course. I'm going to make some more tea. Refills, everyone?"

Gallagher said: "Not for me, thanks. I'd better be getting on. The sooner I get this thing cleared, the sooner we can all go back to a peaceful life." He, too, stood up.

Alicia said: "Oh. Well, all right. I'll give you two some privacy. See you by the car." She left them and went into the house.

He took Rhiannon by the hands and drew her up from her chair. The proximity of her body sent flutters of warmth through his.

"I want you to be very careful," he said. "Take no chances."

"I promise not to."

"Good."

"But I'm very worried about Christopher now. If anything's happened to him, that's it. My whole family will have gone." The eyes were wide with anxiety.

"Let's not jump to conclusions," he told her with gentle firmness. "We don't know what this is all about. Just you concentrate on remaining safe here. I'll handle the rest."

He hoped.

"All right," she said.

He kissed her gently on the lips.

"I hate goodbyes," she said after a while.

"This isn't goodbye." He picked the Nikon up from the back of his chair where he had slung it, then took her by the hand. "Come on. Let's go to the car."

They walked down the terrace and back through the archway to the front of the house. Alicia was waiting. Seated imperiously at her feet, Trebi greeted them with a brief movement of his tail.

"The two numbers," Alicia said, giving Gallagher a piece of paper. "The first is for this house. The other one's for the cottage in Fleet."

He stared at the paper, then returned it to her.

"But I thought . . ." she began.

"I have a way with telephone numbers."

"Of course," she said. "All part of having been on Her Majesty's payroll. The less you carry around with you, the less others are likely to find out."

"Something like that. If I call and ask you to leave," Gallagher went on, "I want the two of you out of here the moment you put the phone down. Don't hang about. Just go." He looked at each in turn. "Got it?"

"Aye, aye, cap'n," Rhiannon said.

Alicia smiled. "To hear is to obey."

"This isn't a joke," Gallagher said. While he didn't want to leave two nervous wrecks behind, he wanted them to feel afraid. Fear aided survival. Rhiannon appeared to have regained part of her irreverent spirit, but he wondered whether this was not some kind of overcompensation, her way of telling him not to worry. Perhaps.

"We'll be all right," Alicia said.

"Just be careful."

"I have to be. I want heirs for this farm."

Gallagher stuck out his hand. "Thanks for everything, Alicia."

"Any time," she said, and kissed him quickly on the corner of his mouth.

Trebi gave a little whine which could have meant anything from approval to disgust. Gallagher patted the dog's head. Its tail beat once.

He entered the *quattro,* clipped on his belt and started the engine. As the powerful motor rumbled into life, Rhiannon poked her head through the lowered window.

"As long as she's not thinking of you," she said in a low voice.

"What?"

"Heirs. She said heirs. She's got that predatory look in her eye."

"She's thinking of good Dorsetshire stock; not me." He grinned.

"Hmm."

"Keep away from strange men with rifles."

"And you keep away from Doria Luce."

"Doria Luce is the last person on my mind." Which was true enough.

"She shouldn't be there at all."

"She isn't. And now, I've got to go. Sit tight until I get back. I want you in one piece. Got it?"

She smiled. "Aye, aye, cap'n." The golden eyes seemed to engulf him; then her lips were soft and warm upon his.

At last, she withdrew from the window and stood back to watch as he drove away.

He looked in the mirror and saw them standing there, looking down the drive. The dog had stood up too. He hoped he would see them again. Alive.

He didn't wave. Neither did they. The time was 17.30.

The man drove the dark saloon into the car park of the small railway station, stopped and switched off the engine. He picked up the briefcase within which the dismantled rifle was once more concealed, and climbed out. The two-way radio was also in the case. He locked the car, pocketed the keys and began walking toward the town center.

It was six o'clock.

With a good three and a half hours of daylight left, the sun made him feel hot. While most people would have regarded the approaching June evening with pleasant anticipation, the man found the sun's warmth an irritant. He was not happy.

He had come to the Hampshire town of Andover in accordance with the instructions he had received prior to the job. It was all part of the planned sequence of events; but one of those parts had not slotted into the pattern.

The most important of all: the job itself.

The man walked down the slope from the station, followed the bend in the road and continued toward the town. His route took him past the Baptist church, across a main road and on to a bridge about thirty feet long which spanned the river Anton. The narrow water was a trifle sluggish here. He glanced down as he passed, more an automatic reaction rather than a look of interest. Some enterprising person had thought it a good idea to chuck a supermarket trolley off the bridge. It had been there for some time, for already strands of green were clinging to it. The man gave a passing thought to the stupidity of whoever had thrown the trolley over; then his mind returned to more pressing matters.

No one had told him the girl would have had company. *Hit the girl.* That had been the instruction. Nothing about a bloody man who would get in the way and cock things up. Who had been her companion? And where had he learned to move with such speed?

Obviously a minder. Someone had known enough to put a minder with the girl. That was the only explanation. Not a boyfriend then.

The man sighed with annoyance that he had not taken the risk and blown her away in Portland.

A sudden burst of laughter coming from a building to his right distracted him briefly. He looked. In a large room young women, it appeared, were being taught how to cook. On a Saturday? Perhaps they were having a party later. He looked away, walked on, his mind in turmoil and losing interest in the giggling students.

The road began to rise, up toward the church of St. Mary. The man walked past it, face grim. It angered him that he had failed. Failure was not the best advertisement with which to impress future customers. He had already been paid the first half of his fee. He liked to deliver. No delivery, and the news would travel fast. Bad news always did.

Against his wishes, he had been given a backup. He had never met the men in the Range Rover before; which was as it should be. In his business, familiarity bred something far more lethal than contempt. After he had reluctantly told them he had missed, they had gone off in pursuit while he made his own embarrassingly hurried departure from the scene. No time to check how they had got on. Not his part of the job. Do the hit and get out. That had been the deal.

Well, it was a screwed-up deal now.

He found himself in a pedestrian concourse, beyond which was a street market. There were many people about. Dotted among them was the olive green of unarmed soldiers. The man felt a brief tightening of his stomach muscles before he remembered this was England and not one of his more usual stamping ground, where every soldier and policeman sauntered about armed to the teeth.

He made his way off the concourse and into the market. Business was brisk and here the crowds were more densely packed. At the end of the market he turned right. The road passed over the Anton, which seemed wider and flowed more freely. It was also cleaner. He paused halfway across, to stare along it. He looked back, then ahead to the bus stops, where he had been told to wait. He glanced at his watch: 6.30. He was on time. He continued slowly across the river.

Within five minutes of his arrival, a pale blue Rover pulled up opposite. At the wheel was a man of about fifty with a thinning mane of silver hair and a neatly trimmed silver moustache. He was wearing what seemed a rather heavy sports jacket for the time of year.

The man crossed the road, went round to the passenger side of the car, bent forward to look through the lowered window. The driver was wearing cavalry-twill trousers. An ex-colonel, the man thought with sour humor. You could always tell. Even in retirement, they wore their uniform.

"I'm Jones," the man said.

"Of course you are," the other remarked, in clipped military tones. "I'm Smith. Get in."

Jones, whose name was as false as that of his new companion, did not show the contempt he felt. He had once served in the British Army and had not risen above the rank of private during his term of service. It had been an uneasy relationship; but he took what they had given him and had turned it to profit: a classic example of private enterprise, he thought wryly.

Jones climbed into the Rover, which began to move almost before he had shut the door. He placed the briefcase in the footwell, next to his left leg.

They drove in silence for some minutes as Smith steered the car out of Andover and on to the A303, heading for Marlborough. Another pale blue Rover took up station some distance behind them. Smith appeared not to notice.

It wasn't until they had branched on to the A342 four miles later, past Weyhill, that Smith said: "Well? What happened?"

The man who called himself Jones found that he resented Smith's manner. Despite the years in his chosen profession and the quite substantial amount of money he had made—enough to buy this cavalry-twilled colonel several times over, he was certain— he still felt a bridling deep within him. He took his time replying, ignoring the several pointed glances he received from Smith. The silver moustache appeared to be bristling with impatience.

"Going to put me on a charge for dumb insolence?" Jones asked with a mildness he did not feel. He was still angry about having missed the target.

Smith tightened his lips, but did not answer.

At last Jones reported what had taken place, in an emotionless voice and in fine detail.

When they were past Ludgershall and had gone right to join the A338, Smith said: "Can't be helped. Mistakes occur."

Jones did not like what that implied. *"I* did not

make a mistake. Nobody warned me about a minder."

"You should have taken him out first."

"I thought he was a boyfriend. No one mentioned taking out a boyfriend. I was paid for one target . . . well, part-paid. I won't ask for the remainder, naturally. I accept full payment only on full completion of the contract."

"That's kind of you. I am certain my principals will look favorably upon your gesture."

The man called Jones glanced suspiciously at Smith, looking for traces of sarcasm upon the slightly reddened features.

Too much port, he thought disparagingly.

"The other two did not make it," Smith said abruptly.

"He got them both?"

Smith gave a tiny shrug. "They have not been in contact for several hours. Given what you have said, we must assume the worst. Interesting boyfriend, that, wouldn't you say?"

Jones said, tightly: "I'll complete the contract. You can have him as a bonus."

"Very generous," Smith said, but then shook his head regretfully. "I'm afraid we must pass this one up. If he is what we now think him to be, you've already been sufficiently exposed. He'll be taking some kind of action. She'll be put somewhere safe, and he'll be alerted to a second try. No, Mr. Jones. We must use different methods, in view of the circumstances. In the meantime, we must get you away. You have left the car as instructed?"

"Yes." Jones searched in his pocket, brought out the keys.

"Put them in the glove compartment, will you?"

Jones complied.

"Thanks," Smith said. "Everything will be taken care of. The car is being moved, even as I speak."

For a while they drove in silence, each to his own thoughts. Some distance behind, the other blue Rover tagged along. Smith still did not appear to notice. He made no effort to elude it.

They drove along the A338 to Burbage, where the road changed into the A346. At Stibb Green, on its outskirts, the road curved left through the tiny village.

Smith said: "Not much longer now. My job's to deliver you. Others will take over."

Jones grunted. It could have meant anything.

Just after Stibb Green, the road came to a narrow bridge that crossed the Kennet and Avon canal at Burbage Wharf. It was then that Smith began to pat his left jacket pocket, as if hunting for something. The bridge required careful negotiation and Jones looked at him with faint annoyance, clearly not liking his one-handed driving.

"Damn!" Smith exclaimed as a car coming the other way nearly scraped them; but he was not thinking of the other motorist. "Never can find the bloody pipe when I want it."

Jones's expression showed plainly what he thought of pipes.

Smith noted it with a glance as they left the bridge. "Hate smoking, do you? Sorry, old boy. Been smoking my pipe for years." His voice indicated he had no intention of stopping. "Look into the glove compartment, will you? I must have left it in there. Always leaving the wretched thing all over the place. Got several at home because of that habit."

Jones waited long enough to register his displeasure before complying. Smith continued to pat away at himself, changing hands at the wheel to do so.

Jones had the compartment open and was foraging unwillingly within it. While he was thus engaged, Smith's hand dived swiftly into the right pocket, came up again with what looked like a child's toy pistol. He brought his hand across his body and fired from beneath his left arm, just once.

The pistol made no discernible noise above the sounds of the car; but its effect was out of all proportion to its size. It had fired a single short dart into Jones's body. The dart, with a small transparent head, had penetrated the clothing to embed itself deeply into the flesh beneath. Once there, the head shattered, releasing a tiny drop of highly concentrated taipan venom into the bloodstream. Toxins of sufficient power to kill a few thousand sheep went to work on Jones. He had just enough time to turn to stare at Smith, eyes wide, lips drawn back tightly across his teeth in the rictus of approaching death, as his nerve centers began to fall apart. He died strapped to his seat, continuing to stare at Smith with undiluted hatred.

Smith completely ignored the man he had just killed, and concentrated on his driving. The lethal little weapon had been returned to its hiding place as swiftly as it had been brought out.

The road took the Rover toward the ancient forest of Savernake. Older than the Norman invasion of Britain, its 2,300 acres of rich woodland was crisscrossed by narrow tracks and footpaths, and was skirted by the A346 on its southwestern border, on the way to Marlborough. The Rover cruised along unhurriedly, shadowed by the second car.

After about a mile, Smith turned right into the forest. The heavy rains the day before had made the track muddy and the Rover gave a brief, jerky slide every now and then on the slippery surface. Jones's grinning corpse made little marionettelike movements with each slide. The face, particularly the lips, had become discolored.

Smith drove slowly. The wheels hissed loudly on the mud, flinging soft lumps against the car's clean bodywork, smearing it so that within seconds it looked as if it had spent all day on such roads. There were no other vehicles to be seen. The condition of the tracks had apparently kept them away.

Smith was pleased. It was as he had expected.

Just before a sharp climbing bend to the right, he came to a parking place of short grass strewn with gravel. He pulled off the track and stopped the car. He looked at the grinning body of the man who had called himself Jones.

"This is as far as you go," he said to it.

He unclipped his belt and reached into the back for a pair of wellingtons that had been placed in the footwell behind the passenger seat. Slipping off his shoes, he put on the rubber boots; then he reached expressionlessly across the body to take the briefcase. He removed the keys from the ignition and put them into a jacket pocket. He searched for and found the dart he had fired. He pulled it out. A red band of blood circled the top of the stem. The detachable head had separated neatly.

He dropped the used dart into the same pocket that now housed the car keys, then he inspected the interior of the Rover minutely. Apparently satisfied, he next fished into the door pocket and brought out a neatly folded, dull-colored plastic bag, which he shook open. He put his shoes into it. Finally, after another quick scrutiny of the car interior, he picked up the bag and the briefcase, let himself out.

He shut the door quietly, walked round to the front. He stooped, reached for the number plate and pulled. It came away with a soft click, to reveal a different one in its place. He put the detached number plate in the plastic bag and went round to the back, where he repeated the performance. The displayed license number now matched the one on the front.

The man who had identified himself to Jones as Smith gave a tiny smile, as if enjoying a private joke. He looked casually about him, without haste. He was still alone; but perhaps not for much longer, he decided. Despite the state of the forest floor, someone was bound to turn up eventually, even at this time of day. A casual motorist could ruin everything.

He listened, but heard nothing to betray the approach of a car. It was time to leave.

Deliberately, he walked round the Rover twice, leaving footprints to give the impression that people had stopped to gape at what was inside; then, choosing his route carefully so as not to leave any tracks marking his departure, he set off into the forest, away from the muddy road.

About twenty minutes later, he was approaching a point that would take him back to the A346, some two miles from Marlborough. He stopped before reaching the road and stood out of sight, in a position where he had a good view of a long stretch of it. There was moderate traffic; but he was not interested in the number of vehicles that passed. His attention was fixed upon the pale blue Rover waiting at the side of the road: the second Rover.

He took his shoes out of the plastic bag, exchanged the Wellingtons for them, then stowed the boots with the number plates. He waited for a long break in the traffic before walking out to the road, choosing a route that left his shoes free of mud. He crossed over quickly and entered the car, which moved off swiftly the moment he had shut the door. Neither he nor the driver spoke as it headed at speed for Marlborough.

Its number plates were exactly the same as those in the plastic bag.

8

Gallagher turned off Holland Park Avenue and into the side road that would take him to the three-bedroomed maisonette he called home. The dimensions of the place were generous, taking up the upper part of the substantial Edwardian house it shared with a garden flat. He considered himself lucky to have found it just over four years before, when he'd been trying to get over Celia. It had its own entrance at the side of the building, with a carport thrown in for good measure. He was comfortable there.

He swung the *quattro* off the road and into the carport, paying a cursory glance at the cars parked in the street as he did so. He saw no white Rovers that would have betrayed the presence of the Department. At least, they had not yet come sniffing.

Directly opposite his home the road forked, branching off to the right and curving out of sight a hundred meters later. He stopped the car, climbed out, gave the curving fork another look. No white Rover. It didn't necessarily mean anything, of course. The surveillance team could well be parked out of sight.

He shrugged. The Department was a constant

irritant in his life, an itch that had to be scratched now and then.

He opened the boot and took out his equipment case. First job was the development of the shots he had taken on the beach. It was just possible he had caught the rifleman in transit, and an enlargement might help toward possible identification. He shut the boot, locked the car and went up to his front door. It was 7.30.

He had just inserted the key into the first of the three locks when he caught movement out of the corner of his left eye. Removing the key, he turned slowly to face his visitor.

A man in a pale brown suit, bouncing cockily on the balls of his feet, was approaching. Gallagher waited, feeling that the itch was ready for scratching.

The man was shorter than Gallagher, and slim; a bantamweight with a long neck and a birdlike face. Short dark hair lay flatly upon his head. Hollow cheeks came down to a pointed chin and a small mouth. His dark eyes looked mean.

He stopped before Gallagher, legs spread aggressively, head pushed forward on the long neck, hands thrust into pockets.

An errand boy, Gallagher thought sourly; not one of the Department's personnel, but someone from an outside section. Police, perhaps. Not from Fowler. Whatever his differences with the Department's second-in-command, Gallagher knew Fowler never used outsiders if he could possibly help it.

The bantamweight said: "Right, sunshine. Someone important wants to see you." London accent, with the faintest trace of the East End.

Definitely not from Fowler, Gallagher was now certain. A summons would have been brought by a bona fide member of the Department. Winterbourne, perhaps? That was more his style.

Gallagher stared at the newcomer, his own eyes cold. If Winterbourne thought he could be pulled in like this. . . .

"Gone deaf, have you?" the birdman said, head jerking backward and forward once. The eyes were beginning to turn nasty. "Not going to give any trouble, are we?" The cheeks sunk more deeply and the mouth got smaller and tighter.

"Tell him to make an appointment," Gallagher said quietly, and turned away. He did not show the anger he was beginning to feel. After what had happened on the beach today, he wanted to hit out at someone. Winterbourne's heavy-handed approach— if it were indeed Winterbourne—through this head-jerking nincompoop was not helping. Calmly, he reinserted the key into the lock, refusing to be goaded.

He was not given a choice.

From behind, tight with its own sense of outrage, came the bantam's voice: "Don't you turn your back on me when I'm speaking to you, sunshine!"

Gallagher knew with resignation what was about to happen and knew, equally, what his reaction to it would be. He prepared himself for the inevitable.

As the quick steps approached, he released the key, leaving it in the lock. His left hand was now free, fingers outstretched, hard edge of palm ready to strike. In his right hand was the camera case.

The bantam's hand grabbed savagely at his right shoulder, intending to pull him round.

Gallagher moved faster. He whirled, left hand cutting across viciously, the camera case swinging at the same time. The slashing hand connected with an exposed upper arm, spreading the flesh beneath the clothing to make painful impact with the thus unprotected bone. At the same time, the camera case slammed into the side of a vulnerable knee.

The bantam screamed with the shock of the double blow and tried to grab at both wounded arm and knee simultaneously. Failing, he staggered back and fell to the ground, mouth wide open in agony. His right arm was now useless and he was having a hard time trying to decide which part of his body was suffering most. His left hand kept shifting frantically from arm to knee, in a vain attempt to ease the pain.

Unmoved, Gallagher watched him, ready for any sudden effort to rise for a further attack; but the bantam had had it.

"You . . . you bastard!" he finally got out through gritted teeth. "You've broken my fucking arm!"

"I don't like being grabbed," Gallagher said calmly. "And your arm's not broken. I only tapped you."

"You lying bastard! It feels broken." The eyes were murderous in their pain.

There were heavy, running footsteps. Gallagher looked away from the fallen bantam to see who it was. A big man, sixtyish, balding, was hurrying toward him. The newcomer seemed vaguely familiar.

Gallagher stood his ground and waited.

The big man slowed, looked from Gallagher to the bantam, then back to Gallagher once more. He made no move to help. He stopped before Gallagher.

"You didn't have to hit him so hard, Gallagher," he said pleasantly. "He was only running an errand."

Gallagher stared at him. "I know you, don't I." It was less of a question than a statement.

The big man smiled. "I'm dormant these days. Creeping old age, you know. We met briefly, once. A long time ago. You were with O'Keefe then."

"Haslam," Gallagher said softly, remembering. "Somewhere in Africa. You were meant to be a newspaperman at the time."

Haslam said, with a touch of wistfulness, "Alas, I am no longer active. I've been reduced to liaison. Youngsters like you run the show now."

"Oh, no, you don't," Gallagher said quickly. "I'm out. And I've been out for some time."

"Of course."

From the ground, the groaning bantam said: "Are you two going to stand there talking about old times or are you going to do something about me, Haslam?"

Haslam stared down at him as if he were a particularly unpleasant bug. "Stand up, Prinknash. You're not badly hurt. There's a good lad."

Prinknash was scandalized. "My bloody arm's broken! He broke it!" He stared at Gallagher venomously.

"Nonsense," Haslam said. "Even from here I can see it isn't."

"It's not your bloody arm."

"You must have done something wrong, Prinknash."

"I only did what I was sent to do."

Haslam looked at Gallagher. "Did he?"

"Why not ask him?"

Haslam looked down at Prinknash, whose hand appeared to have decided that the knee hurt most. "Exactly what did you do?"

After a pause, Prinknash said, grudgingly: "I asked him to come along. . . ."

"Just that? Just 'come along'?" Haslam was skepticism itself.

Prinknash counterattacked. "Nobody told me he was one of ours. . . ."

"I'm not one of yours," Gallagher interrupted coldly.

"And you're certainly not one of mine," Haslam added to Prinknash. To Gallagher, he went on: "No point trying to get anything out of him. You will come, won't you?"

"You're so polite. And if I don't? Are you going to strongarm me, like our little friend down there?"

Haslam said: "So that's what happened." He sighed exaggeratedly. "The trouble we have with the help these days. Strongarm you?" He was amused. "I don't think so."

"Who wants to see me?"

"Winterbourne."

"Ah, yes. Winterbourne. I might have guessed. I didn't think you'd run errands for Winterbourne, Haslam."

Haslam's face remained neutral. "Winterbourne's Head of Department now."

"Everyone knows it's Fowler who really runs things. Does he know about this?"

Haslam chose not to answer. "Look . . . why don't you simply come and talk to the man? That's all he wants to do."

"Come on, Haslam. Pull the other one. Winterbourne doesn't want to talk. Either he thinks I'm involved in something, or he wants to involve me. You know the answer to that already."

Haslam sighed once more. "Well, I've done my job. I've told you. Don't wait too long. Winterbourne might send others who are not as nice as Prinknash."

Suddenly Gallagher knew why Haslam had not warned his younger colleague. It had been his way of getting back at Winterbourne. Covert mutiny in the ranks.

Gallagher said: "You teach a harsh lesson."

Haslam's eyes showed he knew what Gallagher was getting at. He glanced at Prinknash. "As I said . . . the help's pretty ropey these days." He began walking away.

From the ground, Prinknash cried: "What about me? Haslam!"

"You can walk," Haslam said, not pausing.

Prinknash glared at Haslam's receding back, looked round at Gallagher. "You bastards," he said softly, face still pale with pain.

"It's a hard life," Gallagher said. He watched, making no attempt to help, as Prinknash began to struggle to his feet.

Prinknash at last succeeded. His mean eyes looked at Gallagher. "Bastards," he repeated, and began to limp after Haslam.

Gallagher waited until both men were out of sight before he eventually let himself in. Despite the noise, no one had come to look. In London, people tended not to interfere.

He had barely entered when the phone began to ring. The answering machine would cut in at the fifth ring. He did not hurry. The phone stopped.

He went to the darkroom, began to unload the camera. The phone started to ring again. The extension was next to the answering machine. He put down the camera with a sigh, switched off the machine and picked up the phone after the fourth ring.

"Gallagher," he said.

"I think you should come to see us." Fowler. "You might learn something of interest."

"You sound like a lawyer who's just read a will."

"Close," Fowler said dryly. "But I'm not offering you an inheritance. I'm trying to keep both you and your young lady alive. Do come and see us, won't you?" Fowler hung up.

Gallagher slowly replaced the receiver. "Well, well," he said.

He unloaded the Nikon, put the cassette into a pocket and left the house. He would develop the film later. He climbed into the *quattro* and drove slowly into the street, heading for Kensington. At the High Street, he pointed the Audi's nose toward central London and the sleepy square that housed the Department's innocuous offices.

It was 20.15, and the Saturday evening traffic was already quite heavy. Gallagher turned out of the main stream and into a side street where he found a public telephone box. He stopped to make a call to Dorset, having decided not to do so from home. Nowadays, private lines were as secure as those in Iron Curtain countries. The Department, he was sure, would once more be up to their little tricks with his phone.

Alicia answered after the first ring.

"Oh, Gordon," she said brightly. "Are you already in London? That was quick."

"I arrived nearly an hour ago."

"Your car flies, does it?"

"I took it easy."

She laughed. "I know you'd really like to talk to Rhiannon, and she's practically trying to wrap the cord round my neck, so I'd better hand over to her. Be careful. We can't afford to lose you."

There was brief, giggly conversation off the phone before Rhiannon came on.

"I've got to watch that woman," she said breathlessly. Then, more quietly: "Are you all right?"

"I'm fine. How are things down your way?"

"No alarms. Alicia's loaded all the guns. It's like a fort here."

As long as they didn't have to find out just how secure their "fort" really was.

"Nice to know she's on her toes," Gallagher said.

Rhiannon gave a shaky little laugh. "She's being quite ferocious. The warrior queen."

"So's Rhiannon," he said.

"Ah, yes," she said. "But that was in another time . . . and she wasn't really a warrior."

"But she was brave, and she had magic."

"Yes. Yes. She was brave."

He could almost see the golden eyes. "I'm going to see some people now," he said. "The ones I told you about. I'll be in touch. Meanwhile, don't take any chances. Do nothing till you hear from me."

"All right. Gordon?"

"Yes."

"Please be careful. I don't want anything to happen to you, especially if Christopher. . . ."

"Now don't jump to conclusions. Let me find out what I can. I'll get back to you as quickly as possible. Take care of yourself, and I promise to be careful."

The line hummed to itself as each waited for the other to speak, hesitant about whether to put into words what they were feeling.

In the end, he said: "Take care."

"And you," she said quietly.

They hung up at almost the same time.

Gallagher went back to the car and drove off to his meeting with Fowler.

* * *

"Glad you could make it," Fowler said with a straight face. "I don't think we could afford more damaged people."

"*You* were responsible for sending that idiot?" Gallagher began as he took the chair Fowler had waved him to.

"Er . . . no. Haslam told you the truth. I . . . er . . . managed to persuade Sir John I should handle this."

"Convenient."

"Practical. Neither you nor I would really enjoy having a tangle with him. He's better off at his club. Shall we leave it at that? Coffee?"

"Tea, if it can be arranged, thanks."

"Tea it shall be." Fowler spoke into the intercom on his desk to order the tea. "God knows what it will be like. Arundel's away for the weekend."

"I did wonder how you'd managed not to haul her in. I saw her empty room on my way here."

Gallagher liked Delphine Arundel. A widow in her thirties, who had lost her husband—a colonel—in Northern Ireland, she had been Kingston-Wyatt's personal secretary. Now she was Winterbourne's; but her true allegiance, Gallagher knew, was to Fowler since Kingston-Wyatt was gone. She was also Gallagher's friend in the Department, something for which he'd had reason to be grateful on more than one occasion. He was disappointed by her absence. She tended to work almost as many hours as Fowler. No chance now of finding out through her what was really going on. Hearing it from Fowler was not a better option.

Fowler appeared to be smiling. "Sorry about Arundel."

"What do you mean?"

"Come now, Gordon. We both know she has a

soft spot for you. She does not always approve of the way you sometimes become . . . er . . . involved in our affairs."

"Ever since I resigned," Gallagher said, "I have never willingly become involved with this Department. You are well aware of that. Let's get the facts right."

"Whatever you say," Fowler acquiesced smoothly. "But this time, we are not guilty. You did it all by yourself."

Gallagher's disbelief was plain in his expression.

"I have some respect for you, Fowler . . . a little, but it's there. But there's one thing I do know: believing everything you say is more dangerous than playing Russian roulette with all the chambers loaded."

Fowler looked amused. "Such benign flattery."

"You said you were trying to keep me alive."

"Yes. You and Miss Jameson."

Gallagher waited.

Fowler said: "No questions? Don't you want to know how I know of her?"

"What's the point? You're going to tell me anyway."

Fowler's eyes appeared to gleam behind his glasses. "Let's begin with the death and destruction you have already caused this weekend. An hour ago, the Dorset police fished two bodies out of a drowned Range Rover in the Fleet. They don't know who you are, yet; but they did get a description of that car of yours. Seems a fisherman saw you playing silly buggers on the bank. We've told them you're one of ours, so you're off the hook—if you'll pardon the dreadful pun."

"Why do I have the feeling I'm going to have to pay a price for your altruism? Those men were trying to kill us. We were defending ourselves."

"Of course you were. Only to be expected."

Gallagher waited for him to continue.

Fowler said: "Why don't you tell me what happened in Dorset? You can skip the more . . . er . . . intimate details. Tell me what happened when you got to Chesil Beach. I shall want to know about other things, of course; but for the moment, the Beach will do."

Gallagher described the incident on the shingle bank in fine detail, leaving out selected items. He said nothing about Alicia Davenport, or Valley Farm.

"Now tell me what the hell's going on, Fowler," he said.

"Ah, the urgency of youth. Patience, Gordon. Patience. First tell me how you came to meet Miss Jameson."

Gallagher fixed his eyes upon Fowler's. "What are you getting at?"

"Do as I've asked. Please."

Gallagher sighed, and began with the party at Nellis's Thameside home. As before, he left certain things out. He made no mention of his conversation with Chris Jameson.

When he'd again finished, Fowler said: "Now tell me about Jameson himself and how you came to meet him."

"There's nothing much to tell."

"A man allows you to take his sister home after you meet her for the very first time. That requires a certain degree of trust, even in the present . . . permissive climate."

Gallagher shook his head slowly. " 'Permissive.' Now there's a word. It's all right to shoot people but not to sleep with them. I'd expect nonsense like that

from Winterbourne, but not from you . . . especially
in this job."

"I was not declaring my stand on the matter.
You know me better than that, Gordon; or ought to.
But that's beside the point. Go on about Jameson."

So Gallagher told Fowler about the assignment
at Silent Pool. Gallagher decided there was nothing
worth keeping back and filled him in on all the rele-
vant details.

"And that's the lot?" Fowler said.

"That's it."

"Right," Fowler began, then paused as the door
opened.

Haslam had entered with two plastic cups of tea.
Gallagher, who had begun to think the long-offered
tea had first to be picked, now wondered whether
Haslam's entry had been stage-managed. He would
put nothing past Fowler.

Haslam passed a cup to Gallagher, began to
drink out of the other. Fowler apparently wanted
none.

Gallagher said to Haslam: "Your appearance is
a bit on cue, isn't it?"

"Is it?"

"Oh, I see. We're playing games."

"No game, Gordon," Fowler put in. "I'll give it
to you from the shoulder. Naja is here."

"What?" Gallagher said in a soft, disbelieving
voice. He had never come up against the man the
entire world wanted to see dead; but the reputation
was well-known in Intelligence circles, even by those
like himself who had left the field for some years.
"He's still operating?"

"As strongly as ever. He never stopped. But I
suppose that, having joined the massed ranks of the
sheep, you couldn't be expected to know."

"Is that how you see your fellow citizens, Fowler? As sheep?"

Fowler smiled tightly, then went on: "You have other things to worry about . . . such as the fact that Jameson may be involved with Naja."

Gallagher now felt a chill spread through his entire body. Good Christ, *Rhiannon*. Against someone like Naja, neither she nor Alicia stood the remotest chance. Valley Farm was a death trap.

"But that's impossible," Gallagher said.

"What's impossible?"

"Jameson and Naja." Gallagher, remembering his conversation in the darkened Nellis garden, was already trying to find the connection. His expression gave nothing away.

But Fowler's eyes were fixed upon him. "There doesn't seem to be much conviction in your voice. Have you really told me everything?"

Gallagher was not fooled. "You're fishing. I cannot see any link between Jameson and Naja."

"Have it your own way," Fowler said calmly. "Jameson," he went on, "was a Lieutenant-Commander in the Royal Navy. Judging by the clothes you're wearing, it's obvious you're already aware of that." A twitch of a smile. "His sister will no doubt have told you that their father was also a Navy man. What she will not have told you, since she does not know of it, was that her brother was sometimes engaged on sensitive work."

Both Fowler and Haslam were looking keenly at Gallagher. This was beginning to feel more and more like an interrogation.

"We believe," Fowler carried on, "that Jameson was engaged by Naja to undertake a diving assignment. Jameson would not have known it was from Naja, of course. The contract would have been handled in the usual way: through an intermediary. Jameson must have become suspicious and Naja decided to apply a little pressure."

Gallagher was listening with increasing skepticism but gave no indication of it. The only thing Fowler's and Jameson's stories appeared to have in common so far was that diving was involved.

Gallagher said: "So you believe that it was Naja who tried for a hit on Rhiannon."

"It may not have been Naja who did the actual shooting, unless he deliberately intended to miss. Otherwise your young lady would now be as dead as mutton, despite your opportune presence. If that sounds rather cold-blooded, I fully intend it to be. I want you to appreciate the seriousness of the situation. We can help you, if you help us."

"Ah," Gallagher said. "Now it comes." He fought down his mounting anxiety. He wanted to get out of there and to a phone. Rhiannon and Alicia had to be moved.

"It's not what you think," Fowler said.

"It never is."

Fowler ignored the sarcasm. "I was talking about the film you took. Where is it?"

"Why?"

"Obviously, we'd like to see it."

"The thought did cross my mind."

"You used the zoom, you said," Fowler remarked, unmoved. "You may be able to get a reasonable enlargement in your darkroom; but the detail won't be sufficient for your purposes. Here, as well you know, we have the equipment to expand a tiny section of the print several times over, while maintaining resolution. We might get a face. Help us to help yourself."

Gallagher looked from Fowler to Haslam, who

was propping himself up against a wall, then back to Fowler. Much of what Fowler had said was true. Though not taken in by the mutual-aid speech, Gallagher decided to let him have the film.

He reached into the pocket where he'd placed the spool, lifted it out and held it toward Fowler, between thumb and forefinger.

Fowler looked at Haslam. "Can we have this seen to right away?"

Haslam nodded.

Standing up, Gallagher went forward to place the film on Fowler's desk. "I'll be back within the hour." He went out before they could say anything.

Fowler stared at the closing door. A full minute passed.

Then Haslam said: "How much of that do you think he believed?"

Fowler smiled ruefully. "Gallagher has an automatic response to what this Department says, and to me in particular, now that Kingston-Wyatt's gone. He expects me to be devious."

"So what's new?"

"Which means he believed very little." Fowler lifted his glasses to pinch at the bridge of his nose. "It also means he knows a lot more than he's let on. I'm not the only one who's being devious. It seems rather convenient that he was so neatly on hand when the hit was attempted on the girl. Knowing Gallagher, I'm prepared to bet he's got her somewhere safe; for the moment."

"Shall I have him followed?"

Fowler shook his head. "He'd only spot it. He'll be back. He wants to see that film as much as we do. Here's irony for you, Haslam. I believe he would have come to see us of his own accord. He wanted us to develop that film for him."

"Are you going to let him see it?"

"Why not? It's his film."

Haslam shook his head slowly, as if in wonder. "Devious is not the word."

"Not flattery from you as well, Haslam?"

Haslam went to the desk, picked up the film. "I think I'll go and have this done." He paused at the door. "I'm glad I'm retiring soon."

But Fowler was not listening to him.

As the door closed quietly on Haslam, Fowler said to himself: "The question is . . . how much does Jameson really know?"

Out in the street, it was a nine-thirty twilight. Gallagher got into the *quattro* and drove out of town, heading north, to join the M1 at Hendon. He left the motorway at the first service station and went to a phone. He called Valley Farm. This time, it was Rhiannon who answered.

"Gordon!" she began. "What—"

"Get Alicia," he interrupted. "Leave the house."

"Now?" Disbelief. Voice shaky with a sudden fear.

"Right now. This minute. This second. Immediately." *Bloody hell. Move! Don't argue!* Gallagher's mind churned frantic messages at her.

She didn't waste time. "All right," she said. "Here's . . . here's Alicia."

"Gordon? By the expression on Rhian's face I take it you want us to leave."

"Right first time. No time to explain. Just do it."

"Yes. Yes, OK. I'll take the guns."

"Take all. I hope to God you won't have need of them." *If they're frightened, they won't take stupid chances.*

"So . . . so do I. Do you . . . want to talk to Rhian?"

"No. Just go. I'll be in touch."

"Right."

The line went dead.

As he drove back to London, Gallagher hoped he had been in time. He tried not to think of both Rhiannon and Alicia lying in pools of their own blood in the centuries-old house. The last of the Davenports of Valley Farm. He hoped Alicia would one day give birth to her heirs.

He tried not to think of Naja stalking toward the building as night fell upon Dorset; for there would be nothing he could do to prevent the inevitable.

Rhiannon and Alicia ran out of the darkened house toward the Landrover. The guns were already aboard, with spare ammunition. Both women wore jeans and dark shirts, Rhiannon in borrowed clothes that fitted somewhat loosely.

They had barely spoken after Gallagher's call. Now, as they climbed into the vehicle, Alicia said: "He must think those people, whoever they may be, are coming here." She started the engine. It sounded appallingly loud in the approaching night.

"What about Tom Leggatt?" Rhiannon asked.

Their voices were tense with fear of the unknown and the unexpected.

"Oh, God," Alicia said indecisively, "I don't know. We shouldn't tell anyone where we're going. Tom will be all right," she added, as if trying to convince herself.

She drove away quickly, the lights of the Landrover bouncing on the surrounding vegetation, flickering through the hedges.

"He'll hear the Landrover and wonder."

"I know," Alicia said in a worried voice. "But we can't stop."

"I agree."

The back glow of the lights played eerily upon their tautened features. As soon as they'd made it to the road, Alicia kept flicking anxious glances at the rearview mirrors, dreading the prospect of seeing a pair of lights in them.

She drove toward Portesham, retracing the route Gallagher had taken earlier. No one appeared to be following. They made it to the Fleet roundabout safely. The unmarked road to the old village passed through the ruined iron portals of what was once the entrance to a private estate. As Alicia turned on to it, she had to pull in to the roadside for a small police car coming toward them.

The car stopped. The driver had recognized the Landrover.

"Miss Davenport," he greeted. "Good evening." He peered up at her.

"Good evening, Jack. What are you doing here?"

"Had some excitement earlier today, down in the Fleet."

"In the Fleet?"

"Yes. Some people were fooling around in a Range Rover on the bank. They went in. Nasty business. Navy lads from Portland, frogmen, had to fish 'em out."

"You mean they're *dead?*"

"I do mean that, Miss Davenport."

"My God. What could they have been doing?"

"Who knows what people will get up to these days?"

"So who's down at Fleet?"

"Oh, everybody's gone now. I'm the last," the policeman said. "I got the call. First in, last out. Story of my life." He sighed. "Got to be off, Miss. Lots of paperwork for me to do. I shouldn't wonder." The car began to ease away.

"Goodnight, Jack," Alicia said, and continued along the road with relief. "If he had decided to poke around, I don't like to think of what he'd have said about the loaded guns."

"You seem to have got on quite well," Rhiannon said. "Why would he want to search us?"

Alicia gave a shaky laugh. "For the first time in my life, I think I know how a criminal feels on seeing a policeman. I didn't feel I was talking to a man I've known for years. Suddenly, the uniform made Jack a different creature altogether; and all because of those guns and what happened today."

"You sounded absolutely normal."

"Perhaps I should have been an actress."

They smiled at each other in the gloom of the vehicle as the Landrover bounced along the unlit road.

Gallagher stared at the photographs on Fowler's desk. No one had followed him out of London and no one had followed him back. That could mean anything: for instance, that Fowler was sufficiently confident for the time being. Which was not necessarily good news.

Fowler said: "As you see, we've got a face. Damn good shooting, Gordon."

Gallagher picked up one of the enlargements. It was grainy, but the quality was good enough for identification. Fowler's people had managed to expand a small section from one of the sequences and had come up with a three-quarter view of a face partially framed by foliage. All things considered, they'd done a good job.

"Recognize him?" Fowler asked.

Haslam, who was once more giving the appearance of propping up a wall, stared at Gallagher interestedly.

Gallagher shook his head.

"Well, I can tell you it's not Naja," Fowler went on. "Chummy here is well known. Mercenary service in Indo-China, Africa and Central America. He's good, but not up to Naja's standards by a long, long way. So we've got to assume the attempt on Miss Jameson's life was a sub-contract and that Naja, whoever he is, is floating about freely, controlling things like some invisible puppet master. This man, incidentally, is Mike Colthen, formerly of Bootle, Lancs, now of Dayton, Ohio. Why Dayton, I hear you ask? Why not? Perhaps he feels safer there than in Bootle. He was once an Army private. He's been known to do . . . er . . . legitimate work on the other side of the pond. I'll get in touch with a few people over there to see if they can give us anything about his recent movements."

"I doubt if you'll get much," Gallagher said. "Certainly, not enough to lead you to Naja."

"The thought had occurred," Fowler said calmly. "But one must try everything."

There was an unspoken sigh in his voice which Gallagher did not believe for a second.

"Well?" Fowler queried.

"Well, what?"

"What are you going to do now? What's your next move?"

"I haven't got any next move. I'm simply going to stay out of his way. He's your problem, Fowler."

"Yours too . . . now. He'll still be after Miss Jameson. Naja does not know the meaning of giving up. That's why he's so much in demand to those who would employ him."

"I hope that makes him very happy."

"Be careful, Gordon. Don't bite off more than you can chew."

"I like small morsels. I have a living to make: so I'm going home, and I'm going to play my answering machine through to see if there are any jobs waiting for me. Talking of which . . . I suppose you're tap dancing on my phone again." Gallagher walked to the door, turned to face Fowler and Haslam. "I ought to charge the phone people. They're not giving me the service I pay for: a *private* line."

Haslam said: "Prinknash sends his regards." He appeared to be smiling.

"I'll bet he does." Gallagher went out.

Haslam said: "He didn't take a photograph."

"He doesn't need to," Fowler said. "Colthen's face is stamped into his memory. He'll know him when he sees him."

"You expect him to go after Colthen?"

"I expect everything, and nothing," Fowler replied enigmatically.

"Ah, well," Haslam said after a pause. "I'm off to bed. You ought to try it. Works wonders, I've been told."

Fowler's brief smile was tinged with weariness. "Thanks for coming out, George. I'll call you if I need to. Have a quiet Sunday."

Haslam eased himself off the wall. "I'm getting too old for this sort of game. People my age potter in gardens."

"The day you start pottering in gardens I'll take up knitting."

Haslam smiled. "At least, I can cook."

Fowler said nothing. His attention was already occupied by a transcript he had picked up.

"Goodnight, Mr. Fowler," Haslam said, and let himself out.

The transcript had come in during Gallagher's absence, and it confirmed that Selim Antak was a real businessman with relations in Eskesehir. Fowler had studied the information four times, searching for anomalies. There were none that he could detect.

Of course Selim Antak was real, he thought sourly. Naja would not have been so clumsy; but it did not mean that the conveniently placed Mr. Antak had not been impersonated.

Ryszynskow, Antak, Colthen, Jameson . . . all in some way tied to Naja, with at least one being the man himself.

Ryszynskow.

But he would be someone else now. Of that Fowler was quite certain.

"I'm getting closer," Fowler said to himself quietly. He picked up one of the photographs of Colthen, stared at it for long moments. "I'm getting closer," he repeated.

Gallagher decided to go to Chelsea to make his second call to Dorset. No one appeared to have trailed him. He had taken a long circuitous route and now stopped near a phone box on the Embankment.

He got out of the car quickly and entered the cubicle. The phone at the other end rang just once before it was picked up by Alicia.

"Any problems?" Gallagher asked immediately.

"None. We're settled in nicely. All doors and windows are secure."

"Good. Does anyone know where you are?"

There was a hesitant pause.

"Alicia?"

"We . . . we met someone I knew . . . on the way."

Oh, Christ. "Who?"

"Jack Moone. I've known him for years. He's all right. He's a policeman."

Brilliant. "How did that come about?"

She told him, while he shut his eyes in exasperation at the way the unexpected was always waiting round the corner to trip you up. Well, it couldn't be helped now.

"Is that very bad for us?" Alicia was saying.

"We'll have to live with it for now," he said. "Let's see how things go. Are you all right for food?"

"All sorted out. We'll have no need to leave here for a week, if need be; but I'd rather not. There's the farm, and I'm sure Tom will be very worried if I don't turn up in a day or so. He'll. . . ."

"Ring him tomorrow. Tell him you're up in London. You had to leave urgently. . . ."

"In the Landrover?"

Shit. "I'll think of something when I talk to you tomorrow. May I have a word with Rhiannon, please?"

"Of course."

"I'll have to make this brief," he said when she had come on the line. "I've been using this box for too long as it is." He peered through the small panes of glass at the traffic. No car appeared to have cruised past or paused near the *quattro.* "Are you all right?"

"Yes. I'm fine."

It was good to hear her voice.

"As soon as you're up in the morning, I want you to call me so that I'll know you had a trouble-free night." He gave her his home number. "You're not to speak. Let the phone ring once, hang up, ring again in two minutes, and again let the phone ring just once . . . then hang up. Have you got that?"

She repeated his instructions quickly.

"That's it," he confirmed. "Now off you go. I'd better get out of here."

"Gordon?"

"Yes."

A pause. "Nothing . . . just 'Gordon.' "

"Goodnight, Rhiannon," he said gently.

"Goodnight." Her voice was soft, almost inaudible on the line. It told him much. He longed for her presence.

He left the phone box pensively, thinking of a frightened Rhiannon down near the Fleet. His senses, however, were on full alert. He watched the road carefully before reentering the *quattro*. There was still nothing to worry about.

As Gallagher drove home, he wondered where Mike Colthen now was.

2

No one was waiting as Gallagher steered into the carport, and no one came at him as he locked the car and went up to his front door. Everything was so normal, it made him highly suspicious. He entered the house, secured the door behind him.

Anyone trying to break in would have a very noisy job on his hands. The door was the only point of entry at ground level and was thick enough to make a quiet attempt impossible. The only other ways in were through the double-glazed windows, which would remain closed, despite the warmth of the night. Each window was also protected by an electronic beam alarm. Gallagher did not envisage anyone trying to scale the outside walls.

He went into the darkroom to replay the messages left on the answering machine. Some new business calls, but again, nothing urgent. Several clicks: more people who hated these machines. Charles Nellis wanted a meeting at his office on Monday; then there was Doria Luce.

"Here I am again on your dreadful machine, darling." Her voice sounded even more unashamedly sensuous on the tape. "If your little

Welsh pudding has decided to let you off the hook, it would be nice to see you on Sunday. I'm having a little get-together in the afternoon. Lots of lovely people you'd like to meet. Hope to see you." This time she left her address and telephone number.

Gallagher wondered what Fowler's tappers would make of the message. Probably all scribbling down Doria Luce's private number.

No one tried to force an entry into his house that night and at seven the next morning the phone rang once. He timed it. Precisely two minutes later it rang just once again.

He relaxed. At least Rhiannon was still safe. Perhaps the quick move to the cottage had been the right thing to do, despite the meeting with the unexpected policeman. Gallagher remained in bed for a while, trying to prepare himself for whatever the day might bring.

He was not, however, prepared for the call that came at eight o'clock. The phone had begun to ring and there was an imperiousness about it that defied indifference. Reluctantly, he picked up the extension near his bed.

"You'd better come over, Gordon," Fowler's voice said in his ear. "Mike Colthen's dead." Fowler hung up.

Gallagher felt a familiar unwelcome chill come over him as he slowly replaced the receiver. Colthen *dead,* Fowler had said. The assassin assassinated. By whom?

He climbed out of bed.

Take your time about it, sir. If you hurry and you make a mistake, the whole thing will go up in your face. Then it won't matter how much time you've saved, will it?

O'Keefe at his most sarcastic on how not to disarm a booby trap, near leaking aviation fuel.

By the time Gallagher had got out to the *quattro,* he was fully in command of himself. The shock of the news about Colthen's death had dissipated, was just another fact to be taken into consideration. The man must have been dead since at least the night before, if Fowler had just received news of his demise. Gallagher resisted the urge to call Dorset; the two rings on the phone in the pattern he had agreed with Rhiannon proved that everything was still all right down there. Better first to hear what Fowler had to say.

Gallagher checked his car mirrors all the way to the square, without detecting anyone following. Even so, after he parked he went for a walk that lasted twenty minutes before he returned. Still no one was trailing him. This time, he was not thinking of Department personnel, but of an emissary from Naja.

Or perhaps Naja himself.

"I have a theory," Fowler began as soon as Gallagher entered, "that more dead bodies are found by early walkers and children than by police forces." He looked fresher than someone who had spent most of the night awake had any right to be.

"The police would probably agree with you," Gallagher said. "So who found Colthen, and where?"

"Man and wife and child, enjoying a brisk perambulation in Savernake Forest. When most people would like nothing more than to stay in bed on a Sunday morning, there are always those who get up with the lark to commune with Nature. Without them, God knows how many of the world's crimes would go undetected.

"They found a blue Rover," Fowler went on, "with a man in it who proved to be dead. According to the police, the husband had hysterics, the wife fancied herself as an expert in rigor mortis, and the child poked at the body as if that would make it return to life. She was completely unafraid. She'll go far," he added dryly.

"What do your experts say?"

"Colthen was killed by a tiny puncture in the right of his abdomen. Early reports suggest that he was poisoned by a most potent toxin: taipan venom. According to the reports, a dosage sufficient to make a sheep farmer bankrupt was used on Colthen. The state of the body amply demonstrates that, apparently. Not a pretty sight; which must prove that nothing shocks children nowadays."

"Or that particular child. Perhaps she's just ghoulish."

"It's the cinema," came a voice from behind Gallagher. Haslam had walked in. "They see more horrible stuff on the screen."

Fowler said: "Perhaps Bootle would have been safer for Mr. Colthen. Naja does not like failure."

Gallagher said quietly: "When you first heard, did you think that perhaps I was responsible?"

"Not unless you had already developed another film and knew Colthen's identity. Besides, the time factor was all wrong. You're good, but not that good."

"And I don't go in for snake venom."

Fowler ignored the sarcasm. "But you were thinking of going after Colthen, weren't you?"

"All this is news to me."

"I don't think so, Gordon." The eyes behind the glasses stared at Gallagher.

"Can you read my mind as well, Fowler?"

Fowler tried reason. "Look, Gordon . . . you know all about Naja's reputation. Jameson and his sister are within his sphere of interest, with all the unpleasant connotations that brings in its wake. *You* are now within his sphere of interest, by association with those two. Worse, you've cocked up his plans and taken out two of his helpers. The third, he took out himself. Where do you think he's going to strike next?"

Gallagher said nothing.

Fowler replied to his own question: "At Miss Jameson, and at you. You need help, Gordon. Tell us where Miss Jameson is."

"Why?"

"She needs to be kept safe."

"She's safe."

"Are you quite sure? What if, despite all you may have done, Naja is still able to get to her—are you prepared to take the responsibility for what might happen?"

"You tell me what this is all about," Gallagher said. "Why is Naja here in the first place?"

"If we knew the answer to that, we'd be much closer to nailing him."

"I wonder why I don't believe you?"

"It's your suspicious nature."

"That's what kept me alive when I used to work for you lot, plus the fact that I've got good reason. I haven't forgotten what happened to Lauren Tanner."

Fowler sighed. "Are you going to blame us for that forever?"

"Who knows?"

Before Fowler could comment on that, there was a discreet knock on the door and a young woman entered, a message sheet in her hand.

"Hello, Mr. Gallagher," she greeted pleasantly, with an enigmatic smile. She put the paper on Fowler's desk and went out again, after another brief smile.

Gallagher turned to look at the door, before asking: "Do I know her?"

Fowler, who was reading the message, shook his head without looking up. "But she knows of you. Your reputation's quite a legend in this neck of the woods," he added humorlessly. "No prints," he went on. "No bloody prints." He sounded exasperated. He put the message to one side and finally looked up. "They found no prints on any part of the car. He must have worn special transparent gloves, or coated his hands with a spray. Ordinary gloves would have put someone like Colthen on his guard. Damn, damn, *damn.*"

"Well?" Gallagher began. "Are you going to tell me?"

"Tell you what?"

"About why Naja is here. I distinctly remember asking you that same question a few minutes ago."

"And I distinctly remember giving you an answer."

"Oh, well," Gallagher said. "I'd better be going. Thanks for ruining my Sunday lie-in." He turned to Haslam. "How silent you are. Goodbye, Mr. Haslam."

Fowler said: "I'm serious, Gordon. You're in very deep."

"Goodbye, Mr. Fowler."

As Gallagher left, Fowler looked on expressionlessly.

Haslam now said: "Those brief rings he received earlier on, do you think they were signals?"

"Do you?" Fowler countered.

"Yes. I'd lay odds they were from the girl, letting him know she was all right."

"Possibly. But for how long? One thing is certain: they were not from Jameson."

He studied the report. "Stolen car, naturally. It was reported missing from a pub car park in the Norfolk Broads area three weeks ago. Belongs to a doctor."

"That will teach him to drink and drive."

"She," Fowler corrected. "And she wasn't drinking. Went to pick up some friends who had been."

"Whoever did the stealing must have had the false plates handy and since Naja never does anything without thorough planning. . . ."

"They took that particular pale blue Rover for a definite purpose."

"A sister car?" Haslam suggested.

"That's my reading of the situation."

"Which could mean the 'false' plates genuinely belong to the car they're using now."

Fowler nodded. "We could be quite wrong, but it's a thought."

"Do I brief the police? Mark you, with all the pale blue Rovers there must be in this country, they'd have a job finding it."

"No, George. We keep them out of that part of it. In the most unlikely event of their stumbling upon that vehicle, think of the fate of the unfortunate bobby who made the discovery. The population of policemen would be down by one, maybe two, if a pair were on the scene. No; leave it. Naja is teasing us. Let him have his fun . . . for now."

It was all too bloody easy, Gallagher thought, as the *quattro* idled along a virtually deserted Piccadilly. The mirrors showed no one tagging along. No one had touched the car either, to put a trace device on it; the remote in his pocket would have bleeped dementedly. Too easy by half.

He aimed the car into the underpass at Hyde Park, heading for Knightsbridge. Suddenly, flashing lights caught his attention. The mirrors reflected blazing headlamps and twinkling blue beacons. A yelping siren assaulted the quiet morning.

His lips tightened. So now it came.

He drove out of the underpass and pulled into the side of the road, the police car almost on his rear bumper now. It didn't stop. It seemed to launch itself from the mouth of the short tunnel, doing at least 70 miles an hour and still accelerating, a white banded Rover hurtling away with the cry of an injured dog. Its stop lights glared as the driver slowed momentarily to turn left at speed into Sloane Street, across a red light.

Gallagher sat there for some seconds before pulling back into the road. It could have been a genuine patrol car on its way to a call or it might have been one of Fowler's little psychological tricks. The traffic lights were green by the time he reached them. He followed the route the police car had taken, drove to Sloane Square and turned right on to the King's Road. A few hundred meters later, he pulled up at a café that in fancy lettering proclaimed itself a bistro. The aroma of freshly made coffee came pleasantly to him as he left the car.

It was ten o'clock and the early warmth of the sun promised a fine summer's day.

Émile Dujon, the owner of the bistro, was a transplanted Frenchman who had once committed the unpardonable sin of admitting to French friends that he actually liked roast beef and Yorkshire pudding. Gallagher thought it only fair that he should sample Dujon's wares from time to time. The quality of Dujon's simple cuisine was borne out by the fact that the bistro was invariably crowded.

There was another reason why Gallagher used the place. He had once done publicity photographs for Dujon which had so pleased the Frenchman that an easygoing friendship had resulted between them.

"My God," Dujon began as soon as he saw Gallagher, "have you no home to go to?" His English was a mixture of London and Parisian accents. He peered at the *quattro,* noted there was no one else. "The girlfriend has kicked you out? So early on a Sunday?"

"Put your dirty mind away, Émile," Gallagher said with a smile. "I've come for breakfast."

"Full, unhealthy English? Or decent Continental?"

"Since I don't want you to have a nervous breakdown, I'll take the Continental . . . with lots of coffee. I think I need it."

Dujon winked at him. "The night was so bad? All right, my friend. I shall find you a nice quiet table where you can be with your sorrows in peace."

"It's not what you think. . . ."

"Of course, of course," Dujon interrupted soothingly. "A man does not like to talk of these things. Come. I know just the table for you. I will have Clémence bring the order. She will cheer you up. You are her hero ever since the pictures you took of her for the bistro publicity appeared. She has had offers from—" Dujon made a face of disdain—"what I would call not very stylish publications, to appear without many clothes on. I said no, of course, although they offered her plenty of money."

"I'll bet they did."

Clémence was seventeen and had the physical

attributes such magazines liked parting with substantial amounts of cash for. She was also Dujon's daughter. She lived in France with her mother, who hated London, and came over during the holidays. Clémence, unlike her mother, loved London almost as much as did her father.

"There," Dujon was saying. "The table in that corner. Very private for a man with the sorrows of the night." He grinned conspiratorially.

Nearly every table was full of loudly talking people, it seemed; Gallagher wondered how they found the time to eat, so busy were they trying to impress each other. The table Dujon had found him had a row of empty ones separating it from those that were occupied.

"Will this do?" Dujon asked in a pleased voice.

"Perfectly."

"Good. I shall tell Clémence you are here. After that, I must play the Frenchman to my customers. We shall talk later?"

Gallagher nodded as he took his seat. "Thanks, Émile."

"Vous en pris."

Gallagher watched with amusement as Dujon went from table to table, chatting briefly to diners who lapped it up, wanting to show their friends how intimately they knew the proprietor. Dujon was no fool: he knew how to make vanity pay.

From where he sat, Gallagher had a good view of the *quattro*. If anyone came near it, he would see instantly. He could also see a good stretch of the other side of the road, which was gradually filling up with cars belonging to the steady stream of people arriving for breakfast.

He watched them idly, while reviewing the results of his two sessions with Fowler. Something did not have the right smell about it. In a way which was still unclear to him, he believed that Naja, Jameson, Rhiannon and the Department were linked far less tenuously than Fowler had chosen to indicate.

He cast his mind back to the very beginning, starting with the photo assignment from Nellis. Nothing odd there. Nellis was one of his best customers. Gallagher doubted that he knew of what was happening. Although the security services sometimes used people from all sorts of professions on a one-off or even a continuous basis in particular circumstances, the Department had a strict rule: no outsiders. To work for the Department, you had to belong.

So Nellis was out. Jameson?

Highly likely. Ex-Navy, some sensitive job experience; knew of O'Keefe, and thus Gallagher too. But why admit it? And how true was that story about two friends . . . well, one friend with a companion . . . dying in underground waters somewhere in the Midlands? Then there was the approach, and the convenient presence of Rhiannon. . . .

Did Rhiannon work for the Department? It would make some kind of sense, given her background; but he was disinclined to accept that. Someone had tried to kill her; Naja, if Fowler could be believed. The gunman, and the murderous Range Rover, were facts. Gallagher tended to believe that Jameson, having failed to get him as a diving partner, had settled for some kind of protection for his sister.

Was the failed attempt therefore a warning to Jameson to complete whatever job he had been set? Or to keep away? If Jameson was on Department strength, had Fowler set him on Naja's tail? Which was probably as close as one could get to a kamikaze job in peacetime. It still did not explain flooded mines in the Midlands.

The only thing Gallagher was certain about was that Fowler was being less than truthful, if not lying outright; and that would not have mattered, had not his own neck been neatly placed on the line.

And had he not met Rhiannon.

"My crazy father says you have worries, Gordon."

He had been staring out at the *quattro,* his mind occupied by the nagging questions. The smell of freshly made coffee, hot croissants, and Clémence's voice made him look up at her.

A pretty girl with long, dark brown hair that had a natural reddish tinge to it. The genes of an Irish mercenary who had fought in the Huguenot wars, Dujon was fond of saying, were responsible. A Dujon damsel had fallen for the sweet-talking soldier of fortune and now, three centuries later, he was still making his presence felt.

Gallagher didn't know whether to believe Dujon. He smiled at Clémence, who seemed very happy to see him. She was wearing a bright yellow T-shirt and cut-down bermuda shorts. Male heads in the place were turning her way.

"Well, Clémence," he said as she put down her laden tray. "Every time I see you, you. . . ."

"Don't say I look more grown-up. You say that to me always." She began to place items from the tray on the table.

"But it's true."

She gave him a look of censure. "I am not a child, Gordon." Then she grinned as she placed a second cup on the table. "I am going to have breakfast with you. You can tell me all about the woman who threw you out last night."

"Threw me . . . ? Did your father give you that story?"

Clémence was unrepentant. "He told me you would deny it."

But Gallagher was not listening to her. A man who looked like a retired Army colonel was walking slowly round the *quattro.*

The man made no attempt to touch it.

In Portesham, Tom Leggatt was filling up the second of the two Valley Farm Landrovers with petrol. The small police car pulled off the Weymouth-Bridport road and drove on to the forecourt. It stopped behind the Landrover. Leggatt recognized the man behind the wheel.

" 'Lo, Jack," he greeted cheerfully. "Made you get up early, did they? On a Sunday too. Shame."

"A funny man you are, Tom," Jack Moone said, getting out of his car. "A very funny man." He smiled at Leggatt.

"What're you doing here, anyway?" Leggatt queried. "Run out of petrol chasing robbers?"

The banter was almost a set piece between them. When Moone was off duty, they usually downed a few pints together.

"The robbers are behaving themselves for the moment; at least down our way. But others are not."

The Landrover had taken as much as it could hold. Leggatt removed the nozzle, replaced it in the slot on the pump.

"What do you mean?" he said as he secured the petrol cap.

"Didn't you hear?"

"Hear what, Jack? Some of us have work to do. Can't ride along in cars all day, you know, listening to radios."

"Yesterday," Moone began, "two people went into the Fleet."

"You mean they went for a swim?" Leggatt was almost derisory.

"They used a Range Rover to do the swimming in. They drowned, still inside it."

Leggatt stared at Moone. "You mean dead?"

"I mean very dead, Tom."

"Kids?"

"Grown men."

"Why should two grown men want to do a thing like that?"

"That's what my bosses would like to know. I've been going round asking questions."

"Just you?"

"Oh, no. Got other patrols out."

"Hear anything?"

"We've got a few statements." Moone didn't say more. Being a friend and being a policeman were separate things.

He didn't tell Leggatt about the pair of fancy policemen who had arrived from London by *helicopter*. He'd heard someone say they were a Chief Superintendent and a Chief Inspector. They had come by *military* helicopter. Moone didn't think ordinary London policemen would have access to such things. He'd kept his thoughts to himself.

"Talking of the Fleet," he went on, "I saw your boss last night."

Leggatt frowned. "Last night?"

"Yes. On her way to the cottage."

Leggatt's face cleared. "Ah, so that's where they've gone."

"They?"

"Was she in a car?" Leggatt said, putting a question of his own. "Or in the other Landrover?"

"The Landrover. There was no car."

"That's funny."

"What do you mean?" Moone was rapidly switching to policeman mode.

"Well . . . " Leggatt began thoughtfully. "She had some friends up for tea. I saw them arrive. Lovely car. Black, mean-looking thing; but lovely. Rob was in one of the paddocks at the time. He's car-crazy, as you know. Said it was an Audi." Rob was Leggatt's younger son who had once been caught by Moone, for going broadside into a blind corner in a souped-up Mini. "A *quattro,* I think he called it. The rally car. Jack? Are you all right?"

Moone had a glazed look in his eye. "What? Oh, yes, Tom. I'm OK. I just remembered something I should have done. Look, I'll see you later."

Moone climbed hurriedly back into his car, reversed and drove quickly back on to the road, leaving a bemused Leggatt staring after him. He turned left, heading back toward Weymouth.

As he drove, he spoke into his radio.

The man who looked like a retired colonel had made two slow circuits of the *quattro* but had not lain a finger upon it. Now, he stopped to stare into the crowded bistro. He stood perfectly still, eyes probing the gloom.

Gallagher watched, feeling a primeval tension as they searched him out. He knew he could not be seen from outside; but, equally, he knew that the scanning eyes would eventually zero on the very table at which he sat.

Then they were upon him. Despite the fact that he knew he could not be seen, the challenge was implicit. Gallagher was certain he was looking into the eyes of the Cobra.

The man turned away and walked out of sight. Gallagher felt a sudden easing of the strange tension.

Clémence was saying: "Your coffee will get cold. I have poured it out." She looked round the café, obviously wondering what had so claimed his attention. "I hope you are not looking at other women," she added, only half-jokingly.

He gave a brief smile. "No. Not other women."

"Good. Eat your breakfast, then you can take me for a ride in your car. I have already asked Émile. He can spare me for the day."

Gallagher said: "He ought to be ashamed of himself, turning you loose on me."

"You're always teasing me," she said without rancor. "I'm not a child, you know."

"I'm twice your age."

"So?"

"And you're Émile's daughter."

"So?"

"So I behave myself."

"Ah," she said airily. "I know. You have betrayed me for another woman. My back is turned and you *mis*behave yourself."

Dujon came up to the table. "What's this? You two are arguing again?"

"She's arguing," Gallagher said, "and I'm listening as usual." He glanced out at the brightness of the day. The silver-haired man had not returned.

It was to be expected. Naja had already made his point. He had wanted to deliver his challenge in person.

Gallagher found it difficult to equate the man he had seen with the international assassin Fowler had talked about. The strange man had looked as old as

Haslam . . . at least; not at all like what one would have expected such an individual to be.

Perhaps that was why he was so successful.

Dujon said: "Clémence seems to have cheered you up, if only by arguing."

"I'm going to appear rude, Émile," Gallagher began apologetically, "but we'll have to postpone our little chat."

"You're leaving?"

"Of course he is leaving," Clémence said, staring accusingly at Gallagher. "He's going after that woman. I am going to have many, many lovers, Gordon. And you'll be so jealous and sorry that you ignored me for so long."

"Do you always let her go on like this, Émile?"

Dujon gave a good-natured shrug. "Who am I to argue with her? I'm only her father."

Gallagher shook his head slowly in resignation, leaned over to kiss Clémence lightly on the corner of her mouth. "I'll see you soon."

"When she throws you out again?"

"Behave yourself, Clémence. What will your father say?" Gallagher stood up, ready to leave.

"Her father will say," Dujon began, looking down at the table, "you have not eaten much. Don't you like my croissants?"

"I love them, but there's a little matter I ought to have seen to. Here, let me pay. . . ."

Dujon put out a restraining hand. "Don't be ridiculous. You've hardly eaten, and anyway, breakfast's on the house."

Clémence had got to her feet. "As you're determined to leave me here in slavery, I'll walk with you to your car."

"No!" Gallagher said, more harshly than he'd intended. He had nightmare visions of both Dujon

and Clémence coming into Naja's line of fire. It was bad enough with Rhiannon and Alicia, safe for the time being from immediate harm, in Dorset.

He hoped.

They were looking at him puzzledly, and a few heads at the nearest tables had briefly turned in his direction.

"No," he repeated quietly. "There's no need."

Dujon was now looking at him shrewdly. "What kind of trouble are you in, Gordon? Can I help?"

Gallagher smiled fleetingly. "You can't, Émile . . . but thanks for offering. It's nothing I can't handle. I'll be in touch." He gave Clémence a brief squeeze of the hand. "Not too many lovers."

She was looking at him concernedly. "Be careful, Gordon."

"Mr. Careful himself. That's me."

He left them, worked his way between the tables and into the warm, bright sun. He did not look about him, but simply opened the *quattro* and climbed in. He checked his mirrors as he clicked on his seat belt, and saw it.

The pale blue Rover was waiting on the other side of the road, about fifty meters away. For once, he would have welcomed the sight of one of the Department's white shadows but, like policemen, buses, and taxis, they were never there when you wanted them; only when you didn't.

Sod's infallible Law.

He felt the old tightening in his stomach. Would Naja try to take him here in this bright street, with so many people around?

Gallagher doubted it. Naja had not stayed alive for so long by acts of such incompetence. Naja would first be interested in finding Rhiannon. A killing now, while not necessarily counterproductive, would certainly produce nothing to further his plans. Rhiannon, however, was a vital lever on Jameson.

They would want Rhiannon first, Gallagher reasoned.

Which means, they'll follow me around.

Not so good.

Should he tell Fowler about the pale blue Rover and the retired "colonel?"

He sat there, fingers on the inserted ignition key, wondering. He turned the key. The engine burst powerfully into life. He put the car into gear and drove slowly off.

The pale blue Rover followed. It stayed sufficiently far behind so that Gallagher could not clearly see the occupants of the front seats; but he saw enough to tell him neither was the "colonel."

So where had he got to?

Perhaps I've got it all wrong, Gallagher thought.

Was the "colonel" perfectly innocent and had he merely been admiring the car? Gallagher shook his head. The feeling of an inimical presence had been too strong.

He turned right into Dovehouse Street, heading for Fulham Road. A while later, the Rover came into view.

There was no doubt about it now.

10

Jameson sat at the edge of the pond in his wet-suit and made final adjustments to his diving gear. He was going to make a solo dive into underground water, a foolhardy undertaking in any circumstances; but the situation, he convinced himself, warranted it. Besides, he had already made a previous dive.

What he'd seen had scared him; he'd written it all down and had sent the information to Gallagher the day before. With luck, the bulky letter should arrive at its destination on Monday morning. Now, he was going back down for the evidence.

He looked about him and could see no one. The pond was in a depression beyond the edge of which was the larger body of water where people usually came to fish. As yet, no Sunday angler had come. His earlier dive had taken place around 5 A.M. one Saturday, after driving up from London. It had been risky doing the dive but he had felt the occasion had merited it. What he had subsequently seen had amply justified his action.

He intended to make this dive, collect the evidence, then get away from here. Once that was done he'd be off the hook, and Rhiannon would be safe again.

He took another look around. Satisfied, he put on his mask and began to lower himself into the water.

The warning, when it came, was far too late for him to do anything about it. Some instinct of self-preservation urged him to look behind him; but with his attention concentrated on the start of the dive, his avoiding action began much too slowly. Someone landed on his back, pushing him beneath the surface. Another had ripped his mouthpiece away, causing him to gasp and swallow great quantities of water.

Despite the horror of his plight, he retained enough presence of mind to shut his mouth tightly and to try and release his air tanks. The assailant on his back seemed to be using them for purchase. Perhaps if he could get rid of the tanks that would cause the unseen person to lose his grip, temporarily leaving only one person to deal with; then maybe. . . .

But Jameson suddenly found his desperate struggles being effectively hindered. The second man had now got hold of both his legs and had wrapped vicelike arms about them. Unable to pedal his way back to the surface and the blessed air, he felt himself being dragged inexorably down. His chest began to hurt, but he continued to fight, mouth closed, using up whatever oxygen he had left.

Soon he could do no more. His mouth opened in a desperate last gasp and the water rushed into it, filling his lungs. Eventually, his struggles ceased.

The killers, who had alternately used the mouthpiece for taking in air, held on to the body and made their way back to the surface, dragging it up with them. They hauled it to the edge of the pond and left it there half in, half out of the water. They were in wetsuits, but without flippers or tanks.

They ran away from the body and disappeared into the woods that began a short distance from one side of the pond.

For over two hours they had been hiding there, waiting for Jameson.

Gallagher had been towing the blue Rover all over the place. He had never attempted to lose it, reasoning with a sense of wry acceptance that if they knew of the Jameson cottage in Owermoigne, they would know of the Gallagher maisonette in Holland Park. They were not interested in his home address, but instead wanted to know where he had hidden Rhiannon and assumed he would eventually lead them there. Then would they make their move. So far, they had appeared content to follow him at a discreet distance.

He wondered if they realized he was aware of their presence.

He had still not made up his mind whether to let Fowler know. Some instinct was pinging away inside of him, making him reluctant to do so. He chose to be guided by it. He would tell Fowler when it felt right.

One o'clock saw him, after a stop to fill up the *quattro*'s tank, on the A3 Esher bypass, heading toward Guildford. By now, his followers had become settled into the routine, and the Rover was cruising six cars behind. Gallagher decided the time had come for evasive action. The Oxshott exit of the motorway-standard trunk road was coming up, and he set his left indicators going in plenty of time to warn them. He took the road to Oxshott, knowing they would follow.

He kept his speed low until he came to a railway bridge, where he turned sharp left on to the B280 for Epsom. He accelerated gradually. Those in the car behind would think he was approaching his destination. A glance in the mirror showed the Rover had perceptibly increased speed. There were two cars in front of it, and it could not pass; which suited Gallagher perfectly.

Once out of the built-up area and entering Stoke Wood, he stamped on the accelerator. The turbo cut in, and the *quattro,* giving its imitation of a Phantom on afterburners, leapt ahead. The Rover was stuck, temporarily balked by the two cars filled with Sunday motorists. It was desperately trying to get past and with gleeful satisfaction Gallagher saw that it could not. Anytime now, it would do something risky and frighten the life out of the solid citizens having their quiet drive in the sun.

He intended to be well out of the way before they successfully managed to complete the maneuver. There was no one more infuriating than the self-righteous driver who hogged the crown of the road and tended to ignore the rest of the world about him; but today Gallagher loved those two drivers.

He came to the Malden Rushett crossroads and turned right, in the direction of Leatherhead; but he had no intention of going there. The road was virtually a 3½-kilometer straight before it ended in a fork with the A244. Gallagher let the *quattro* have its head. The digits on the speedometer blurred as the speed climbed. A quick look in the mirrors showed no sign of the Rover and he silently thanked the Sunday drivers. He hoped they would continue to balk his pursuers until he reached the fork, at least.

Once the Rover got to the crossroads, its occupants would have to guess his route from a choice of three directions. If they came down this way, he hoped they'd think he had taken the M25, heading east for Sevenoaks and Maidenhead.

He passed three cars before he got to the fork where he went right, back toward Oxshott; but only for about a kilometer. He turned left along a narrow road that connected a mile later with the A245 to Cobham. He went through Cobham and past the garage that kept the *quattro* in constant and fine tune, to rejoin the A3, going south.

He took the next exit five kilometers later, took the roundabout beneath the road bridge and doubled back. A short while later, he turned left into Wisley Common. He drove through Wisley village and followed the road round to the left until he came to a pub near a hump-backed canal bridge. There was a graveled car park off the road to his left, with plenty of room. Driving in, he parked the car as far away as possible. He climbed out, locked it and went across to the pub.

The place was right next to the water, a navigable canal, and had a patio with seating and tables for customers who liked to do their drinking in the open. There were only two occupied tables, one with a family group that spanned three generations. Gallagher hoped the men in the Rover would not find him here. If they decided to play rough and started shooting, he didn't want these people caught up in the crossfire.

As he entered the pub, he decided that it was unlikely he would be found. The Rover had not been in sight when he had taken the fork near Leatherhead. It would be searching all over the place for him, and he thought it likely that its occupants would head for the M25. They would reason he would go for fast lanes of the motorway.

He hoped.

From the pub, he made a quick call to Fleet. Rhiannon and Alicia were all right. No alarms there. Feeling easier, he ordered some food and spent a relaxed two hours on the patio watching boats, arriving from both directions, negotiate the canal lock.

After that, he drove home and, despite a careful lookout, never saw the blue Rover again. No one followed him at all. It was four o'clock when he arrived at the maisonette.

He chose not to get in touch with Fowler. Instead, he decided to go to Doria Luce's little get-together, as she'd called it. Later, perhaps, he would call Fowler. Gallagher still did not know how he was going to play it.

He took a shower, changed into black trousers with pouched side pockets, a plain T-shirt and lightweight pale gray jacket. They would have to do. He wore his soft black boots.

He drove to Doria's north London home in Totteridge, unsure of what to expect. Had the Rover been following him, he would have been quite happy to lead it there; but no hostile car appeared in his mirrors. Perhaps they were still on the M25.

Doria Luce's was a large house, secure within a walled garden. There was even a gate, with a man in attendance. Gallagher knew she was a popular actress, but never realized she made enough to live in such style. Maybe she had inherited. Still, it was none of his business. He had come in a bid to get away from both Fowler's and Naja's prying eyes; if only for a few more hours.

Gallagher would have to start his own countermeasures soon.

There were long lines of cars, some very pricey, parked on either side of the road, and he began searching ahead, looking for a likely slot within which to squeeze the *quattro*.

But the man at the gate was coming toward him. "Mr. Gallagher?"

Gallagher nodded, surprised.

The man smiled. "She said I wouldn't be able to miss your car. It's a beauty. There's a space reserved inside for you."

"VIP treatment," Gallagher said.

Now the smile had a knowing look about it. "You know Miss Luce, sir. She has her ways."

"I do indeed." He gave the man a little wave and drove through the gate.

Five other privileged cars were parked in a neat row along the wall, to the left of the gate. Gallagher reversed the Audi next to a bright yellow Ferrari two-seater, climbed out, and looked about him. Doria Luce's idea of a "little get-together" was a full-blown garden party. There were people everywhere; all over the garden and in the house, where they seemed to be bulging out of open windows and doors. The babble was unbelievable.

A small group was standing by the cars, some leaning against two of them. A brightly pretty young woman, in denim shorts, negligible blouse and bare feet, had turned to stare at him, then at the car.

"Wow!" she said.

Unsure whether she meant the car, Gallagher stamped on his vanity, and decided he had lost out to machinery.

An equally pretty young man had also turned in curiosity. "Wow!" he echoed.

"Definitely not me," Gallagher muttered to himself.

The couple detached themselves from their group and came toward him. Their companions turned to stare briefly before taking up their conversation once again. It was obviously not done to get excited about cars.

"Wow!" the girl said again as they reached Gallagher. She stroked the bonnet of the *quattro.*

Gallagher watched her with mixed feelings.

She smiled at him. "It's all right. I won't scratch it."

"Stroke her as much as you like."

She raised an eyebrow at him. " 'Her?' Mmmm. That says a lot."

"Does it?"

This was a ridiculous conversation. Both the girl and her companion appeared to have already had generous helpings of whatever alcoholic liquids were flowing at Doria Luce's gathering.

The man was saying: "I'm Peter Lassiter, and this is Jenny Pryce . . . with a 'y' of course."

"Of course. I'm Gordon Gallagher."

They shook hands, Lassiter surprisingly firmly and Jenny Pryce softly and lingeringly.

"So you're the one Doria's been talking about," Lassiter said. His eyes wandered over the car. "Bet she's fast."

"She is."

Jenny Pryce said: "Doria? Or the car?"

"Miaow!" Lassiter said. To Gallagher, he went on: "Professional jealousy. Jenny and Doria are friends and rivals."

"And you?" Gallagher asked him.

"Me? I'm in your line of business." Lassiter paused. "I'm a photographer."

"So we're rivals? Professionally, I mean."

"Good Heavens, no. Doria swears by you. I've never worked with her."

"I've only recently started."

"So she said. But you're obviously well-favored. We're parked outside with the rest of the plebs."

"Oh, come on, Peter," Jenny Pryce said. "There isn't the room in here."

"I was just making a joke," Lassiter said casually. "Can't you take a joke?"

Oh, great, Gallagher thought. *Just what I need. A lover's tiff.*

But he was saved by Doria Luce herself.

In an outfit that was as brightly yellow as the Ferrari and was just big enough not to be called a bikini, she came strolling up to them, tawny legs striding as if she were some great feline on the prowl. The dark eyes sparkled greenly.

"I see you've met Jenny," she said with studied unconcern. She put an arm through his possessively, glanced pointedly at the car. "No one with you?"

"No."

"Oh, good. 'Bye, Jenny. 'Bye, Peter." She steered Gallagher away, leaving the other two staring blankly after her. "I want you to meet some people," she went on to him. "I've been telling them about your work. They'll want you to do some for them too. Did Jenny ask?"

"Er . . . no."

"She'd have got round to it, the little minx. Can't keep her hands off anything."

Gallagher took refuge in silence and allowed her to get him a drink, which he intended to nurse throughout, and to introduce him to various people. He put his mind in neutral, tuning himself, building his resources to enable him to cope with the hornet's nest he had blundered into when he had taken the Silent Pool job for Nellads.

He recognized many faces from television and some minor ones from the wide screen. Doria Luce kept close to him at all times. At last, she dragged him away to a relatively quiet corner.

"I'm glad you decided to come," she said. "I was afraid the Welsh princess might have got her hooks in too deeply. Can't be too careful with these Celtic women." She smiled slowly, flecks of green showing in the darkness of her eyes. "So where did she give you your freedom? Does she know you're here?"

"No." An innate caution made Gallagher add: "She said something about having to see her brother."

"The monster from the deep?"

"The very same. God knows where she is. I didn't think it my place to ask. I've only just met her, after all."

"Don't I know it," Doria Luce said. "Well, her loss is my gain. Most of these people will be leaving soon. Why don't you stay for a while? And if you refuse me, I shall throw a tantrum."

"No, you won't, and I must refuse." He saw her eyes grow darker. "I am not turning you down."

"Is there another word for it?"

"I'm going to have to work tonight," Gallagher said carefully. "Charles Nellis wants to see me tomorrow morning. I'll lay odds he's after the rest of the shoot we did. You're in competition with your own publicity campaign. Do you think I want your wonderful manager Mr. Tramm on my neck? I had enough of that the last time. Where is he, by the way? Sulking?"

She smiled suddenly. "You really love him, don't you?"

"The feeling's mutual, I'm quite sure."

She sighed theatrically. "Oh, all right. Since you've put it that way, I suppose I've got to let you. I don't want any hassles from dear Mr. Tramm either. He hates my parties. That's why he's not here. But what about your Welsh pudding? What if she calls?"

"She'll get the same answer."

"In that case, let's mingle." She gave him a quick kiss on the lips.

"Right," he said, and suffered himself to be led back into the throng.

Rhiannon was safe. He could afford to relax a little.

Tom Leggatt heard the approaching car as he walked back from the main house. He always checked it when both Alicia Davenport and Betty were away, especially if the hound had also been taken.

He paused, waiting for the oncoming vehicle to make its appearance. In a few moments, a dark Jaguar saloon came up the drive toward him and stopped a few feet away. He walked up to it, stopped by the driver's door. He took one look at the man at the wheel and his past military conditioning made him assume he was looking at a retired officer.

"Can I help you, sir?" he inquired politely.

The stranger smiled. "I do hope you can."

Leggatt was now convinced he was in conversation with an ex-officer. "I'll try, sir."

"Is this the Davenport place?"

"It is."

"Ah. Thank God! I thought I must have got my directions scrambled." The man got out of the car and stood close to Leggatt. "Name's Petrie. Don't suppose you'll have heard of me. Family friend of the Jamesons'."

"Oh, yes, sir. You mean Christopher and Rhiannon."

"Yes, yes. That's it. Called at Owermoigne, but there's no one at the cottage. I was told they sometimes come up here. Someone was there yesterday, apparently. Haven't seen them in years, and, as we're down in the area for a spot of holiday, I thought we'd look in on them. My wife's down in Abbotsbury hunting a few trinkets, so I thought I'd pop up here. . . ."

Leggatt was nodding sympathetically. "I'm very sorry, Mr. Petrie, but you've missed them. Miss Jameson was here yesterday. . . ."

"Ah! Was she? We're in luck, after all. . . ."

"But she's with Miss Davenport."

"And, of course, they're not here."

"No, sir."

"Ah. . . ." Disappointment.

Leggatt, wanting to help, went on: "You could try the cottage."

"Cottage?"

"Miss Davenport's got a small cottage in the old village at Fleet. I believe she may have gone there with Miss Jameson. On days like this, she likes to be near the water but away from crowds. The Fleet's a favorite spot of hers."

"Very sensible. You suggest I try Fleet?"

"It's a thought, sir. I'm sure Miss Jameson would be quite pleasantly surprised to see you." Leggatt gave detailed instructions on how to get there.

The man smiled. "It's been some time since I saw her. One does not move around as often as one would like during retirement."

Again Leggatt nodded, understanding. "I know what you mean."

"Well, thank you, Mr. . . ."

"Leggatt, sir. Tom Leggatt. I manage this farm."

"Thank you, Mr. Leggatt. You've been of great

assistance to me. Saved me trundling about the countryside needlessly." The man who called himself Petrie looked about him. "You do a fine job here, Mr. Leggatt. You seem like a military man to me. Ex-Army? Navy?"

"Commandos, sir."

"I'm impressed." Petrie returned to his car.

"You've been a great help, Mr. Leggatt. Now I'd better get back to the wife before she works up enough steam to brain me." He smiled, full of friendliness.

"One other thing, sir."

"Yes?"

"Miss Davenport's got an Afghan hound. He can be quite fierce if he doesn't know you. If you see him outside the cottage, wait for her to talk to him. If Miss Davenport's not there, wait for her, if you've got the time. She may have gone for a walk with Miss Jameson. They like using the coastal path."

Again Petrie smiled. "I shall remember."

He turned the car around while Leggatt stood back to watch him; then, with a casual wave, he drove sedately away.

Leggatt watched the Jaguar until it had gone out of sight. It was as easy as that.

It was six o'clock.

Gallagher climbed into the *quattro* and started the engine. The timer glowed 20.10 at him.

He smiled to himself as he remembered Doria Luce's rearguard action. She had not wanted him to leave, but career interest had won in the end. She wanted her photographs on Nellis's desk as badly as Nellis himself.

"Leaving us?" someone called.

Gallagher saw Lassiter approaching. The *quat-*

tro rumbled quietly. He liked the slightly offbeat thrumm of its five-cylinder engine, despite the fact that many people he knew preferred the sewing-machine smoothness of a six. It didn't matter. This was just one of the many things about the car that appealed to him.

Lassiter came up, stopped clear of the car. "So she finally let you off," he said with a smile.

Out in the street, there was the sound of revving engines as a few early leavers tried to get out of their parking spaces.

Gallagher said: "Work to do."

"Ah ha. So that's how you're able to afford a car like this. Dedication."

"Something like that," Gallagher said.

From the street came the sickening crash of bumper on headlamp.

Lassiter gave a laugh of pure glee. "Oh, dear. Some poor bastard's had one too many. Or two, or three, or more. . . ." He let his words fade with a grin.

"Might have been yours," Gallagher suggested.

"Not a chance. I parked well away from here. I expected this. There'll be more. It happens every time."

"So you've been before."

"Oh, yes." Lassiter ran his hand through his blond hair. "I've known Doria since the days when she used to model bras."

Bully for you, Gallagher didn't say.

Something appeared to be wrong with Lassiter's eyes. Gallagher wondered why he hadn't noticed before. Lassiter appeared to be weaving slightly; but the eyes had nothing to do with being drunk. Then Gallagher realized what it was. The day was still bright enough for him to see. Each of Lassiter's eyes was subtly different. One had a tinge of green, the other of blue and, in certain lighting, both could appear to be either: green-eyed or blue-eyed.

"Where's Jenny?" Gallagher asked.

"Probably being screwed somewhere," was Lassiter's offhand reply.

Then, reading Gallagher's expression accurately, he added with some amusement: "Bloody hell, you didn't think I'd had anything to do with that little tart, did you?"

Gallagher shrugged. "You seemed close."

Lassiter gave another peal of laughter. "Jenny is close to anyone who stands still long enough. Given half the chance, she'd have screwed you in your fancy car."

Gallagher decided he didn't like Lassiter, but he kept his feelings to himself.

Another crash came from beyond the wall.

"What did I tell you?" Lassiter remarked with pleasure. "This is going to be fun."

"I'd better leave before they block the gate," Gallagher said. "See you around."

"I'm sure of it," Lassiter said, and stood back for the *quattro* to pass. "Nice," he added with appreciation. "Really nice." He raised a hand in a brief wave as Gallagher drove away and out through the gate.

Gallagher saw him standing there in the mirrors, watching, until the posts hid him from view.

On the way home Gallagher stopped at a phone box in Finchley, to call Rhiannon. He was still not being followed. He smiled at the thought of the Rover still cruising on the M25.

The phone at the other end began to ring; and continued ringing. Gallagher felt his heart miss a beat. *Come on, come on, one of you. Answer.*

He held the receiver to his ear, praying for a

reply. Christ. Where were they? He'd told them not to leave the cottage.

The phone rang forty times, and Gallagher found himself trembling. It just wasn't possible. No one could have got to them. He couldn't understand it.

On the forty-fifth ring, a breathless Rhiannon answered.

"Hullo. . . ."

"*Rhiannon,* for God's sake! Where have you *been?* I'm having kittens up here."

"Oh, Gordon . . . just a minute. . . ." She coughed, seemed to take a deep breath. "Sorry about that. I've had to run to catch the phone before you hung up."

"Why did you leave the house?"

"We . . . we didn't go far. Just up the road a bit, to give Trebi a run. I'm sorry, Gordon. I didn't mean to worry you. But Trebi needed to . . . well, you know . . . before we settled down for the night, and Alicia didn't want to leave it too late, for obvious reasons."

"Couldn't he do it alone? He's a big dog now . . . oh, I'm sorry. I suppose you both wanted a little air yourselves; but I can't begin to stress to you how important it is for you to stay out of sight."

"I know," she said contritely. "I'm sorry . . . oh, here's Alicia now."

"Gordon?" Alicia began. "Have you been bawling Rhian out? My fault. I dragged her out of the cottage for a breather. Sorry. It was a silly thing to do."

With all the bloody guns left uselessly and dangerously behind them. He said nothing about that.

"I promise we won't do it again," Alicia was saying, "but we'd left Trebi at the farm and this morning he turned up here."

"He *followed* you?"

"Oh, he's done it before. That's not so unusual. Animals do it all the time. A cat once walked for miles to find its owner who'd been taken to hospital. It even found the bed, jumped on it and promptly went to sleep."

Gallagher said: "All right, Alicia. But this has got to be the only time until the matter's settled."

"It won't be repeated."

"I'm sorry if I'm sounding harsh. . . ."

"I do understand. It's nice of you to worry about us."

"I wouldn't put it quite like that. . . ."

"You know what I mean," she interrupted gently. "I'll give you Rhian. Goodnight, Gordon."

" 'Night." Then Rhiannon was again on the line. "Have a good night," he told her, "and call me at eight tomorrow, exactly as you did this morning."

"Eight. All right."

"Take care."

"Yes," she said softly.

He hung up and left the phone box. He'd told her eight o'clock in case Fowler was hoping for a repeat at seven.

He got back into the car and continued his journey homeward. Something was nagging at him; something he'd wanted to ask. Ah, well, it could wait till morning.

But the feeling of unease wouldn't leave him.

He passed several phone boxes on his way back into town and, with each one, his worrying increased. He eventually gave in to his anxieties in Golders Green and stopped opposite a phone box in the high street.

He rushed out of the car and crossed the road. A middle-aged woman was in residence. She gave him a defiant look, turned her back on him and continued speaking. Five minutes later she was still there, while Gallagher's frustration grew. Her back remained resolutely turned.

He toyed with the idea of going further up the road to the tube station, but rejected it. The phones there were probably all vandalized. At least he knew this one was working.

He moved round the box to make urgent signals at the woman. She again turned away and went on babbling into the phone. Another five enraging minutes passed. At last, she hung up, taking her time about replacing the receiver. Then there were her plastic bags, in which were a couple of potted plants. She wasted a good thirty seconds trying to maneuver herself out of the cubicle with them.

Gallagher could not restrain himself from saying: "You should have bought the box, then you could have taken it home with you."

She glared at him, walked past stiffly to a spanking new Mercedes parked a few yards away, as Gallagher rushed into the box and began punching buttons. The woman put her plants carefully into the car, then got in and drove off on the wrong side of the road. It took the frantic hooting of an oncoming car to cause her to swerve dangerously over to the left, nearly clipping the nose of another car that had come up behind. That driver let rip with his own horns.

Gallagher shook his head in resignation as the phone in Dorset began to ring. Rhiannon picked it up almost immediately.

"Gordon!" she said in surprise when she'd heard his voice. "Is anything wrong?"

"No. Nothing wrong . . . just something I forgot to ask. Remember that policeman Alicia spoke to on your way down?"

"Yes." She was clearly puzzled.

"Have you seen him again? Has his car been patrolling the area?"

"No," she replied. "Surely, you don't believe. . . ."

Gallagher had shut his eyes briefly with a sense of relief. "No, I don't," he interrupted. "If Alicia's known him for years, I doubt very much we've got to worry about him; but the fewer people who know where you are, the better."

"Even Jack Moone?"

"Even Jack Moone, if that's who the policeman is. Jack Moone's got friends and colleagues who themselves have got friends and colleagues. Do you understand what I'm saying?"

"Yes, yes. I do." There was a pause, then she said: "Oh, dear."

"What do you mean?"

"Well . . . we did speak briefly to someone, but I don't think it's anything to worry about."

Gallagher found he was gripping the phone tightly. "Who was it?" he asked carefully. *Don't panic. Don't scare her. She must be all right. She's talking calmly to you on the phone.*

It didn't help. He was still trying to throttle the receiver.

"Just someone who stopped to ask us the way," she was saying. "Nice old man, really. He was completely lost. Looking for Bridport. . . ."

"Rhiannon! What was he *like?*" Gallagher felt himself trembling once more. It was silly. People got lost every day when they're out driving. Bad map-reading.

Even so.

"What was he like?" she repeated. "Oh. . . . He

looked just like everyone's idea of an ex-Army colonel, I suppose. Blimpish. . . ."

But Gallagher was not listening. His blood seemed to congeal, and a strange clanging seemed to have filled his ears.

"Rhiannon!" he was yelling into the phone. "Call Alicia and get the hell out of there! Call me at home when you're clear." It didn't matter now if Fowler got to know. *Naja was in Fleet. "Do it!"* he heard himself shout. *"Go!"*

"All right, Gordon." Her voice had become shaky. "I'm. . . ."

The line went dead.

There was a sudden silence in his ears. She hadn't hung up. She'd been about to say more and had been cut off in mid-sentence.

Oh, sweet Jesus.

Gallagher replaced the receiver, picked it up again, and again punched out the number of the cottage. The continuous tone of the "unobtainable" signal sounded like a death knell in his ear. With the horror of what might be happening down there forming itself into an increasingly tightening vice that seemed to wrench at his stomach, he slammed the phone down, picked it up for a third time. His fingers stabbed at the buttons as he called the Department.

Sod's Law being what it was, he thought bitterly, Fowler would at this of all times be unreachable.

The call was answered.

"This is Gallagher," he said. "Get me Fowler."

Already, the anger he felt was coalescing into something he would eventually use to terrible effect. He could feel the adrenalin pumping through him. His body was going cold; but it was no longer the chill of fear, or terror for Rhiannon's and Alicia's safety. It was the iciness of the organism preparing itself for the kill. If Naja harmed Rhiannon, then that was it. Whatever the purpose of his presence in the country, it had ceased to matter.

Naja's mission had been Fowler's concern. He had the whole Department with all its technology, its funds, and its personnel at his disposal, to enable him to cope.

Nothing to do with me, dammit, Gallagher thought savagely.

But it did concern him now.

He wasted no energy railing against the futility of trying to get from London to Dorset in a few seconds. Cold reason had already told him there was nothing he could do to prevent what might be happening at the cottage; but he knew what he was going to do. In his present mood, Gallagher was at his most dangerous.

Fowler was on the line. "Yes, Gordon."

"Use every lever in your network, Fowler," Gallagher said in an emotionless voice, "and get some people to Fleet, in Dorset. Naja's down there. Don't interrupt, for Christ's sake. Let me finish! He's down there, and he's going to kill Rhiannon Jameson and Alicia Davenport. You'll be too late to save them, but if you move quickly you just might catch the bastard." Gallagher gave Fowler the location of the cottage. "You'll probably miss him, anyway."

Fowler said quickly: "What are you going to do?"

"What do you think? I'm going back down there."

"George Haslam's getting things organized. You'd better come up. . . ."

"Didn't you just hear what I said?"

"I did, Gordon . . . but unless you think that car

of yours is faster than a helicopter, I suggest that you accept my invitation."

"I'm on my way."

Gallagher slammed the phone down and left the phone box at a run, forcing himself not to think of Rhiannon.

He wasn't having much success at it.

Rhiannon had stared at the phone, then put it down puzzledly.

Alicia was looking at her. "Well? What is it?"

"Gordon wants us to leave right away. I was still speaking when the line went dead."

"Then it's already too late," Alicia said. She had picked up the hunting rifle. "They're here. You'd better grab yourself a shotgun. Perhaps if we make enough noise, they'll think twice about doing anything."

Rhiannon picked up a weapon. She held it with the assurance of someone who knew how to use it.

"Do you really think they were responsible for cutting the line and that they're out there now?"

"How did Gordon sound?"

"Frantic."

"There's your answer."

"You'll never guess who it is."

Alicia looked at her, waiting.

"The man who stopped to ask for directions," Rhiannon went on. She smiled ruefully, almost philosophically.

"The colonel? That old man?"

"He wasn't so old. Sixty, perhaps. Yes. The colonel. Gordon became frantic after I told him."

Alicia shut her eyes. "My God. If only we hadn't taken Trebi. . . ." The eyes snapped open. "Trebi.

He's not here." She looked about her. "Trebi?" she called softly. "Trebi?"

Silence answered her.

"Oh, no," she said. It was a moan of pain. "They wouldn't harm him, would they? Trebi?"

"Don't . . . don't go outside, Alicia. Trebi's probably chasing rabbits. He'll be back."

"You don't really believe that."

Rhiannon said nothing.

"Oh, Trebi," Alicia said softly. "I'll make them pay. The windows," she went on to Rhiannon. "Let's shut the windows. You take upstairs."

The cottage, a small two-storied stone building, was close to the shore of the Fleet and a short distance from the rest of the other houses in the village. The water's edge was itself about twenty meters away, down a gentle slope. Alicia Davenport had liked the slight isolation the position of the cottage afforded; but now she found herself wishing it were not so.

The upper floor was taken by the two bedrooms, while downstairs housed the bathroom, kitchen and small lounge. Carrying the shotgun, Rhiannon went up the short flight of stairs. Alicia first bolted the door, then went into the kitchen. There were three windows: one overlooking the Fleet, the other two set into opposite walls.

The Fleet window had a fine view of the water and of the high bank beyond. Alicia went over to it, intending to shut it first. She held the rifle in her right hand and leaned forward, reaching for the window with her left.

What happened next did so with a sudden and brutal rapidity.

She was well-extended and had actually got her hand on the window hook when the man appeared in front of her, silhouetted against the fading light of the day. In his hand and pointing directly at her was a strange-looking pistol.

The intruder was the man who had pretended to have lost his way.

Alicia felt a bolt of fear go through her; but even so, she tried to get out of the way and to bring the rifle to bear. It was a forlorn effort.

Though she felt she was moving quickly, she was far too slow. The pistol gave its almost spiteful cough, and the venomous dart plunged through clothing and flesh to pierce her heart. She was dead before she hit the kitchen floor. The rifle clattered as it fell from her lifeless hand. Valley Farm would have no heirs.

Face expressionless, Naja climbed through the window and went past the body to the lounge, pistol seeking a second target.

He did not even glance at his victim.

Rhiannon was in the bedroom she had used the night before—the one above the lounge—and was in the process of shutting the second of its two windows, when she heard the clatter of the rifle. She paused, listening.

"Alicia?" she called. "Are you all right?" When there was no reply, she called a second time: "Alicia?"

Again, silence greeted her.

She passed her tongue slowly over lips which had suddenly gone dry, and came away from the window. She picked up the shotgun, brought the hammers back. They clicked loudly in the stilled gloom of the cottage. She froze, listening more intently this time.

"Alicia!" Her voice carried fear, but she fought

down panic, silently praying she'd be able to use the weapon when the time came.

She began to move cautiously. A floorboard creaked so suddenly, she jumped and nearly dropped the shotgun. Then she realized it was she who had made the noise. She shivered and moved away from the spot, the gun pointing ahead of her.

The stairs from the lounge ended in a landing that led straight to Alicia's bedroom, the door of which was partially shut, virtually killing all light from that direction. The landing then doubled back upon itself to reach the room in which Rhiannon now stood apprehensively. She had paused once more, to listen. Silence still greeted her.

She moved warily forward, pausing on the darkened landing, midway between Alicia's room and her own. She peered down the stairs. Nothing.

Another shiver passed through her entire body. Where was Alicia? What had happened?

Shotgun held ready before her, she went carefully down the stairs, expecting attackers to jump out of the shadows. Nothing happened. The lounge was empty.

She went through to the kitchen and saw Alicia's body.

"Alicia!" she screamed, eyes widening with horror.

She retained enough presence of mind not to drop the weapon as she hurried forward.

A cold, emotionless voice behind her made her jump to a sudden halt.

"Stay exactly as you are, Miss Jameson, and you will not be harmed. You are of greater value to me alive, but I shall kill you if you do not do precisely as I tell you. Release the hammers carefully and put the gun down. *Do it!* I have neither the time nor the inclination to tell you anything more than once. Don't keep me waiting."

Body stiff with fright and the expectation of a bullet in the back, Rhiannon did as she was told.

"Now turn around," the voice ordered when she had straightened up again.

She turned and found herself staring disbelievingly at the man she had taken for a retired officer. In the bad light, she could not properly see his eyes, which seemed hidden in dark patches in his face; but there was still sufficient illumination for her to note the dull metallic gleam of the odd-shaped gun in his hand.

"You, Miss Jameson," he said, "are going to give me the benefit of your company for a while. And I won't take no for an answer."

He seemed to be smiling.

It occurred to her that both his stance and his voice belonged to a much younger man.

11

Gallagher drove the *quattro* fast, down the Finchley Road. He was lucky with the lights at Swiss Cottage and entered the left fork of the one-way system with barely a reduction in speed. Traffic was light enough to enable him to do so. The fading day had caused him to switch on his headlamps, which he kept dipped. His eyes were cold, face expressionless as he aimed the car down Avenue Road, toward Regent's Park.

The police car lurking in Adelaide Road near the intersection was lying in wait for unwary prey. Its crew noted Gallagher's passage with great interest.

"Did you just see that?" the driver exclaimed with anticipatory pleasure. "Went over like a bloody rocket."

"Right," his partner said. "Let's get the bastard."

The headlamps and flashing blue lights came on, and the white Rover gave chase, screeching round the corner, its siren yelping with distinct eagerness.

The partner spoke into his radio. "In pursuit of suspect car . . . black Audi *quattro,* registration number. . . ."

He was interrupted by an incoming message. "Do not apprehend or follow. Repeat . . . do *not* apprehend or follow."

"Say again?"

"Do *not* apprehend or follow."

The partner signed off. "Shit."

The driver was already slowing down. He took the first side road they came to. "Wonder what that was all about," he said. "Some VIP in a hurry?"

"How should I bloody know?" the other said disgruntledly, feeling deprived.

The driver cruised slowly toward Primrose Hill, and kept his silence.

Gallagher had seen the police car behind him, all lit up like a Christmas tree, and, remembering the earlier occasion at the Hyde Park underpass, had wondered whether he was the object of their attention. He'd been half-expecting it to be when he saw the Rover peel off to the left like a fighter aborting an attack.

Thankful for small mercies, he pressed on and thought no more about it. Fifteen minutes later, he was in Fowler's office. Haslam was not there.

Fowler said: "That was quick. No trouble with the police?"

"So it was you who had the hounds called off," Gallagher said. "I might have guessed. Where do we meet the helicopter? Battersea?"

"You're not going anywhere."

"You said . . ." Gallagher began, outraged.

"I know perfectly well what I said," Fowler interrupted evenly. He stared at Gallagher unblinkingly. "We already knew where Miss Jameson was and my people down there were preparing to move in, to give her cover."

"What do you mean you *knew?*"

"A conscientious policeman called Jack Moone."

"I bloody well knew that copper was bad news," Gallagher said bitterly, "as soon as Alicia said she'd seen him."

Fowler's expression was unnaturally still. "Moone ran into Miss Davenport's farm manager. During the conversation the manager, a Tom Leggatt, mentioned having seen your car on the grounds. Moone drew the right conclusions and reported to his superiors, who passed the information to us. Moone was sent to watch the place until we'd organized cover. Moone is now dead, killed the same way as Colthen. There's more," Fowler went on inexorably, and Gallagher watched as he reached toward a small cassette machine to press the play button. "Listen."

The machine began to speak.

"A message for you, Mr. Gallagher," the unknown voice began. "Miss Jameson is safe—for the moment. I am afraid, however, that her companion is dead. . . ."

Gallagher felt the blood drain from his face. He stared disbelievingly at the machine.

"So is that policeman," the voice went on with a metallic lack of emotion, "left uselessly on guard. You are to remain at your home, Mr. Gallagher, until contacted. You will do nothing that I have not first instructed you to do. You will suffer no harm should you decide to ignore my instructions. I shall, however, kill Miss Jameson. You would not like that, I believe. You will go to no one for help. To any listeners on this line, I would advise extreme caution. Any moves against me, or to attempt a rescue of Miss Jameson, would swiftly result in her death.

Do not doubt that I mean it. Wait until you hear from me, Mr. Gallagher."

The message ended abruptly. Fowler stopped the tape.

"That's it," he said. He removed the cassette and pushed it toward Gallagher. "We've got copies."

Gallagher felt sick. Alicia Davenport dead and Rhiannon taken by Naja, whom he had himself seen earlier that day. Dear God.

"No use flaying yourself," Fowler said. "You should not have tried to go it alone. That point having been made, I'm not going to rub salt into the wound. If your face is anything to go by, you're suffering enough as it is."

Wanting to hit back at something, Gallagher heard himself say: "You are tapping my bloody phone."

Fowler was unrepentant. "Just as well."

"You're tapping my bloody phone!" Gallagher repeated tightly. "You have no right, damn you!"

Fowler said nothing, while Gallagher glared hotly at him.

After some moments, Gallagher said: "Where's Haslam?"

"Off to Dorset to sort out the pieces."

"Why should I believe you?"

"Whether you believe me or not is now purely academic," Fowler replied calmly. He pointed to the cassette. "He's the man you've got to believe. I'd take it with you . . . just to make quite sure you've missed nothing."

"My own machine will have recorded it."

"This is a better copy than anything your commercial version could come up with. Take my word for it."

"Oh, yes. Your word."

"It's no use directing your anger at me, Gordon. I haven't got Miss Jameson."

Gallagher said: "If, as you've told me, Jack Moone's superiors passed the news of Rhiannon Jameson's whereabouts on to you, why did it take so long to organize good cover?"

"We didn't get the news in time. That's why Moone was sent to keep a lookout. He was told to stay well out of trouble."

"Fat lot of good that did him."

"Why don't you tell me what the man you saw looks like?" Fowler suggested.

"You heard the tape. No interference."

"We may be of some. . . ."

"No bloody interference!"

"I can get you a gun, if you think you need one." Fowler was still trying.

"No bloody gun either. I'll handle it my way."

"Suit yourself."

Gallagher, who had been sitting across from Fowler, now stood up, picked up the cassette.

"I don't know exactly why, Fowler," he said slowly, eyes locked on the deceptively benign face, "but I'm still finding it hard to believe everything you've so far told me. Perhaps, as you've said before, it's my suspicious nature. Long may I have it. Don't bother to get up."

He went out, leaving Fowler staring expressionlessly at the closing door.

Haslam entered Fowler's office a few moments later.

"I used to think Kingston-Wyatt was a hard nut," he began dryly, "but you're beginning to make him look like a pussycat, as the Yanks would say. You've been hiding your light under a bushel all these years, and no one was the wiser."

"More flattery, George?" Fowler gave one of his fleeting smiles. "Naja is an extremely dangerous animal. To get him, we need someone as dangerous."

"Or someone worked up to an equally dangerous pitch."

"Something like that."

"I'm glad I'm getting out of this business."

"So you keep saying, George. But you keep coming back."

"For my sins . . . yes."

Fowler smiled.

Gallagher was in his darkroom when the phone rang. Thinking it might be Naja, he picked it up quickly. It was Fowler.

"We have confirmation about the way Miss Davenport died," Fowler said. "Same method as for Colthen and Moone."

Gallagher said nothing.

"Look, Gordon . . . I'm sorry about the way this thing has turned out. . . ."

"Of course you are."

"I'd like to help."

"Take the tap off my phone. That would be a great help."

"It's been done."

"That's all right then." Gallagher was unsure whether to believe Fowler or not, and chose not to.

Fowler said: "We can give you cover. It can be made very unobtrusive."

"Forget it. He would know. Goodbye, Fowler."

Gallagher hung up. He had no intention of taking chances with Rhiannon's life.

He went back to his developing and printing.

When he'd returned from Fowler's office, he had listened to the tape several times. He had also played

back the one on the answering machine. After a
while, he began to think there was something familiar about the voice; a quality to it that teased at his
memory. He reasoned that was unlikely. He had
never heard Naja's voice before, and in any case, the
voice would have been disguised. A simple harmo-
nizer attached to the mouthpiece of the phone would
have given any level of distortion desired.

Despite having done a good job of convincing
himself, he was still finding it difficult to ignore the
nagging in his mind. Eventually, he gave in and
went back to listening to the tape, after leaving a
fresh batch of prints to dry.

He played the tape five times on the stereo, listening to it on the headphones, but was none the
wiser. Giving up in disgust, he poured himself a
brandy, turned off the lights and settled himself in
his favorite chair. It was a high-backed, well-upholstered recliner with integral foot stool that he'd
picked up in an antique market for a giveaway price.
The vendor had been only too pleased to get rid of it,
but Gallagher found it very comfortable and called
it his thinking chair.

But he was not doing much constructive thinking. He kept seeing Rhiannon's face. He drank his
brandy and tried not to imagine what might be happening to her.

When he had emptied his glass, he placed it
carefully on a low table next to the chair, and remained in his seat. The glow of the streetlights came
in through the windows and projected bizarre shapes
upon the walls. He stared at them, mind in neutral.
He let his body relax, forcing the tension out. In
moments, he was asleep.

He dreamed of Rhiannon, seeing her wrapped
within the sinuously moving coils of a cobra.

He came awake with a start, a film of sweat glistening upon his face.

He went into the bathroom to splash his face with cold water. He patted it dry then returned to the living room to stare out of one of the windows, but staying in cover. The clock on the mantelpiece had told him it was three o'clock; an hour or so before dawn.

The street was still, as if waiting for something; or perhaps recovering from it. Gallagher wondered why he had come awake at this particular time. On impulse, he went down to the front door, putting on the stairwell lights as he did so. He paused midway.

On the mat was a white envelope.

He stared at it for some moments before descending slowly to pick it up. There was no address.

He felt it gingerly, searching for minute protrusions that might betray a booby trap. There were none. He went back up the stairs and turned off the lights before going into the kitchen, where he slit the envelope carefully open with a knife. He need not have bothered with his caution, for within the envelope was nothing more sinister than a neatly folded sheet of paper. He extracted the paper, slowly unfolded it.

Upon it were precise instructions.

Gallagher arose at eight o'clock. After receiving Naja's message, he had gone straight to bed and slept dreamlessly. It was like waiting to go into action. When the fireworks started you were still afraid, of course, but you were no longer plagued by uncertainty. You knew what you had to do. Despite the training so efficiently implanted into him and his own inherent capabilities, Gallagher found he still hated certain aspects of waiting.

In combat, waiting was part of the strategy. It was altogether a different matter if your subsequent actions depended on instructions from your enemy.

But that didn't mean you couldn't make your own plans.

As Gallagher went to take his morning shower, he felt in tune with himself. He had put Rhiannon out of his mind. She was a distraction and that would jeopardize his efforts to do anything to help her; but he hung on to his anger, turning it into a force that would drive him powerfully.

He dressed and had a leisurely breakfast, during which he mulled over the implications of Naja's demands. Naja had ordered him to go on a dive, in underground water near Mansfield—the very spot where, according to Chris Jameson, Donlan and Millar had disappeared; and which had so excited Jameson's interest.

So what was the connection?

All sorts of alarm bells were ringing in Gallagher, but none of them signaled anything specific. He was being dragged deeper and deeper into someone else's mess; and that someone else, he felt sure, was none other than the Department. He sipped thoughtfully at his coffee.

The Saturday and Sunday newspapers had been delivered during his absence, but he had not yet read any of them. He now picked up a Saturday issue from the pile on the table and browsed through it. The usual national and international mayhem: countries trying to pound each other or their own citizens into insensibility. Leafing through the almost predictable stuff, he skimmed an article about an explosion in a Bayswater hotel; the paper blamed a faulty gas system. Losing interest, he returned it to the pile. He'd have time to read later. He paused.

If he was still around. . . . He began to clear the table, and smiled without humor.

He had every intention of surviving; Naja or no Naja.

Gallagher went downstairs to collect the morning mail, then, settled in a chair in the living room with some fresh coffee, he began to sift through the assorted envelopes.

Most were subscribed magazines; some were bills, which he decided to leave to last, and others he identified as checks—always good news.

There were also three that looked like personal letters. Two he recognized as being from people he knew abroad. The third was fat, and a mystery. This he chose to open first; and he soon began to wish he hadn't.

It was from Chris Jameson and was handwritten.

Dear Gordon,

This is by way of explaining the subterfuge I have played upon you, but I trust that when you have read my letter through, you will understand.

I shall start at the beginning.

Some months ago, I was approached by a man I can only describe as belonging to a shady department like the one you used to work for. In any case, he seemed to know all about my service record. Who knows? Maybe he was even one of your lot.

He suggested that I might want to do a spot of work for them; nothing illegal—whatever that means these days! On the face of it, all I had to do was be available for someone who would approach me to do some diving. This person was someone they apparently desperately wanted to catch. . . .

Gallagher felt his blood go cold. He was already anticipating what the rest of the letter would say, but he was still unprepared for the full horror of its revelations. He continued to read:

I was assured that I would be given full cover all the time. I accepted, partly because the fee was good and partly because the idea excited me. I suppose they knew it would. . . .

The rueful comment struck a chord of sympathy within Gallagher's mind. He knew how Jameson felt.

He turned to the second page.

. . . but there it is. I began to smell something fishy when, after Jack Donlan's death, I got a call requesting the dive in the same place where Jack had gone in. I decided to do my own dive first. What I discovered made me realize why Jack and Millar had died. They had blundered into a well-prepared trap. At least, that is what I now think. You may be able to prove me right or wrong, though that scarcely matters now.

All I know is that once I had made the discovery, I had truly stuck my neck out. I was upsetting applecarts. That job with Nellads was one of those coincidences in life, as was meeting you. . . .

"Don't you believe it," Gallagher muttered bitterly, seeing the Department's manipulatory hand looming large.

. . . the result of which you now know. I will quite cheerfully admit that I steered Rhiannon your way in an attempt to give her some protection, although I did not expect the two of you to take to each other so quickly! Why did I want her protected? I wanted out, and I felt she would be used as a lever to coerce me. I found out very quickly how right I was.

When I saw you at Nellis's home, I already knew what was beneath that water, for I had seen it all. I wanted photographs as proof, but, more than anything else, I wanted a corroborative statement from someone I felt I could trust. I knew that in approaching you I could be making a grave mistake—you might, after all, have still been working for them—but I had to take the chance. I had known of your photographic work before, and I risked the chance that you had left that sort of business for some time.

Nevertheless, I felt you could look after Rhian, even if you decided not to go on the dive with me. . . .

The irony of those words hit hard. Look after Rhiannon indeed. With Alicia Davenport dead and Rhiannon herself now in Naja's hands, the hope expressed in the letter looked a very forlorn one.

. . . so I hope that, at least, is a correct decision on my part. I was told that I would be asked to bring an item up from its subterranean hiding place, and that I should comply, whatever that item turned out to be. Everything would be under control. Which was fine, until I realized what had to be brought up.

But the time you receive this letter, I shall

have made the second dive. I am not, as you may have supposed, on my way to Cornwall in Nellis's boat, although the boat is itself there by now. Nellis wants new sequences in Cornwall with Doria Luce, so he'll probably be on the phone to you about it. If all goes well up here, I shall be joining you. If not. . . .

Gallagher again paused. Was Jameson already dead? It would amply explain why Naja wanted him in Jameon's place. Rhiannon was still the powerful lever of coercion.

He sighed, stared at the letter in his hands, then turned to the fifth page, reading on to find out what had so frightened Jameson.

. . . I shall probably be down there in the water, for good. In which case, do what you can for Rhian; but I have a feeling you don't need to be told.

I have kept you waiting long enough. What I have found down there, in an air chamber beneath the ground, is a store of chemical and biological weapons. If I tell you I have seen Tabun, Sarin, Soman, Hydrogen Cyanide, to name but a few, your own background will tell you what that means. . . .

Jesus Christ, Gallagher thought with horror. Was the Department so determined to get Naja that they were prepared to risk tempting him with the theft of some of the deadliest nerve and blood gases in the world? Some of those could kill within six minutes, through convulsions and suffocation. It was incredible that Fowler should take the chance of turning Naja loose on such a stockpile.

Yet everything that had happened so far pointed to just that. Gallagher was appalled and stunned by the complexity of the scheme. His feelings urged him to upset Fowler's plans; but Rhiannon's quite certain fate if he did anything but obey Naja gave him no choice.

. . . However, even these are child's play by comparison with one particular batch of new stuff whose lethality I can barely guess at. I have an acquaintance who knows about these things, and whose name I shall keep out of this letter. He was able to identify the serial numbers I had memorized. He has said they belong to a particularly potent nerve gas, the manufacture of which was stopped not only because it was too unstable—time to take effect is *ten seconds*—and a danger to user as well as target, but also because it had a persistence of six months in dry conditions, and five in wet. Imagine the effect on soil and vegetation—assuming anyone survived the first dose.

I don't know who this person is who rates such a risk; but he must be bloody dangerous. I have only spoken to him (if he's the one who contacted me) on the phone. Whoever he is, he's got a very efficient network. He knew exactly how to find me. Incidentally, my knowledgeable acquaintance says he may well be wrong about the lethality and that it could easily be more potent and unstable than he believes. He cautions against handling. I did not tell him about the store.

I am going to bring back photographs. They won't be as good as yours, but they'll do. If the man they're after gets his hands on a canister, he'll sell to the highest bidder, who will then no doubt attempt to manufacture it. There are enough daft little governments around, as we all know, who would love to get their grubby hands on something like that.

I hope to see you later. If not, do what you think best, and look after Rhian. Do not tell her what happened.

Attached is a sketch I have drawn to show you how the things are stored, and the access to them.

Jameson's signature, like the writing on the pages of the letter, bore distinct signs of haste, as if he had been afraid of being caught in the act.

Gallagher stared at the sketch for a long time. There was the price of Rhiannon's continuing survival, as well as Naja's capture; and it had all been dumped right in his lap.

He cursed both Fowler and Naja savagely in his mind. Was his past life with the Department going to haunt him forever, like some dogged specter?

He folded the letter carefully, returned it to its envelope and decided to hide it in the darkroom. He was not going to tell Fowler about it. Jameson's letter was private and that was how it would remain. He could not pass it on to Rhiannon when this was all over, for Jameson had himself forbidden him to do so.

At ten o'clock, the phone rang. Fowler.

"Gordon," Fowler began, "we've found Jameson. He's dead."

Gallagher said nothing.

"Gordon?"

"I'm here."

"I said. . . ."

"I know what you said."

"Is that your reaction?"

"What did you expect? Tears?"

There was an uncertain pause as Fowler tried to interpret Gallagher's attitude.

"Are you all right, Gordon?"

"I'm perfectly all right. Are you?"

"I don't understand."

"I'm sure you don't," Gallagher said sarcastically.

"Are you trying to tell me something?" Fowler's voice was calm, but there was a guarded edge to it.

"As if I would."

"You're being enigmatic again, Gordon."

When Gallagher remained silent, Fowler was forced to continue. "Have you heard anything?"

"No," Gallagher lied.

"Can I believe you?"

"Can I believe *you?*" Gallagher countered.

"Don't forget, we are here to help."

"I'll remember," Gallagher said, and hung up.

Fowler replaced the phone slowly, looked up at George Haslam.

"He was very calm about it," he said. "Either he already knew or he's even colder than I thought."

"Didn't O'Keefe once say he was emotional?"

"Yes, but O'Keefe also said he knew how to control his emotion and use it as a weapon. That's what makes him special. Most people are called emotional because they show no control. For Gallagher, in certain circumstances emotion becomes a source of energy which he chooses to direct into selected focal points. . . ."

"You're talking about him as if *he* is the weapon."

"When he's primed . . . he is, George. He is."

Haslam said, after a while: "How much do you think he really knows?"

"Not as much as we fear, or more than we think."

"That's a strange answer."

"It's my way of saying 'I don't know.' "

Haslam sniffed. It could have been an attempted chuckle. "We could follow him, I suppose."

"Hardly necessary. We already know where he'll be going."

"Yes, but not when."

"Patience, George. We'll know soon enough."

"The thought has occurred to me," Haslam went on, "that Naja is already well aware of the trap, which is why he had Jameson killed: to let us know."

Fowler said nothing.

"And where does that leave Gallagher and Miss Jameson?" Haslam queried softly.

Again, Fowler made no reply.

Gallagher picked up the phone and called Nellis's office.

"Ah, Gordon!" Nellis began brightly. "How was the weekend?" There was a wealth of meaning in the words.

"Passable."

Nellis laughed. "Passable, the man says. He leaves my party with a most gorgeous young woman and he says 'passable.' Believe in understatement, do you?" He laughed again, then added: "How does the idea of Cornwall grab you? Assuming you can bear to be parted from Chris Jameson's sister, of course."

Gallagher forced some levity into his voice. "I think I can manage it. When do I have to go?"

"The boat's already down there. We'll be doing

a few shoots on it and some in the water. It's moored in the Camel estuary. Doria Luce is on her way down and should be there by early afternoon. She wants a day or two to wander around Padstow and Wade-bridge and to sun herself on the boat; so you don't have to be there till Wednesday. See? You've got some more time with your lovely lady. Now don't say I'm not kind to you."

"All right. I won't."

"By the way, dear Doria is most miffed you passed her up for Rhiannon Jameson. You'll have to make your peace."

"I did. I was at her binge yesterday. She didn't mention Cornwall, though."

"You know how she is, dear boy. The menials make arrangements. Party time is party time. Full stop."

"I know what you mean," Gallagher said, re-membering. "Is Chris Jameson going down?"

"Yes. I expect him about the same time as you. I shall myself be joining you on Thursday. Might as well have a long weekend while I'm at it."

"So who took the boat down?"

"Would you believe Mr. Sourpuss himself? Tramm."

"Gerry Tramm? That weed? Wonders will never cease."

"I shared your disbelief, till he showed me his Master's ticket. The man's an expert sailor. I had been hoping for Chris Jameson, but he cried off at the last moment. Had to do some checks on his div-ing gear apparently, so Tramm volunteered. He took his driver with him as crewman. They've apparently sailed together several times before. Tramm's on his way back by train. The driver's staying to look after the boat till we get down."

"Do I still need to come to the office?"

"Well, I had hoped to discuss the program with you, but if you've got a heavy day on, perhaps we can leave things as they are till Cornwall."

"Thanks, Charles," Gallagher said, putting relief into his voice. He knew what Nellis would think.

True to form, Nellis said: "Don't use too much of your strength."

"You've got a dirty mind."

"People are always saying that to me. I wonder why? See you in Cornwall." Another laugh, and he hung up.

Gallagher dialed the number of the gallery where Rhiannon worked. A man answered in supercilious, fruity tones.

"Miss Jameson won't be coming in today, possibly not for a few days," Gallagher said.

"Oh? Why not?"

Gallagher felt himself become suddenly hostile, but retained control. "She has a very high fever. Summer flu."

"Oh." Recoil sounded in the man's voice. "And how long will she be away for?"

"She won't be contagious when she returns to work," Gallagher said with malicious relish, "but of course with these summer attacks, one is never too certain." He hung up.

He glanced at the darkroom clock. His instructions had said he was to be at the Mansfield site at four in the morning. That left him seventeen hours to play with. He switched on the answering machine, turned the volume up. He could listen in to the message being recorded, then call back if he felt like it. Meanwhile, he would occupy his time with catching up on his printing and developing. The work would relax him, enable him to prime himself over the hours.

There were some incoming calls about jobs. He left those alone. The day passed uneventfully. Then at six o'clock, a call jolted him.

It was from Rhiannon.

He stared at the machine as if it had suddenly turned into a living thing while he listened to her voice coming out of it.

"I didn't want to do this, Gordon," the strained voice said, "but . . . but he said if I didn't. . . ." There was a long pause. "He said if I didn't, he would. . . ." The voice ended suddenly.

Then another voice, Naja's, cut in: "I just wanted you to hear Miss Jameson speak, Gallagher. She is in good health, for the moment. Your complete cooperation will ensure she remains so."

The call ended.

Gallagher forced himself to remain calm. Naja was playing with him, trying to destroy his self-control. Gallagher refused to let such a blatant ploy work. He replayed the tape several times, trying to guess from background noises where Rhiannon was being held; but that was a non-starter. Background noises could be faked by using sound-effects tapes.

Rhiannon had not been talking directly to him. The entire message was a recording that could have been made at any time. Naja had simply gone to a phone box and played the thing through.

Gallagher turned the volume on the answering machine right down. He would listen to no more calls.

He left the darkroom, made himself a light snack, then went off to bed.

By seven o'clock, he had fallen into an untroubled sleep.

12

At midnight, Gallagher awoke feeling re-freshed. He spent the next hour unhurriedly getting ready, then let himself out of the house, carefully locking it.

He took nothing with him that could conceiv-ably be mistaken for a weapon. He was certain he would be searched; but he brought a spare key for the *quattro*. It was encased in a sheath with a power-ful magnet, which he attached under one of the wings. He deactivated the remote and hid that too, in the same way, beneath another wing.

No one had come near the car. He looked about him casually as he drew on his black gloves, and saw nothing to cause alarm in the quiet of the night. Once, the sound of a single vehicle traveling fast came to him from the direction of Holland Park Ave-nue. He entered the car and started the engine.

He drove slowly on to the road, turned left to go round the block and eventually joined the tree-lined avenue. He turned right, beginning the first leg of his journey to Mansfield.

Scrutiny of his mirrors showed no one following, even after he'd taken a series of deliberate turnings, in an attempt to flush out a possible shadower. He drove through the empty streets of the city, feeling as if he were the only person in the entire world.

A light rain had fallen, leaving the road surfaces gleaming like polished metal in the amber glow of the street lamps. When he'd joined the M1 to head north, he pushed a cassette into the stereo. The thumping rhythms of the beginning of "Self-Control" slammed out of the four speakers. The car seemed to leap along the motorway, as if urged on by the song. ". . . Creatures of the night . . ." the sensuous, haunting voice sang to the driving pulses of the music.

Creatures of the night. Gallagher smiled grimly. *We're certainly that, Naja and I.*

The motorway sped beneath the fat wheels as the music pounded. The digits on the speedometer flickered, settled at 100. The car rushed into the night.

Some miles later, Haslam stood within the confines of an enclosed service station motorway bridge and watched as the black shape hurtled beneath him. He turned to follow it with his eyes. Already, only the taillights and the glow of the headlamps, growing fainter by the moment, were still visible.

"Was that Gallagher?" his companion asked.

"It was," Haslam said. Several hours of waiting were at last over.

"Going bloody fast, wasn't he?"

Haslam gave an unseen smile. "So would you, in his place. Go and warn the others, then join me in the cafeteria. I think I'll risk the coffee again."

"I thought we'd be chasing after him."

"He'd be ten miles up the road by the time we

got on to the motorway. Besides, there's no need. Just warn them, will you?"

Haslam's companion left to go to the car park, where a white Rover was waiting. He got in, and began speaking softly into the radio.

Gallagher left the M1 at junction 27 and took the A608 to Mansfield. A mile and a half later, he took a sharp left on to the A611. There followed a five-mile stretch of deserted road that enabled him to maintain a high cruising speed. He came to the A60 from Nottingham, turned left, then right on to the B6030 a mile further, to Clipstone.

He was nearly there. Another five miles and that would be it.

The cassette, with its assortment of songs and classical pieces, had kept him company on the way up. Now, he turned off the stereo as his destination drew closer. A swift pulse of pre-combat tension shot through him. It was like a switch being thrown. He was ready. Primed.

Through the windscreen, he noted a perceptible lightening of the sky. The time on the instrument panel showed 03.30: just over an hour to sunrise. He cruised through the sleeping mining village that was Clipstone and almost missed the turning.

He braked sharply. The *quattro* stopped dead. He reversed for a few feet until the peripheral glow of the headlamps caught the sign planted on the opposite side of the road. VICAR'S WATER, it announced; the place mentioned in Naja's instructions.

Gallagher turned right, into the newly tarred lane. A short, wattle fence leaned drunkenly away from the corner, near the sign. Behind that was another fence—of chicken wire—that began out of sight, but did not reach beyond the wattle. The lane itself sloped gently downward and was neatly curbed, here and there indented by lay-bys and passing places. On the left-hand side, solid wooden stumps were planted into the ground at regular intervals.

In the gloom, to his left and ahead, the ground rose in undulating mounds, landscaped slag heaps he could not as yet see properly.

The lights followed the lane in a gentle curve to the right; then the tarred surface ended abruptly in a hard unpaved track that formed part of a roundabout. He turned left along the track, as per instructions. The track led to a short tunnel from whose mouth the slag heap rose perpendicularly; and on either side, the ground seemed to funnel steeply downward. It was like the entrance to an amphitheater, Gallagher thought, and he did not like the unwelcome associations the comparison brought with it.

The stumps had disappeared, but, to the right of the track, a fence of four parallel crosspieces, fixed to evenly spaced uprights, reached to the tunnel. Gallagher drove slowly and entered. The rumble of the *quattro*'s exhaust echoed resoundingly.

The track continued out of the tunnel. The wooden stumps were now on both sides and he saw why. To his right, a darkly shimmering body of water came into view. The stumps were to prevent cars from going off. He scrutinized them carefully as he drove past. If he had to get out in a hurry, hitting one of those things at speed would not be fun.

The narrow track took him along the edge of the water, curving right for a few meters before ending in a wide parking area on the left. Gallagher turned into it. There was a car already waiting: a big two-door Mercedes. The instructions had informed him that he'd be met and that all the gear he'd be need-ing for the dive would be supplied.

He was quite certain he'd be accompanied. Naja would not leave anything to chance.

He parked close to the Mercedes, but left a rea-sonable distance between the cars. A man was sit-ting at the wheel of the waiting vehicle. He did not turn to look at Gallagher.

Gallagher shut down the engine and turned off the lights. The ticking sounds of the cooling engine and the whirring of the fan counterpointed each other from the engine bay as his eyes began to adjust to the sudden change in lighting.

The driver's door of the Mercedes opened and the man climbed out, pushed the door shut and walked over to the Audi. In the gloom, he appeared to be wearing tight-fitting clothing. As he came nearer, Gallagher saw it was a wetsuit. Someone would be coming down with him. Despite the high risk inherent in a solo dive, he would at least have had some room for maneuver; but it appeared that Naja had squeezed off the options.

The man, having reached the car, now stood by the door, looking down on Gallagher.

Gallagher's mind reeled in shock. The blond hair, slate-gray in the faint light, was unmistakable.

He climbed slowly out of the car.

"Yes," Lassiter said with a soft laugh, taking a cautious step backward. "It really is me. I did tell you I was in the same sort of job. You're nice and early. Good."

Gallagher continued to stare in Lassiter's direc-tion, trying to understand the other's presence in this place. Giving himself time to absorb the implica-tions of this totally unexpected development, he glanced about him slowly.

Vicar Water, obviously a man-made lake, stretched away, a dog-legged shape to the right, at the base of the continuing slag heap. As his gaze moved leftward, Gallagher saw the dark forms of thickly clustered trees that grew in a seemingly impenetrable screen right up to another high mound, beyond which was the tower and wheel of a mining shaft. There were lights in the distance and between the trees, pinpricks that made no difference to the gloom. Down the slope from the parking area, he made out the dull glisten of a much smaller patch of water.

"I wouldn't think of it," Lassiter said. "There are people waiting in the trees if you should decide to try anything."

"I have no intention of trying anything," Gallagher said calmly. He was back in control. "And for your information, we don't have the same job."

Lassiter's soft laugh came again. "I wasn't talking about photography. I was talking about your real job. This sort of thing." He went on, before Gallagher could make comment: "Just so we get things in perspective and know exactly where we stand, I shall answer some of the questions I'm sure are buzzing about in your head. No . . . I'm not Naja. Never met the man and don't want to. People who have seen him have a dodgy habit of not lasting very long afterwards. I have a great liking for my own skin. So you could say I'm a sort of sub-contractor. My instructions are delivered . . . I do the job. The arrangement suits me perfectly." Another mocking laugh. "Pay's good, too. Next question. Where is Rhiannon Jameson? Answer: I don't know, and I don't care; but I have a message for you. If you don't do exactly as you're told, she'll be dead faster than you can blink.

"What was I doing at Doria Luce's place?" Lassiter went on. "Apart from the fact that I know her, my real purpose was to keep an eye on you, of course. Does Doria know of my . . . ha-ha . . . moonlighting activities? Naturally not. Not the thing to discuss in bed, is it?"

Gallagher let Lassiter talk. The man seemed to like the sound of his own voice. As for that remark about taking Doria Luce to bed, he doubted she would have given him the time of day. Lassiter seemed to have a need to impress, even in a situation where he apparently held all the advantages. A weakness that could probably be later exploited.

Gallagher maintained his silence.

"Behind you, in a hollow," Lassiter continued, pointing briefly, "is a pond. We dive there. If you're a good boy, we'll do it with as little fuss as possible. We go down, you collect the item, then we get out of here before the locals start getting out of bed. All the gear you need is here."

The light was continually improving and Gallagher could now see him better. There was something in Lassiter's left hand.

A gun.

Lassiter shifted it into his right hand and pointed it at Gallagher who, in the increasing light, recognized it as a big Colt .45 automatic.

"The first thing you do is give me the keys to your car." Lassiter held out his left hand.

Gallagher said: "What for? I'm not going anywhere."

"Let's say I don't like leaving things to chance."

Gallagher stood his ground. It would not do to give in too easily. "I'm hardly likely to risk Rhiannon Jameson's life. I wouldn't be here otherwise."

"That may well be so, but let's not waste any more time, shall we?" The hand was still waiting.

"Look," Gallagher began, "this car is very special to me. I don't want anything to happen to it."

"You'd better begin to worry about what might happen to *you*," Lassiter said in a harsh voice. "Then *I'll* take it. It's your decision."

Gallagher sighed with apparent resignation. "Oh, bloody well all right, then. If it will make you happy." He reached into the *quattro*.

"Careful!" Lassiter cautioned. "Take it nice and easy."

"For God's sake," Gallagher said, putting the right amount of irritation into his voice. "I've told you I'm not going to do anything stupid."

"Perhaps, but I'm still not taking chances with you. You have something of a reputation, I hear. You put two of Naja's people out of action. He warned me about you."

Gallagher removed the key, handed it over wordlessly.

"One key?" Lassiter queried.

"That's it. It opens the lot."

"Right. Let's go to the Mercedes. The gear's in the boot. You can take it down to the pond. After you."

They went to the other car, where Gallagher was made to open the boot and unload the diving equipment. It took three trips to ferry everything down to the pond.

Under the menace of the Colt, Gallagher stripped to his underpants and, shivering slightly in the early dawn air, began to put on the wetsuit provided for him.

While Gallagher was thus occupied, Lassiter changed the automatic for another weapon, which looked like a foreshortened, single-barreled shotgun.

He had placed the automatic in a waterproof bag that was now attached to his waist.

Gallagher paused to stare at the new weapon. The dawn light was now a uniform gray, but details stood out plainly. The woods about him were still, as if holding breath. Far away, Gallagher could hear the lonely hum of an engine.

"What's that for?" he queried, keeping his voice calm.

"That," Lassiter began, "is something to discourage any nonsense while we're under. It's a compressed-air dartgun, pump-action loading. It has a magazine of seven darts, each of which has an explosive tip. Very nasty. It can stop a shark. I'm sure it can stop you."

Jesus, Gallagher thought.

He smiled fleetingly at Lassiter. "Makes you feel safe, does it?"

Lassiter's expression stiffened, then he gave his soft laugh. "Naughty, naughty. Continue putting your kit on. We haven't got all day."

Gallagher obeyed.

Lassiter had himself already completed his own preparations, having taken care to do so at a safe distance from Gallagher, with both weapons close to hand. Now he stood in wetsuit and flippers, air tanks secured to his back, helmet with twin integral lights, face mask resting on the helmet, mouthpiece with its attendant air tubes dangling on his chest. The dartgun pointed unerringly at Gallagher.

When Gallagher had eventually kitted himself out similarly, he said: "I hope you realize my diving skills are minimal . . . and I've never dived underground before."

"I'm sure you'll cope."

"I can't understand why he needs me to do this,"

Gallagher went on, chattering as if nervous. "Why didn't he use you?"

"It's not in my contract. Naja has his reasons for everything he does. I'm not about to query his decisions. Besides," Lassiter went on with studied malice, "you may be expendable. I'm not. Right. Shall we go? Don't forget the little box."

The "little box" in question was a cylindrical container five inches long and just over two in diameter, about big enough to take a 50-gram coffee jar. It was air- and watertight. Lassiter passed it to him, and Gallagher fastened it to his belt.

"The lights have a duration of one hour each," Lassiter said as they eased themselves into the water. "Since we won't be spending enough time on the bottom to require decompression on the ascent, running out of power won't be a problem."

Gallagher had done swift final checks of his equipment, and, as he now felt the water seeping through the neoprene to form a warm layer about his body, he could not dispel the feeling that he was not intended to make the return trip alive.

Lassiter was surely under orders to kill him in the darkened waters beneath, with that vicious dart-gun even now still pointing his way. Naja's plan would be to get the canister of deadly gas, have Rhiannon killed as well, and make a clean exit out of the country; and Fowler would be left with egg on his face.

Gallagher was not inclined to become Naja's victim; directly or indirectly.

"I'm ready," he told Lassiter. He lowered his face mask, switched on the helmet lights by briefly pressing the rubber-sealed power pack attached by the belt to his right hip.

Lassiter nodded. "Watch out for the silt at the

bottom of this shaft. It will hang about for ages if stirred up, blotting out visibility. I'd be so nervous about losing you, I might shoot. So don't even think about it. Right. Down you go." He adjusted his mask, then secured his mouthpiece.

Gallagher clamped his own mouthpiece between his teeth and allowed himself to sink before turning over and heading downward, Lassiter trailing within gun range.

From above, their plunging lights seemed disembodied beneath the surface of the water, made steely gray by the reflection of the lightening sky. The myriad broken pieces caused by the disturbance of their departure were rapidly rejoining each other as the water settled over them. Soon the lights disappeared and the surface of the pond became still once more.

Save for the pile of Gallagher's clothes, it was as if the two men had never been there.

Gallagher swam through the clear water of the flooded mine tunnel, trying not to think of Lassiter following close behind with the loaded dartgun; trying not to think of Rhiannon; trying not to think of what it would be like to die in such a place.

Beyond the flare of the helmet lights, the darkness closed in with an almost solid permanence, the tunnel itself paradoxically appearing to stretch to infinity.

The fat gauge on his left wrist, with the dive timer strapped next to it, showed the depth as 30 meters—100 or so feet—and time into the dive two minutes, with perhaps a minute of that at the present depth; a good nineteen minutes left to avoid a decompression stop during the ascent. Better cut that to fifteen minutes as a safety margin. Five minutes to get to the chamber, a minute to somehow disarm Lassiter—two at the outside. Any longer and things would get messy, as the exertion required began to use up the available air. Five minutes to get away from the chamber. Eight minutes left to get to the top and in some way avoid Lassiter's waiting colleagues.

Time to think about that later. If he succeeded with Lassiter, at least he'd be armed.

A shadowy form, like a predator on patrol, had appeared at his side. Lassiter wanting to know why Gallagher was looking at the gauges. Gallagher spread the fingers of his right hand at Lassiter three times, then tapped at the dive timer. Lassiter nodded, seeming to understand, then fell back to his old position.

Gallagher swam on with leisurely leg strokes, maximizing the effect of his fins, conserving his strength and his air. The water caressed his body, whispering at him. His expelled air bubbled away in a globular trail. Yet, for all that, there was a strange tomblike silence that seemed, like the bordering darkness, to hang just out of reach.

The tunnel was wide and high, with straight sides and a flat ceiling. The scourings of its construction were clearly visible as the lights moved along it. Here and there, cracks ran like aged veins across its surface. There was enough room, Gallagher judged, for six people to swim abreast.

A sudden clanging made him look slowly round, treading water gingerly so as not to disturb the sediment on the floor of the tunnel.

Lassiter was in the process of bouncing off one of the walls. He seemed to have temporarily lost his bearings.

Narcosis? Gallagher wondered. From 100 feet

onward, some people tended to become drowsy, or euphoric, depending on their tolerance. Was Lassiter thus affected?

But Lassiter was urging him on vigorously, indication that whatever had occurred was not a serious impediment.

Continuing to swim, Gallagher decided on how he was going to get Lassiter. It would involve some risk, the level of which would depend upon Lassiter's psychological state when they eventually got to the chamber. All would hang upon that. If Lassiter had just suffered a brief attack of narcosis, so much the better.

Gallagher felt no compunctions about what he intended to do.

They came upon the chamber entrance two minutes later and nearly swam right past it. The circular door had been so well camouflaged, it seemed like part of the tunnel wall, even to the added detail of having cracks etched upon it. The directions he had received from both Naja and Jameson had enabled Gallagher to spot the barely visible circular outline of the flush-fitting door.

He paused, anchoring himself by one hand to the tunnel wall, and looked at Lassiter, who had joined him.

Lassiter reached down to his left leg and unsheathed a big diving knife that was strapped there. He handed the knife to Gallagher and moved quickly out of reach, dartgun pointing. He motioned to Gallagher to use the knife to prize open the door.

Gallagher obeyed. The door came open easily with a slight, petulant grumble, like an underworld monster disturbed in its sleep. There was hardly any sediment disturbance, suggesting that it had recently been used. Gallagher guessed it was Jameson who had earlier been this way.

He swung the door fully open so that it lay flat against the wall. It disclosed a dark tube just wide enough to take a diver and his equipment. He peered along it, noting that it appeared to reach well beyond the limit of the lights.

He turned to look at Lassiter, who was gesticulating for the return of the knife. Gallagher handed it over without fuss. Lassiter slipped the knife back into its sheath, then motioned toward the tube with the gun.

Gallagher entered the narrow passage, heard a brief scrabbling as Lassiter followed him.

The tube was lined with smoothed concrete, and every so often Gallagher came across a sectional joint as he swam past. Handy to remember, should he lose his lights on the return journey. He touched one surreptitiously, to see whether he would be able to navigate by feel.

Yes. There was a definite sensory break between the sections.

He had counted twelve such when the tube came to an abrupt end and the bottom dropped away. Taken by surprise, despite what Jameson's rough sketch had indicated, Gallagher could not believe what his lights showed as he looked down.

There was simply no bottom to be seen, although the water was still crystal clear. It had to be a good 200 feet deeper. At least. That meant 300 feet down from the outside world; if not more. *Christ.*

He swam further over the abyss, as Lassiter came out of the tube behind him. He saw Lassiter look down, then jerk back in shock.

Good. The more shaken Lassiter became, the better it would be when the time for action arrived.

Gallagher looked up and saw a slowly shifting patina in the glow of his lights. He swam upward, taking it at an even pace. Ten feet later, he broke surface.

He trod water, turned slowly to look about him. The chamber was wide, almost perfectly circular, with a high vaulted ceiling that echoed even to the slightest of his movements, despite the dampening effect the water should have had. The sculpturing of the ceiling showed it to be natural, rather than man-made. Man had, however, made his mark in other ways.

Protruding about four feet above water level and in the middle of the chamber was an island. It had originally been cone-shaped and its base was somewhere far below on the unseen bottom. The top of the cone had been lopped off to create a large, natural platform. A short flight of concrete steps was set into it and from these a metal railing curved in full encirclement. On the platform was stacked a huge pile of what looked like ammunition boxes of varying sizes.

Bingo, Gallagher thought without enthusiasm.

He hoped none of them leaked, otherwise breathing the air in the chamber would be about as wise as poking his head into a gas oven; except that the result would be terminally far swifter. With a gas oven there was still a chance of survival if someone found you in time. In this place, ten seconds and that was your lot.

Gallagher surveyed the chamber once more, before returning his attention to the apparently innocent-looking boxes. This, he decided, was his vision of hell.

To do what he needed to, if there was to be the slightest chance of his getting out of this hellhole alive, he would have to risk breathing the air. It wasn't much of a choice.

Hearing Lassiter rise noisily away to his right, Gallagher turned to look. Lassiter had removed his mouthpiece and was gulping in air. Stupid bastard; but it indicated signs of stress.

"Get on with it!" Lassiter commanded, too loudly. He obviously found the place unnerving.

Gallagher reasoned that Lassiter had not enjoyed the swim either, and was probably not looking forward to the trip back; alone.

Taking comfort from the fact that Lassiter had not slumped dead in the water, Gallagher continued to breathe from his tanks and swam just below the surface to the island which was some ten meters away. Lassiter followed, remaining above.

Gallagher reached the steps, removed his mouthpiece and raised his mask. The steps went down into the water, enabling him to turn and climb out backward, and so keep his fins on. Removing them meant putting them back on again. There wasn't time for that.

He glanced at the timer. Nine minutes remaining, according to the limit he had set himself.

He reached the uppermost step, turned, and began to flip-flop his way along the perimeter, using the railing as support.

"Stop!" Lassiter ordered.

Gallagher stopped, turned again to look.

Lassiter had reached the steps, but had chosen to remain in the water, one hand holding on to a railing support. The gun poked up at Gallagher, from the other hand.

No wonder Naja had remained successful for so long, Gallagher thought. Trap or no trap, Naja would never have come to this place. There was always the risk of being snared. Better to use greedy expendables, none of whom would know his true identity. It would not be surprising if Naja expected him to take Lassiter out, Gallagher thought.

Lassiter had also raised his mask. The man looked jumpy as he said: "All right. Where is it? Which one?"

"How should I know? I was just about to look when you stopped me."

"I don't want you out of my sight."

"Well, come up then. Unless you like hanging there with two or three hundred feet of dark water below you. I wonder if there are all sorts of things down in those depths, that nobody's ever seen or heard of; like big, poisonous water snakes. . . ."

"Don't be stupid! Adders are the only poisonous snakes in this country, and they wouldn't be down here. . . ."

"Why not? A big species, specially adapted to deep-water existence, nasty as hell. . . ."

"Shut up!"

"Or maybe a few drowned bodies. . . ."

"*Shut up, damn you!* Otherwise I'll blow you away with a dart." Lassiter's voice echoed around the chamber, a touch of hysteria plainly audible.

"I wouldn't," Gallagher cautioned reasonably. "This pile of stuff has enough poison gas to kill off the whole of London. If you hit one of these containers with your little explosive toys, I wouldn't give much for your chances. Some of them can kill in ten seconds."

Lassiter glanced fearfully up at the stockpile. "Get on with it!" he said tightly.

Gallagher wanted to smile but did not. Lassiter should have climbed to the platform first. That way, he would have retained the psychological advantage. Gallagher was grateful for the unexpected bonus.

He turned once more, his lights playing eerily about the chamber. The platform, from what he could judge, seemed about six meters across—perhaps twenty feet—with the island itself about another ten meters away from the other side of the chamber. That gave the entire place at water level a rough span of nearly ninety feet: plenty of room to get lost in, should the need arise. The important thing was to remember where the entrance to the exit tube was. A lifetime measured in minutes could be spent looking for it; and if there were more than one. . . .

More than one. He had not considered that. If there were more exits, at the end of which were firmly closed doors. . . .

He drove the terrible thought out of his mind. *Concentrate, concentrate. Remember the position in relation to the steps.* An imaginary line led directly from their center to the tube.

Lassiter had not brought guidelines, obviously feeling these would not be needed. Lines could also get lost, entangle a diver, dragging him to the bottom. . . .

Shut up, Gallagher ordered himself in his mind. *You're supposed to be scaring the shits out of Lassiter, not yourself.*

Another quick scrutiny of the timer showed him eight minutes to go. Had only a minute passed? It had seemed like hours.

Then he found one of the boxes he was looking for. There were no serial numbers upon it; no identification marks save for a yellow, black-bordered disc within which was a black skull-and-crossbones logo.

Its message could not have been clearer. Several such boxes were stacked together.

Gallagher began to work on one that was at chest height. It had two clasps, one at each end of the oblong box. He lifted the first gingerly, then the second. He held his breath, wondering how fast he could get back into the water if there had been leakage within, before he needed to draw breath again. Once beneath the water, he could easily put on his mouthpiece. Water was a safe barrier, but it was no bloody good if the stuff had already got into you.

Ten seconds to bloody oblivion.

He lifted the cover. Eight little canisters, in twin rows of four, gleamed up at him. Each carried the death's-head label. They were black, with yellow spiral stripes, reminding Gallagher of the grab handles on ejector seats. He wondered why he had made such a strange connection, then concluded that his subconscious was screaming at him to get out, fast.

Eject, the screaming brain was saying. *Get us out of here.*

The canisters seemed intact. Gallagher released his breath slowly. Carefully, he picked up one of the canisters. There was a seal around the joint between lid and body.

Ten seconds had passed and he was still alive.

He went back to the steps. Lassiter was looking up at him, gun still pointing.

"Is that it?" Lassiter queried. "That little thing?"

"Yes, Lassiter. That little thing can kill you in ten seconds flat. That's the one I was talking about."

Lassiter said, uncomfortably: "Put it in the case and give it to me."

"I thought you'd say that. Sorry; not a chance." This must be the moment when Lassiter was meant to kill him. Gallagher knew. Bringing him down here had merely been with that object in mind, and then the man would take the canister back up, leaving Gallagher's body in this underground chamber. Gallagher was not about to let that happen.

"Do as I say," Lassiter snarled, "or I'll. . . ."

"You've got a bad memory," Gallagher said admonishingly. "Didn't I just tell you what would happen if you hit one of these boxes? The one this little item came from is wide open and very vulnerable. There are seven more like it in there. You wouldn't have time to get your mouthpiece on before the gas hit you. Just imagine," he went on with relish, "what would be happening inside you as you struggled to breathe. It'd feel as if you were trying to swallow your lungs. All that, with three hundred feet of nothing under your feet. It's dark and cold down there, Lassiter. How long would it take to reach bottom, do you think?"

"Shut up, you bastard! *Shut up!*"

"Of course, you could try for a hit and hope I won't drop the canister and break the seal. See, here? That's the seal. Maybe I'll just have a go at—" Gallagher touched it speculatively with a fingernail—"picking it. . . ."

"No!" The man's cry of horror, almost a sob, echoed in the darkness of the chamber beyond their lights.

"Right," Gallagher said firmly. "First, you push the gun slowly up the steps, or I will open that seal. You were going to kill me anyway, so I've got nothing to lose. *Do it!*"

Seven minutes.

Lassiter reluctantly obeyed.

Gallagher reached forward with one hand to

take the weapon. "Now remove your fins and climb out of the water. Hurry!"

Lassiter seemed to be trembling as he complied. When he was on the platform, Gallagher made him drop the fins.

"Now the knife, and the pouch with the pistol. In that order." When Lassiter handed the knife to him, Gallagher threw it into the water, then clipped the pouch to his own belt.

"Now the tanks."

Lassiter's eyes were now wide with a very real fear. "*What?* You can't. . . ."

"Take the bloody things off!"

"Jesus, Gallagher . . . you can't. . . ."

"Don't you believe it."

"Gallagher, for God's sake, *please.*"

Gallagher picked up the dartgun. "The gas or the gun. Take your choice."

Lassiter's face seemed to crumple. "You're mad," he said in a shaky voice. "You're bloody mad!"

But he removed his tanks.

"Put them down, and move away."

Again, Lassiter complied. "What . . . what are you going to do, for Christ's sake?" His voice was almost breaking by now.

"You'll see. The helmet's next. Off with it, then put it down. Move away, but stay within range of my lights."

Lassiter did as he was told. Gallagher put the canister close to hand on a box, picked up the helmet and smashed one of its lights with the butt of the dartgun.

"That should be enough for your needs." He reached upward and perched the helmet high on the boxes. "I'd be very careful if you try to take it down. . . . Don't try to rush me." Coldly. "You wouldn't

make it. Now, where was I? Oh, yes. Be very careful
if you try to take the helmet down; I've balanced it
very finely. Two things could happen. You could drop
it into the water; in which case, bang goes your lighting. Or you could bring all these boxes tumbling
down. . . . Or both. The consequences don't bear
thinking about."

Six minutes.

Gallagher dragged the tanks and the fins one-
handedly to the steps. Then he went back for the
canister.

"You're not going to leave me here without air!"
Lassiter's cry rose to a squeak.

"All the air you want in here," Gallagher said
flatly.

"But I won't be able to get back. *I'll die here!*"

"Don't move! Don't . . . move. I'm going to give
you the chance you wouldn't even have given me. It's
a slim one, but it's a hell of a lot more than you
deserve. I'm taking your tanks to the tube. You've
still got your helmet and mask. No fins, though." He
tossed them into the water. They disappeared in the
darkness.

Lassiter seemed to be sobbing. "This is murder!
You're murdering me!"

"You could always use one of the gas canisters.
That would be quick."

"I won't be able to find the way out! There are
no lines. . . . Oh, God, Gallagher, you can't do this!
I won't be able to find the tube! *What if there's more
than one?*" He suddenly screamed in full horror, seeing himself forever going down the wrong passage as
his air and lighting ran out.

Gallagher had placed the canister by the steps
to prevent a mad rush from Lassiter as he dragged
the air tanks down to the water. It had been awk-

ward going, for he was carrying the dartgun as well; but now that he was back in, buoyancy made things a lot easier. He hooked the straps round his left arm, pulled down his mask, then chomped on the mouth-piece.

"Gallagher! Gallagher!" Lassiter was screaming dementedly, trapped in the near-darkness with the boxes of invisible death. "Wait! I'll tell you where I was to take the canister. To Nellis! *To Nellis, Gal-lagher! Gallagher! Wait, you bastard!"*

Then Lassiter was suddenly running, desperate fear galvanizing him into action. Gallagher saw him coming but, encumbered by the added weight of the spare tanks and the dartgun, could not move out of the way in time. He swore at himself. He had under-estimated the extent of Lassiter's desperation—a stupid mistake he should have been able to avoid. God, he was bloody rusty.

He began evasive action as Lassiter launched himself over the railing. Gallagher found he could not bring the dartgun up to bear on the darkly mov-ing target. Lassiter had misjudged his leap, but his clawing hands snatched at Gallagher as he landed heavily in the water. The smack echoed loudly round the cavern.

Gallagher lost the dartgun as the alternately whimpering and snarling Lassiter struggled to rip away his mask. He fought Lassiter away with his free hand; but it would be a one-sided battle if that continued for long. He would either have to jettison the tanks and thus give himself the freedom to com-bat the maddened Lassiter, or he could try to drag the man beneath the water. Without equipment, Lassiter would not stay below for very long.

Gallagher was reluctant to drop the tanks, de-spite the other's original intentions to kill him. Las-

siter would suffer a thousand deaths in the chamber
before summoning the courage eventually to go for
the tanks; or when desperation drove him to do so.
It was a more fitting punishment. Killing the bastard
at once was too quick a fate.

They grappled like ferocious water beasts in the
eerie chamber: Lassiter grunting, snarling and
whimpering alternately, while Gallagher fought to
slow his own breathing, keeping his teeth firmly
clamped on the mouthpiece as Lassiter tried to tug
it away.

Gallagher's jaw began to ache with the effort of
resisting Lassiter. They rolled and thrashed in the
dark waters of the chamber. Perched upon the boxes
on the platform, the single light from Lassiter's helmet stabbed through the gloom, a small searchlight
beam fixed blindly upon its vaulted ceiling; while in
the water, Gallagher's lights described crazy arcs
both above and beneath the churning surface as he
and Lassiter fought. Their frenzied splashings
sounded like thunderclaps within the subterranean
cave that could easily become their tomb.

Gallagher had no intention of letting that happen. Lassiter's tomb perhaps; but that was it. Besides, time was running out. How much air had he
used in the struggle? He preferred not to think about
it.

He managed to grab Lassiter by the hair and
mercilessly dragged the other down as he dived. He
heard a sudden bubbling sound from his adversary
as the pain forced Lassiter's mouth open and the
water poured in. Lassiter now began to struggle for
breath, forgetting all about trying to wrench Gallagher's mask off.

Gallagher could see his distorted face an arm's
length away, appearing to dissolve as the lights

played upon it. Lassiter's eyes were staring. Now was the time to release him.

Gallagher let go of Lassiter's hair.

Lassiter propelled himself desperately upward. Gallagher watched the dark shape rise, before surfacing himself some distance away. He needed to get his bearings, not certain of where the fight had taken him in relation to the position of the exit.

He need not have bothered about surfacing too close to Lassiter. His would-be killer himself had managed to struggle back to the platform, but had not found the strength to climb the steps. Lassiter was hanging on to a railing support half out of the water, his head drooping, breath rasping loudly in the gloom. Every so often, it was punctuated by a hacking cough as he tried to clear his throat.

"Gallagher!" It was a long, drawn-out plea with barely any strength in the voice. "For God's sake. Don't leave me here!" Another hacking cough echoed within the chamber.

Gallagher said nothing, the twin lights of his helmet fixed upon Lassiter's drooping form. He felt himself shiver slightly. Lassiter's posture reminded him of a tableau in some bizarre religious painting; a vision of a condemned soul forever doomed to remain in an eternal purgatory.

"Gallagher! Have mercy, for Christ's sake. Have mercy. . . ."

Gallagher lowered himself beneath the surface once more. Lassiter's weak cries came muffledly to him until as he went deeper, they faded completely.

But his mind was reeling in shock over what Lassiter had shouted before the fight.

Nellis?

It was a difficult thing to believe. Given the circumstances, it was equally difficult to believe that Lassiter would choose to lie.

He found the exit, but slightly misjudged his approach and was pulled downward past the lip by the extra weight of Lassiter's tanks. He went down a good ten feet before he was able to stabilize his descent and begin to push his way upward again.

For one terrible moment, he remembered a nightmare experience in a waterhole in the Australian desert, and had visions of being dragged inexorably toward the bottom. He fought the panic and regained control of himself.

Strange, he thought, that he had not lost such control during the fight with Lassiter. Perhaps this was a form of delayed shock.

I ought to drop the bloody things, came the thought; but Gallagher knew he wouldn't do it. Not after he had just fought so hard to keep them.

He made it back to the lip and swam in, pulled the tanks after him. He left them halfway along the tube, then swam on. He finned his way out of the tube, but did not shut the door. Once more in the wide tunnel, he felt curiously alone in the alien world without Lassiter's malign company. He swam with speed but without haste along the drowned corridor, his lights marking his progress through the watery dark with ghostlike sinuosity.

He knew the fight had lasted barest seconds, a far shorter time than it had seemed, but he was taking no chances. He finned strongly on.

His return to the shaft was without incident. None of Lassiter's colleagues had come down to check. A good thing too. Without the dartgun, things would have been a bit tricky.

Daylight gleamed brightly down the shaft, and

Gallagher turned off his lights. No point in warning Lassiter's friends of his impending arrival.

He rose slowly, staying close in against the flank of the shaft. The timer told him he had exceeded his limit by one minute, though not the full bottom time. Even so, he decided to stop at five meters for five minutes, giving himself time to decide how best to leave the water without running into the rest of the opposition.

He looked upward, saw no shadows that would indicate a watcher. He worried about the rising bubbles from his expelled air, but could only hope they would surface among the pond-side weeds.

His five minutes up, he continued his ascent. He surfaced cautiously. . . .

And saw a pair of nondescript brown shoes.

13

"Well, well, well."

Haslam.

Gallagher controlled his surprise; he raised his mask, pulled his mouthpiece out and hauled himself on to dry land. He began to remove his fins; then he took off his helmet, released the tanks and stood up. His clothes were still where he had left them.

Haslam said: "You don't seem surprised."

"Oh, I'm surprised, all right. I'm waiting for you to tell me why you're here." He peeled back his hood, unclipped the pouch from his belt and began to remove the wetsuit.

Haslam handed him a towel. "Better use that. We found it in the Mercedes."

"We?" Gallagher looked round and up, saw two men by the cars. A white Rover was next to the *quattro.* "I see." He toweled himself and began to dress quickly. "You still haven't told me why you're here."

"Good thing we were. We immobilized a reception committee waiting in the trees over there."

"I knew about them."

"Oh?"

"Lassiter told me. He didn't expect me to return."

"Yes. We were beginning to wonder whether to send a search party down."

"That's nice to know . . . except you'd have been too late."

"But you made it OK. Speaking of which, where is he?"

"That depends."

"On what?"

Gallagher had finished dressing. He stooped to pick up the pouch with the automatic in it; he removed the gun and let the pouch fall to the ground. The Colt was dry and in perfect working order. It had been well looked after, beautifully kept; a killer's gun. It was also fully loaded.

Nellis, he thought grimly. He still felt reluctant to believe it; but if Lassiter had spoken the truth. . . . He had to check it out to find the answer, one way or the other.

He looked up from the gun and asked Haslam: "You're not going to take it away from me, are you?"

"I have no such instructions."

"And just what are your instructions, Mr. Haslam?"

"You were telling me about Lassiter."

"He's either dead, coming up, or is quietly going insane in a dark cave."

"I don't understand."

Gallagher told him what had happened.

Haslam said slowly: "Remind me never to get in your way. You should have killed the poor bastard. It would have been kinder."

"Send a couple of frogmen down. He should still be there."

Haslam was staring. "And Fowler said you were emotional."

"Oh, I am. I am. Talking of Fowler . . . get on to him and tell him I want an exact dummy copy made of one of those yellow and black joys you've got stashed away down there. I want it by the time I get to London. It must feel like the real thing. I'll collect it at his office. You lot got me into this, now you're going to work to get me out . . . *and* Rhiannon Jameson—*alive.*"

"Anything else?" Dryly.

Gallagher stooped again to pick up the dartgun, which he handed to Haslam. "Present. Oh, yes. Another thing . . . if you do find Lassiter, he's got one of my car keys on him. I'd like it back."

He turned away and walked up the slope to the *quattro.* Haslam's colleagues looked expressionlessly at him as he approached.

"Good morning, gentlemen," he said to them brightly.

They nodded their unspoken acknowledgment and watched interestedly as he poked beneath the car for the spare key and the remote.

"Magic," he said to them as he got in behind the wheel. He glanced up at the cloudless sky. "Going to be hot. Nice day for a swim."

They looked at him stolidly as he started the engine. The *quattro* growled throatily, matching the simmering anger he felt at the way he had been used by Fowler. Haslam was still by the pond, in no apparent hurry to send someone down for Lassiter.

Gallagher smiled falsely at the two silent men. "Cheer up!" he shouted, and drove away so vigorously they had to jump out of the path of the surging car.

They didn't look pleased.

Gallagher aimed the car carefully between the rows of stumps as he made his way back along the track, at a greater speed than when he had arrived. A glance at the timer showed him 0500. Hard to believe one and a half hours had passed.

But now he knew more . . . and he was still alive.

He suppressed a shiver as memory of his near descent to the bottom of the deep underground pool came rushing back. For a very brief moment, he felt sorry for Lassiter; but Lassiter had been about to kill him, cold-bloodedly. The feeling of sympathy vanished.

He drove through the short tunnel and was soon on the metaled section of the lane. Pausing at the junction with the main road, he turned left, back through the still-sleeping Clipstone. The road was empty of other traffic. He gave the car its head.

He intended to make it to London by seven.

He parked in the square at five minutes past. For once, the stretch of the M1 from Luton down into town had been relatively free of early commuter traffic. He had been lucky with his time slot.

The first thing Fowler said when Gallagher entered the office was: "How do you like our service?"

"What service?"

"You were seen by three police patrols on the motorway—'flying,' as one of them reported—but they had been called off. Haslam got to me in time."

"It's the least I'd expect in the circumstances."

Fowler was unrepentant. "How much do you know, Gordon?"

"Enough."

Fowler nodded. "Haslam told me about Lassiter."

"I got nothing from Lassiter," Gallagher lied. "I just prevented him from killing me."

Fowler did not look as if he believed that. "But you left the stuff down there and asked for a dummy to be made. It means you know something."

"I said I got nothing from Lassiter," Gallagher corrected.

Fowler seemed to smile as he reached into a desk drawer to bring out a small canister exactly, in outward detail, like the ones Gallagher had seen underground.

He stood it on the desk. "This what you asked for?"

Gallagher stared at it warily. "It's not the real thing, is it? I may need to break the seal to make a point to someone."

"Anyone I'd like to know about?"

Gallagher did not reply, but continued to stare at the canister.

Fowler said: "It is a dummy. You'll have to take my word for it."

"Oh, yes. Your word." Gallagher looked at Fowler, hazel eyes cold. "We'll have a long chat about that one day, you and I. But right now, I'm more concerned about getting Rhiannon Jameson back alive . . . if I have to kill Naja to do it. That's what *you* want, isn't it?"

"Now, now, Gordon . . ." Fowler began soothingly.

"For Christ's sake, Fowler!" Gallagher interrupted, his anger as cold as the look in his eye. "Don't play the politician with me. Save that for your sessions with whatever minister you deal with these days. What I don't understand, is why you didn't use dummy canisters in the first place, instead of taking risks with a gas as lethal as that."

"How do *you* know what gas it is?"

Gallagher stared silently at Fowler.

Fowler nodded once more, seeming to accept Gallagher's refusal to answer. "I see. Why not use dummy canisters?" he went on. "The answer to that is quite simple. Someone of Naja's caliber would not have fallen for it. Everything had to be genuine. We made sure Naja was well aware of the lethality of the gas."

"He didn't fall for it even then."

"Didn't he?" Fowler queried mysteriously.

"He sent a legman to take the risk for him."

Fowler appeared to be smiling again. "You mean Lassiter. Well-known killer, Lassiter," Fowler continued, as if to himself. "Known about him for some time. Sub-contractor. Petty stuff."

Petty stuff, Gallagher thought grimly. "*If Lassiter had killed me in that chamber, it would have been 'petty stuff.'*"

"But he didn't, old boy. Did he?"

Gallagher was momentarily surprised to find he had spoken his thoughts aloud. "Am I supposed to feel better about it?" he asked harshly.

"Lassiter was no match for you. I was not worried."

"*You* weren't worried. That's nice." Gallagher took the canister off the desk. "I've got work to do."

"Need any backup?"

"Would you listen if I said no?"

"We'll be discreet about it. Be on hand if you need us. That sort of thing."

Gallagher shook his head slowly in feigned amazement. "Sometimes, Fowler, I think even Genghis Khan would have crossed the road if he'd seen you coming."

"Now there's a much-maligned figure in history." Fowler was quite unperturbed. "Besides, I have no dreams of empire. Haslam says you've managed to acquire a gun from our friend Lassiter."

"Yes," Gallagher said, and went out.

When he reached the street, there was no yellow wheel clamp on the *quattro*. Either it was still much too early at seven-forty for the predatory traffic wardens or Fowler had again warned them off.

Gallagher drove toward Covent Garden where he made a choice from the unoccupied parking meters. He fed the machine for the full time allowed, then went into a coffee shop that had opened early. He ordered a light breakfast and took his time over it. He wanted to think about Nellis.

Charles Nellis could not possibly be Naja. Otherwise, who was the retired army officer type? A killer employed by Nellis? All sorts of people had a variety of militarily taught skills that sometimes found their way into the open market in a multitude of forms. Could the mystery "officer" be one such?

Gallagher finished his breakfast none the wiser about Nellis. He had put off the unpleasant task for long enough. He would have to face the man who had given him many lucrative photo assignments, and whom he had grown to like.

He left the coffee shop, decided to walk to the Nellads offices. It would give him time to compose himself for what was to come. He persuaded himself that a parking space would have been difficult to find close by, even so early in the working day. It was a good excuse, even if he didn't really believe it.

He arrived at the offices at eight-fifteen. Nellis would not yet have arrived; neither would have most of the staff. That suited perfectly.

He climbed the stairs of the well-kept Regency building to the second floor, not hurrying. In one

pocket of his bomber jacket the big Colt reposed. In
the other was the canister.

The wide double doors to the reception were
open, but the place seemed deserted. Gallagher entered. A wide curving desk, flanked by two huge
cheese plants that grew almost to the ceiling, formed
the focal point of the familiar room.

He went up to the desk, paused to listen. Faint
movements could be heard. Mandy Turner, perhaps.
She was the receptionist and was always first in.
Nellis swore by her total reliability.

Gallagher moved swiftly away from the desk
and down a short corridor, to Nellis's own polished
door. Mandy would have already unlocked it, he
hoped. Nothing confidential was ever kept in the
offices, for all client files were locked away daily in
a special room which was never opened until one of
the partners had arrived. Gallagher felt certain,
therefore, that Nellis's office stood a high chance of
being open.

He reached the door, pushed at it gently as it
gave to his touch. It would certainly not do to find
Nellis already in residence. He wanted the element
of surprise to be in his favor.

No one was in.

He entered and shut the door quietly behind
him. Nellis's desk was free of clutter, save for a single telephone. Gallagher sat down in the high-
backed chair to wait.

In the event, it was not Nellis who came in.

He had been waiting for some five minutes when
he heard Mandy Turner's voice.

"Oh, hello! You're early. Mr. Nellis is not in
yet."

The reply could not be heard properly, but it was
a man's voice; low, indistinct.

"Oh, I see." Mandy Turner again. "Well, his office is open, but there's nothing on the desk. Though I could be wrong. I didn't actually go in."

More murmurs, then footsteps approaching. Gallagher quickly got out of the chair, to press himself against the wall near the door. He was just in time. He took the automatic out of his pocket, as the door was being slowly pushed open. He held the gun down his side and kept perfectly still.

The door opened further, and whoever it was made a sound of annoyance. Whatever had been expected to be waiting on the desk was obviously of great value. The sound of annoyance carried much more within it. There was anger.

And Gallagher suddenly knew what it was.

The canister.

Naja had come for the canister in person!

Gallagher felt his mind do a somersault. It was not Nellis at all, but someone else entirely, using the empty office as a drop. Someone who was known to Mandy Turner and obviously to Nellis, and who also knew the office routine.

Naja was Nellis's friend?

It still didn't make sense. The barest fraction of a second had passed and the door had opened still further. The unseen person was coming in, to search more thoroughly.

Gallagher had brought the gun up in his right hand and was cautiously inching the canister out with his left as a long two seconds passed.

Now!

He moved swiftly, away from the wall. "Looking for this?"

The intruder whirled in shocked surprise. Gallagher himself was shocked.

Tramm.

Tramm recovered very quickly. "My God, man! You startled me. What . . . what are you doing with that thing?" He stared at the gun, then at the canister, before looking at Gallagher once more. "And what's that funny can you've got there?"

It would have worked if Gallagher had not already heard the hiss of annoyance mixed with anger. It would have worked, if he had not seen the briefest spark of feral light in Tramm's eyes before self-discipline had effectively veiled it out of existence; and it would have worked if Tramm's stance had not become that of someone ready to do battle, rather than that of a cringing potential victim. It was subtly done; but the signs were all there, if one knew what to look for. Gallagher realized he was not looking at a soft, arrogant showbiz manager. He was looking at a very dangerous enemy.

"Close the door very slowly and quietly," Gallagher said. The big Colt pointed squarely at Tramm's forehead.

Tramm continued to play his role. "You're . . . you're mad." There was the right amount of fear too. "I . . . I don't know why you're doing this. A gun! My God! What . . . what do you think you're doing? You can't be after money. . . ."

"Shut up, and close that door. Quietly! You're not going to get the chance to use Mandy Turner as a shield."

"Mr. . . . Mr. Gallagher . . . you're making a crazy mistake. I . . . I don't know what you think I'm here for. I came to look for . . . for something I left here yesterday. . . ."

"Bullshit."

"I . . . I'll shout. . . ."

"Do that and your head will reach the ceiling in

several pieces. Recognize the gun? It's Lassiter's. Now . . . do you close the door?"

It had all been there in Tramm's eyes throughout: a savage gleam of hatred behind the glasses. Tramm was about as frightened as a tiger about to spring upon a tethered goat.

Tramm shut the door, and seemed to have grown in stature within the passing seconds. It was all in the stance and the manner of moving. He smiled as he turned away from the door, removed his glasses.

"Fake," he said. "So, Mr. Gallagher, you are no longer fooled."

"No," Gallagher said, gun unwavering. "I still don't know how you did it, Tramm . . . or should I say, Naja?"

Tramm laughed. "Naja? I'm sorry, Mr. Gallagher. I am not Naja."

"Then who? Nellis?"

Another short laugh. "Dear Charles. No, not him. He's been useful . . . unknowingly, of course." Tramm looked slowly about him. "I suppose we'll have to close this part of things down. Still, it had a good run."

"What are you talking about?"

Tramm smiled. "I'm talking about subterfuge, Mr. Gallagher . . . elaborate, complex, years in the making. I'm talking about the fact that you won't be leaving here alive."

"Neither will you."

"Oh, you won't shoot me. You need to know where Miss Jameson is. How are you going to get that information out of me?" Tramm's right hand was now in his pocket. He smiled when Gallagher made no move to stop him. "Besides, that thing will make the noise of a cannon."

Gallagher raised his left hand. "This gas kills in ten seconds; very nastily. If you shoot me—if that's a gun you've got in that pocket—I'll drop it. The seal will break. You won't even reach the door. Ten seconds to kill, but a lot faster to contact. Do you want to risk it?"

Tramm was visibly shaken. "You wouldn't dare. You would eventually kill everyone in this building, the street. . . . It lasts for months. . . ."

"You know all about it, I see," Gallagher interrupted, his own eyes hard. "Lassiter didn't think I was serious either."

"You killed him with *that?*"

"I've got his gun. I'm here."

"How did you survive?"

"I had a mask," Gallagher replied with a straight face.

"You haven't got one now. You can't make me believe. . . ." Tramma's words died as Gallagher dropped the canister. His mouth opened wide in naked fear and he rushed for the door.

But Gallagher had moved too. He barred Tramm's way, hand reaching into Tramm's pocket. He pulled out a strange-looking gun, shoved Tramm away and moved back out of lunging range.

Tramm, surprised to be still alive, stared at the canister.

"Seal's intact," Gallagher said. "They build them to withstand handling by the clumsiest squaddie, I've been told. Personally, I don't believe that. I think we were just lucky." He went up to the desk, where the canister had rolled, put a foot close to it. "I'll stamp on it next time. That should do it." He glanced at Tramm's gun. "Weird-looking thing. Quieter than Lassiter's cannon, I'll bet." He pointed it at Tramm, who cringed.

Tramm was not playacting; but the eyes were full of open hatred.

"You've got a choice, Tramm," Gallagher went on. "The gas or the gun. *Your* gun, this time. I want to know where Rhiannon Jameson is, and I want to find Naja."

Tramm, Gallagher knew, was no weakling. Fear of the gas, and now of the strange gun, had wrought the change in him. Tramm was a killer who was afraid to die, not by gunshot, but by the lethal gas . . . and by whatever was in that gun. He would talk.

"You are mad," Tramm said in a low voice. The hatred was still there, despite the change.

Gallagher knew that to give Tramm the slightest opportunity would be to sign his own death warrant. Tramm was never going to get it.

Gallagher said: "Not half as mad as I'm going to be if you don't give me answers. Who is the man I saw outside the bistro? The one who looked like a retired officer?

Some kind of pride made Tramm speak before he realized what he was doing. He actually smiled.

"I was that man."

Gallagher looked at him in disbelief. "Don't play games with me, Tramm. The person I saw was taller, with silvery hair, and walked with a straight back."

"A wig, the right makeup, slightly taller shoes, different clothes. It's what you see, or think you see, that counts. I used to be an actor. I have been many different people for many years."

Gallagher was staring at Tramm. "The voice on the bloody tape. There was something in it that sounded familiar, even though it had been disguised."

Tramm was obviously beginning to think he would be able to bargain with Gallagher. He said, almost conversationally: "The voice is more difficult, even with electronic aids."

"You're the bastard who killed Alicia Davenport, and that policeman Jack Moone."

Tramm saw his mistake. "Look," he began. "You want Naja. I'll give you Naja. The whole thing's finished now, anyway. I was hoping to get out after this. We've had years of good fortune. The end had to come sooner or later. This might as well be the time to stop."

"What about Rhiannon Jameson?"

"I'll tell you where she is."

"All right. Tell me."

"She's in Cornwall . . . at Padstow, on Nellis's boat. She was taken there, from Dorset."

"Who's with her?"

"Two others."

"Armed?"

"Yes."

"All right," Gallagher said again. "Now we come to Naja. Who is he? And where is he?"

Tramm seemed to be smiling once more. "Naja is also in Cornwall."

"On the boat?"

"Yes."

"But you said. . . ."

"Naja is one of them. Naja . . . is Doria Luce."

"What!"

"It's true. Can you think of a better disguise? Everyone, yourself included, expects Naja to be a man. We deliberately created the illusion. I was the visible invisible man, if you get my meaning. Naja was always a man to the outside world. Our network was run on that belief. Who would suspect Doria Luce, darling of the screens? We would travel together quite legitimately as manager and client

when on a job, while a false trail would be laid somewhere else entirely. If the people you work for would
care to run a check over the last five years, they
would find a consistency: the presence of Doria Luce
and her constant companion and jealous manager
where every job was pulled."

Gallagher felt himself going cold once more as
he listened to Tramm.

*Doria Luce . . . Naja. And Rhiannon was on a
boat with her!*

"I carried out much of the organizational work,"
Tramm was saying. "We have several companies
worldwide, none of which can be traced to us. It's
been tried. People who work for us don't know who
we are. We've even got shares in Nellads." Tramm
smiled again. "All the really tough assassinations
were carried out by Doria.

"As I've said," Tramm went on into Gallagher's
aghast silence. "Who could possibly suspect her?
She's killed people with guns, knives, poison . . . you
name it, she's done it. I'll give you an example. Once,
someone had to be taken out in France. We studied
him for months. Doria was his favorite actress,
though they'd never met. One day he was driving
along a back road with two bodyguards. Doria used
the classic, oldest trick in the book: the conked-out
motor. The man's car stopped, suspicion giving way
to eagerness when he saw who it was. What was
Doria Luce doing all alone on a back road in France?
Her answer was plausibility itself. She just wanted
to get away from that cloying manager of hers . . . me
. . . the poor misunderstood darling. Her reputation
for impetuosity is well known, as is the constant
battle between the two of us. You can personally
testify to that. I'm certain she's already told you how
she can't stand me." Tramm's smile came on again

briefly. "So the man ordered his bodyguards to help
her. While they were thus engaged, she shot all
three. Simplicity itself.

"She has carefully managed not to become too
famous as an actress, but hovers somewhere in a
limbo between starlet and star. No one really both-
ers if she disappears for weeks on end. Given what
people think about actresses, they invariably imagine she's having yet another secret affair behind my
back, or an abortion. The kind of world we live in
makes such things easy to use as a smokescreen. I
can give you a complete breakdown of the whole
organization. In return, I want a nice quiet life, free
from hunters sent by people like your bosses."

"I have no bosses." Gallagher found his voice
had grown hoarse and he had to clear his throat
twice.

Doria bloody Luce! The ghostly princess of Silent Pool, with death in her eyes.

"She expects me to call her," Tramm said, "with
news of the canister."

"When?"

"Two o'clock. She'll be at a phone box in Padstow. If I don't make it, she'll know something's gone
wrong and will take off in Nellis's boat. Strictly
speaking, it's ours too, being company property.
She'll kill Miss Jameson and throw her overboard, or
just throw her overboard alive, when they're well
out to sea. Doria's like that. I've seen her do it in the
Aegean. We've got a place on Kythira that no one
knows about but the locals. Doria always disguises
herself when we're there—except in private, of
course. She's very good at her disguises. She could
pass you in the street and you'd never know."

Gallagher had already made up his mind, calcu-
lating on the time it would take him to drive to

Padstow. Asking the Department to lay on a chopper was no good. Doria Luce would be instantly suspicious if she saw a helicopter hovering above the boat; after which, he wouldn't give much for Rhiannon's chances.

"Why two o'clock?" he asked Tramm. "Why not immediately you picked up the canister?"

"Doria never panics. Why should she? No one's looking for a female Naja, and certainly not for a sexy actress. She'll expect me to have carried out my part, and will be catching up on her suntan till she's ready to take my call. It's that kind of discipline that has made us so successful."

Tramm could quite easily be lying, Gallagher argued with himself, waiting for a drop in the level of concentration; talking continuously to establish familiarity. Then. . . .

Tramm could also quite easily be Naja, despite the story about Doria Luce.

Yet, certain pieces were beginning to fit. The boat *had* gone to Cornwall. Jameson had already confirmed that in his letter, a fact Tramm could not possibly have known. Jameson had also mentioned that Doria Luce would be down there, for a session, as he'd thought. But. . . .

Gallagher pointed the strange gun at Tramm. "You could be lying. You could be making this all up to save your skin."

Tramm backed away, face pallid. "Why should I?" There was a sense of desperation in his voice. "I've told you the truth. I am not Naja. Doria Luce is the one you're all looking for."

"What will she do when she finds out you've ditched her?"

"Kill me if she can," Tramm said philosophically. "I can give you all the help you need. I'll even make that call, to keep her in Padstow and, incidentally, save your girlfriend's life."

Gallagher made his decision.

"Tramm, he began, "you may be Naja, or you may not be . . . but you killed someone I liked very much. She'd done nothing to you, but that didn't stop you, did it? You took her out, because she just happened to be there. . . ."

"Look, Gallagher," Tramm began in a hoarse voice, moving backward until he had come up against a wall. His hands went up, palms outturned as if to push Gallagher away. "Be careful with that. You've no idea what it can do."

"Did you kill Alicia Davenport and Jack Moone with it?"

"Miss Davenport was an accident. . . ."

"Bullshit," Gallagher said, and fired.

The gun coughed and a dart plunged into Tramm's stomach.

"Christ . . . !" Tramm began in terror; but that was all he had time for.

Gallagher watched, horrorstruck, as Tramm's body seemed to rear on tiptoe, stretching until it could stretch no more. Then it took two steps forward, still on tiptoe, before collapsing like a suddenly unstrung puppet to the floor. The body stretched to its full length once more as the toxins continued to ravage it. The face twitched spasmodically. Discoloration began to set in. The lips drew back from the teeth, trying, it seemed, to pull each corner as far back as the ears. The eyes, popping, appeared to glare with an all-consuming hatred. The arms jerked uncoordinatedly on drumming elbows. Once, unbelievably, Tramm actually tried to push his dying body off the floor. The effort threw him on to his stomach and, finally, he became still.

Gallagher inspected the gun slowly. If that was how Alicia Davenport had died, he did not regret what he had just done.

He stood for a while, listening. There were no sounds of hurrying footsteps. Mandy Turner could not have heard. It was usually her practice to spend some time in the small room set aside for tea-making, before properly starting her day's work. She liked the peace of the empty offices, before the incoming rush of the rest of the staff. She would probably be boiling a kettle. The noise would have drowned any sounds coming from Nellis's office. Besides, the tea room was itself far enough away, down another corridor.

She could also be looking after the plants, Gallagher reasoned, as he continued to listen. Another of her routines was the daily round of all the offices. The monster cheese plants had benefited wonderfully from her ministrations.

Grateful though Gallagher was for her continuing absence, her horticultural enthusiasm would eventually bring her to Nellis's office, and her early mornings at work were never going to be the same again. He had to get going.

Swiftly, he put a gun into each jacket pocket. The canister went inside the jacket itself, which he then zipped up. There was a slight bulge, but nothing overtly suspicious. He did not touch Tramm's body.

He opened the door carefully, peered out. No one seemed to be moving in the outer offices. Mandy Turner must still be having her tea.

Quickly, but without haste, he left Nellis's office, walked through reception and out of the door. He went down the stairs with apparent casualness, but was out of the building within seconds. No one had passed him on his way.

He walked calmly back to where he'd left the car, pausing briefly at a phone box to tell Fowler about Tramm. Fowler wanted to know more, but Gallagher hung up.

There was still time left on the parking meter, but some bright spark had stopped inches from the *quattro*'s front bumper. Expecting the spaces to be full by the time he'd got back, Gallagher had deliberately chosen an end space. The thoughtless parker had blocked his exit.

Gallagher climbed in to the car and put the guns in the glove compartment. The canister dropped neatly into the map tray in the door. He strapped himself in, started the engine. The timer showed 08.50. Five hours and ten minutes to make it to Padstow. He couldn't sit here and wait for the illegal parker to return.

Gallagher slowly eased the *quattro* forward until its solid rubber overriders had touched the car in front; then he used the turbocharged power of the 275 Treserized Audi horses to push the offending vehicle out of the way. He reversed, then set off for the long drive to Cornwall.

Fowler picked up a phone and made a call.

"Get some people in ambulance gear to the Nellads offices," he ordered, and gave the address. "There's a body in the senior partner's room. It will not be a pretty sight, so cover it up before the staff see it. . . . No, none of them has as yet. If you hurry, they won't. There's a young woman there at the moment. Receptionist. . . . No, she hasn't seen it either. She'll be a bit startled to see you so tell her you got a 999 call. Make it look as if it was from the person who is now dead. Felt he was falling ill and all that, but too late for help to reach him. Got it? Good. Get going."

Fowler hung up just as another phone rang. He picked it up.

"Ah, George. Found Lassiter, have you? Good. . . . Won't he?" Fowler smiled. "Gallagher must have thrown a real scare into him. Sounds like it's going to be a long job. Have you closed the place off? . . . Good. Leave Quinn in charge. He'll cope. He's the underwater expert anyway. I want you back in London."

Fowler listened as Haslam spoke, then: "Gallagher got someone called Tramm, showbiz man. . . . Yes, I was surprised about that, but Tramm had the gun that killed Colthen, Moone and Alicia Davenport. . . . Yes. He used it on him." Another pause. "We must assume Naja is not Tramm, and that Gallagher has found the trail. We, however, have not got Gallagher's. I've alerted the motorway patrols. We must also assume he knows where the girl now is and will want to get there as fast as possible. In that car of his, it means the motorways. . . . What? Of course he may expect us to do that, George, and keep off all motorways. Stop making life more difficult. We'll just have to chance it. The patrols have orders to observe but not to detain. I'll have a chopper waiting for you. . . . I know you don't like helicopters, George, but there it is. Get a move on. Gallagher could be going anywhere. The chopper will be working with the patrols. As soon as they've found Gallagher, it will be diverted to pick you up. He's warned us not to come near if we do find him. He's afraid for Miss Jameson, so the chopper will have to be discreet. Pity you couldn't get anything out of Lassiter. Can't be helped, I suppose, if his mind appears to have gone."

Fowler hung up. "The wolf is on the scent," he murmured, looking very pleased.

The intercom bleeped.

"Yes, Arundel," Fowler said.

"Sir John wants to know if you're in." Delphine Arundel's voice had a conspiratorial edge to it.

"What do you think, Arundel?"

"I think you haven't arrived yet, Mr. Fowler."

"Precisely."

"Mr. Fowler!" Arundel's voice was suddenly agitated.

"Fowler!" came Winterbourne's outraged snarl over the intercom.

The bastard must have sneaked in on Arundel, Fowler thought with distaste.

"Shit," he said uncharacteristically, and closed his eyes with weariness.

Gallagher kept off the motorways.

He did not trust Fowler to hold shadows at a discreet distance. He also had a very strong feeling that Fowler would call up a helicopter. Whether civilian or military, any chopper coming near the boat would give Doria Luce all the excuse she needed to take Rhiannon out. He was not prepared to risk that.

It was all right for Fowler, sitting back in his window-starved office, pushing his pawns across the board as the fancy took him; but it was altogether different when the life of someone who had become very special was on the line.

It was also the holiday season, and motorway traffic had a habit of becoming quite horrendous when you were in a hurry; given the number of cars that would be heading south and west, not to mention assorted roadworks.

He therefore went south of the river, and his

route took him through Basingstoke to Andover, from where he joined the A303 all the way to its junction with the A30 near Honiton. He made good time, most of the traffic having chosen to stay on the motorways. With only one stop for petrol to fill up the tank in Ilminster, the *quattro* ate up the miles, launching itself along the roads with seeming eagerness, its exhaust roaring deeply.

From Honiton, Gallagher went on to Exeter, where he lost valuable time going through the city instead of taking the bypass. He still felt certain the patrols would be out looking for him.

At last, he left Exeter, heading out on the twisting, climbing B3212 that would take him across Dartmoor, deliberately avoiding the A30 holiday route to Bodmin. He knew he was risking being caught in a jam of summer sightseers, but luck was with him. There was not enough traffic to balk him.

Luck was not with him, however, in other ways. A patrol coming off the A30 spotted the low black car as it sped toward Longdown.

Oblivious, Gallagher went across Dartmoor, turned right at Two Bridges for Tavistock, on a route that would take him through Liskeard to Bodmin, and eventually to Wadebridge.

Then it would be the final run to Padstow.

Gallagher was going through Tavistock when Fowler got the call.

"Where did you say?" He smiled, almost fondly. "On the way to Dartmoor. Well, he certainly covered some ground. Concentrate on Devon and Cornwall. Shouldn't be too difficult now. Get through to Haslam in the helicopter. Tell him to see if he can pick up the trail, and warn your boys to keep back . . . but not too far, of course."

Fowler felt good as he hung up. It almost made up for the row he'd recently had with Winterbourne.

Strictly speaking, it hadn't been a row. Winterbourne had gone on and on about proper channels and insubordination, while Fowler had listened patiently, infuriating Winterbourne even further.

Fowler had eventually excused himself from the office to which he had been imperiously summoned, pleading pressure of work, and leaving a frustrated Winterbourne behind him.

The big Aerospatiale *Dauphin 11* civilian helicopter was beating its way westward over Reading, when the message came for Haslam. He'd already been airborne for half an hour, and was not happy about it.

"Devon or Cornwall," he said to the pilot from the second pilot's position. "Probably Cornwall. How long will it take us?"

"We've got a high cruising speed. Under an hour."

"Thank God for that," Haslam said with feeling.

The pilot smiled and thought about the poor souls who didn't appreciate flying.

Gallagher took the sharp left on to Thomas
Lovibond's fifteenth-century bridge and crossed the
Camel into Wadebridge. It was 1.30. Half an hour to
go before Tramm's expected call to Doria Luce. With
only eight miles to Padstow, there was plenty of time
now; but he had no intention of taking any chances.

Despite his sense of relief, he would press on as
fast as he could. Better to arrive ahead of time. He
went through the town, following the road in a wide
curve to the right. There was some traffic, but nothing that held him up for more than a couple of minutes: then, a mile or so outside town, his luck
vanished.

He had come round a left-hand bend to find himself in the kind of traffic jam he'd been dreading all
the way down. Over to the left, some kind of fair was
going on and the road was jammed with holidaymakers in cars and on foot.

Gallagher sat in the car in mounting frustration
as laughing, chattering people sauntered past, while
the digital timer inexorably counted away his margin.

Fifteen minutes later, he had at last managed to

inch his way out of the jam and when the road forked right to Padstow, half a mile further on, he found it blissfully clear of traffic. He drove as fast as the road conditions allowed toward the ancient fishing town; but it had become more of a holiday spot and, as he drove through narrow streets looking for somewhere to park, he saw the inevitable crowds.

He eventually found a space a few streets up from the little harbor. The timer glowed 14.04 at him just before he shut down. Four minutes adrift. Christ. Doria Luce would have gone back to the boat, having assumed that Tramm had not made it. Rhiannon's life could now be measured in minutes.

As the engine ticked and cooled, Gallagher took the guns out of the glove compartment, put one in each pocket. He ignored the canister.

It had been a bright day all the way down, and, as he got out of the car and quickly locked it, he felt appreciably warmer. He kept the jacket on and hurried down to the waterfront.

The people he passed all seemed to have come from London and as he made his way along the curving harbor frontage, he saw the gleaming white boat in the middle of the estuary. He felt his heart lurch. Faint wisps of smoke were coming from the twin exhausts. They had started the engines.

Gallagher ran, frantically dodging past people who had all day to while away the hours. Many scenes etched themselves upon his mind.

On either side of the estuary, several small boats—skiffs, dinghies and outboards—rode at anchor. There were a few cabin cruisers, a couple with flying bridges. An open-decked ferry was crabbing across from Rock, while at the sea wall another was taking on passengers. Tall signs offered fast boat rides, with prices brightly tabulated. Out in the estuary, a speedboat was charging in the direction of the open sea.

But among all that, Gallagher had eyes only for the sleek white boat now hauling up its anchor.

He stopped at the harbor wall, peered down. A bright red speedboat was grumbling at idle, fresh splashes on its rakish prow. It had obviously just returned from a run. It was warm and primed to go.

Gallagher pushed his way past a group of people waiting their turn for a ride, and hurried down precarious-looking steps to the speedboat. A blond, youngish man, with a heavy sea tan and crow's-feet about the eyes, looked up in surprise.

"There's a queue," he began. "Can't you see?"

The accent was not Cornish. This was probably a seasonal job. Maybe it was his own boat, Gallagher thought. If so. . . .

"I've got thirty pounds on me," Gallagher said quickly. "It's all I've got for the moment. It's yours if you take me over to that white boat over there." He glanced anxiously to where the object of his interest burbled, beginning to move forward, he was sure. The curve of the sea wall partially hid it from view, and he could only see from midships to stern. The bloody anchor was probably up by now. "Please," he added. "I'll get some more when we get back."

The man was still looking at him, unmoved.

Gallagher decided he wasn't going to argue. He'd tried the nice way. Any time now, the people up above would start coming down; but worse, the engines on Nellis's boat would be opened wide, and that would be it.

Goodbye, Rhiannon.

Gallagher surreptitiously showed the man the butt of the big Colt. "I did offer you money first."

The crow's-feet seemed to disappear as the

man's eyes grew round with shock. He paled under his tan. Gallagher could almost see the thoughts chasing across his face. Some kind of colored man with a gun . . . a terrorist, perhaps . . . maybe Arab. . . .

"I'm not any of the things you're thinking," Gallagher said briskly, "but you'd better take me across pretty bloody quickly."

"Yes, yes. Of course. Of course. Don't get angry. It's no problem. No problem at all."

The man got down to it immediately and threw the speedboat into astern. The maneuver nearly tossed Gallagher overboard, and he barked his shin painfully.

That's right, he thought sourly. *Break my bloody leg. That's all I need.*

Up on the pier, people were beginning to shout in annoyance.

The man swung the boat round and headed at speed into the estuary. The boat raised its prow half out of the water and seemed about to take off, its engines screaming.

But the bigger boat was definitely on the move now, heading for open water. A white moustache was growing at the bows.

Shit.

"What do you want me to do now?" the unwilling helmsman shouted above the roar.

"Follow them and catch up! What else?" Gallagher looked away from the fugitive boat. "How fast can this thing go?"

"I've got twin Mercruisers. She'll do forty knots at least."

Some encouraging news that was good to know if they had a chase on their hands.

"Well, that's something," Gallagher shouted

above the sounds of slipstream, sea, and engines. "If they open up their bloody great turbo diesels before we get close, we'll have a hell of a job catching up."

"Looks like an RAF launch . . . those air-sea rescue types."

"She used to be, but she's faster than normal."

"Looks pretty."

"A lot of money's been spent on it." He spoke bitterly, knowing where most of that had come from.

Even as he looked, the stem began to rise out of the water. The powerful engines were beginning to build to maximum revs. Before long, the familiar skyward tilt would become apparent and the boat would give the impression of planing on its transom as it hit top speed. He had to get aboard before that happened.

"Why do you want to catch them?" the blond man queried, curiosity getting the better of his fear of his "terrorist" passenger.

Gallagher said: "I'm sorry about the gun, but I had to get you to move this boat quickly. I work for the . . . er . . . government. There's a young woman on that white boat. If I don't get her off, she's dead. They'll dump her overboard once they get to sea."

"How do I know you're telling the truth? You threaten me with a gun. . . ."

"You don't know. But I promise you one thing: if I miss that boat and she dies, you're a dead man."

Something in Gallagher's eyes made the man say: "Why didn't you tell me that in the first place? Girlfriend, is she?"

Gallagher said nothing, and turned to watch the fleeing vessel. The speedboat gathered speed and seemed to leap out of the water.

Gallagher crouched down to keep out of sight. "They won't be expecting anyone to attempt boarding," he shouted. "They'll have seen you going up and down all day. They won't suspect anything until it's too late. . . ." *I hope,* he added to himself.

"When you're close enough," he continued to the blond man, "make a quick run-in. I'll have to take my chances then. Once I'm aboard, pull out of the way. I don't want them shooting at you. . . ."

"They've got guns?"

"Yes," Gallagher replied. *They'd be bound to.*

"Fucking hell," the man said. He went pale once more.

"If you keep out of the way, you'll be all right; but hang about to pick us up. We'll probably have to jump for it. We'd look pretty stupid if we had to swim against the current. Could be nasty." He took out the .45 and cocked it.

The man stared at the gun as if mesmerized.

"I can't do anything to make you wait," Gallagher said, "so I suppose I'll have to trust you. What's your name?"

"Jeff . . . Jeff Dyson." Dyson looked away to see where he was going.

"This boat must have cost you a bit."

"I don't own it all. I've got a quarter share, but I do most of the driving. We've had it for three years now. Done well out of it so far."

"Well, I hope this won't cause any damage . . . but in case something does knock it about, I know some people who will pay for repairs, with a bit on top into the bargain."

"Government people?" Dyson looked as if he wasn't sure whether to believe that.

"Sort of."

There was no talking for about a minute, then Dyson said: "We're coming up to Gun Point now. . . ." He gave a shaky laugh. "Funny that. Gun Point.

They haven't quite got the speed yet, but it won't be long. A man's at the wheel, with a blonde woman . . . that your girlfriend?"

"No."

"They've just looked us over, but only casually. I'm closing in now. They're ignoring us." Dyson had lowered his voice, as if expecting those on the boat to hear him. "I'm still closing in, and they're still not bothering. Any minute now, though, they'll be telling me to get out of the way. You'd better get ready if you're going to do this."

"Thank you, Dyson."

"Don't thank me. I've seen what being crushed between two boats can do to a man. I hope she's worth it."

"She is."

The speedboat had begun to buck like a skittish young horse.

"I've entered their wake now," Dyson said. "Here we go!"

The speedboat seemed to find yet more urge and in fleeting seconds, Gallagher found himself looking up at the superstructure of the racing launch.

He leapt up, flung himself up and outward as, for the briefest of instants, the two craft matched speeds. Then the red speedboat was winging away to starboard, going round in a wide sweep.

Gallagher found himself hanging by his left hand to a grab rail on the right side of the superstructure, being buffeted by the speed-induced breeze coming off the bows, and drenched by flying spray.

A tableau had been fixed upon his mind, at the instant of his leaping aboard.

The big dark-haired man on the bridge had turned at his sudden presence, startled and momentarily frozen. But it was Doria Luce who grabbed his attention, even as he was bringing the Colt to bear.

Surprised though she undoubtedly had been, she had recovered swiftly, dark eyes with their flecks of green flashing at him even as she moved. There had been no emotion in them; no anger, no hatred, no acknowledgment of him. The eyes of a killer.

Her palm had slapped hard upon two switches just as the Colt roared twice and the man at the wheel, in the act of pulling a gun out of his own pocket, was flung away from it, the weapon spinning out of his hand to fall to the deck.

The man collapsed in a heap in one corner, the great holes in his side flowering redly all over the white of his T-shirt; but Doria Luce was moving with all the swiftness of her reptilian namesake. She had grabbed the discarded weapon and was pointing it at Gallagher. In a yellow T-shirt and shorts, she looked stunning.

"Well, darling," she said. "We appear to have a stalemate. Your gun or mine?" The beautiful mouth smiled. The eyes of death did not. "I must say I never expected to meet you in such circumstances. You must have taken out poor old Jerry, who played his role very well over the years. And Lassiter too. I'm impressed. Very impressed. We could perhaps have worked together. Who knows?"

Gallagher, still precariously balanced on the outside of the bridge of the speeding boat, shook his head. He dared not make a sudden move. Doria Luce, propped for support against the instrument panel, did not appear to have a shaky hand.

She said: "No. I suppose not. You go for Welsh puddings. Now that you've risked life and limb to come for her, it's a pity you won't ever see her again . . . but you will be together. I promise you that, at least. You see, I've just primed one switch and turned another on. The first is an explosive device that will rip this boat apart. The second locked the steering. You'll be sailing on one heading, forever." Again, the smile with the lips only. "Your little darling is below, but you'll die up here."

Gallagher said nothing, keeping the Colt trained upon her.

"What about me?" she went on. "That's what you're thinking, I know. I'll be jumping off soon, before the boat gets too far. I'm a very strong swimmer. I'll get ashore at Daymer Bay, and disappear. Doria Luce will cease to exist. As for you and your Welsh pudding, you will die in a boat explosion. Such a terrible tragedy."

Gallagher still said nothing.

Doria Luce studied him pointedly. "You don't look very stable . . . like a man trying to control a runaway horse. Any moment now, you'll lose your balance and I shall have my chance. I did warn you to stay away from Celtic princesses. Very bad for the health."

Suddenly, the boat hit a swell. It reared, then plunged sickeningly. Gallagher had no choice but to reach out with his right hand to steady himself, otherwise he would have toppled helplessly. Unfortunately, he lost the gun.

But as it skidded over the side to flop uselessly into the churning water, the boat hit another swell, catching Doria Luce off-balance.

Gallagher flung himself into the wheelhouse, clawing desperately for Tramm's dartgun in his other pocket. Mercifully, it was still there; but Doria Luce was quick.

The gun in her hands roared above the sounds of the boat's engines and the smashing of its stem into the sea. A bullet tore into the deck, inches from Gallagher's head. Slivers of wood erupted from the point of impact to sing past. One seared across the back of his left hand, leaving a raised weal in its wake.

Gallagher froze, making no further attempt at the dartgun. It was just possible she had been too busy regaining her balance to shoot, to notice what he had been trying to do.

"I did not miss because I'm a bad shot," her voice came from behind and above him, "but because I'm very good. Turn around, very slowly, but stay down on the deck."

Nothing about the gun. So she hadn't seen.

Gallagher wasn't at all sure whether that fact improved his chances in the slightest.

He did as he was told, taking care to keep the pocket containing the dartgun out of her line of sight.

Doria Luce had braced herself securely against the movements of the speeding vessel, her gun pointing unerringly down at Gallagher.

"Properly," she commanded. "Turn over properly."

"I . . . I don't think I can. I landed badly. My side. . . ."

"Oh, Gordon, really. You don't expect me to fall for that, do you?"

"Come and check for your bloody self then!" Gallagher said irritably, putting pain into his voice. It helped that the hand with the weal was stinging ferociously.

She laughed, eyes of death unsmiling. "You've got to try something, I suppose. Stay where you are, then. I can attend to you from here. I'd have loved to stay and play with you a little before bidding you a fond but permanent farewell; however, time is not on our side."

Gallagher stared at the gaping snout of the gun in a kind of dream.

Do something! his mind screamed at him in something disquietingly close to panic. The organism wanting to survive.

Great. What the hell could he do?

Doria Luce said: "You seem to be waiting for something. The cavalry's not going to come riding over the hill. We've seen your friend in the speedboat all day. I know he's local, so he's not going to risk his neck for you. Besides, he'd lose it before he got close enough. The same trick won't work twice. I won't kiss you goodbye. You might take advantage of me." She laughed as she steadied the gun.

She pulled the trigger.

A click that seemed inordinately loud was all that followed. *The gun had jammed!*

"Jesus Christ!" Doria Luce screamed in sudden rage. There was no fear on her face, only a suffused anger that distorted the beautiful features; an anger directed at the gun that had dared jam on her.

As she slammed the cocking lever backward and forward in an attempt to free it, Gallagher grabbed his opportunity. He rolled to free the pocket which held the dartgun. His hand scrabbled for it, pulled it out just as she looked at him.

Her eyes widened as she recognized it for what it was and, for the first time, fear entered her eyes.

He fired.

The poisoned dart entered her throat. Her eyes strained to their limits in horror as she dropped the gun to claw at the embedded dart. Her beautiful face became hideous as the venom began its deadly work, destroying her in fleeing seconds. She staggered, chest heaving, eyes seeming to pop out of their sockets, the approaching death in them now very real.

Gallagher rolled away from her stumbling path, and stood up.

She fell heavily. "Empty," she croaked. *"Bloody empty."*

The magnificent legs twitched once and were still forever.

Empty? What did she mean?

The gun.

Gallagher picked it up, inspected it swiftly. The magazine was indeed empty. The gun had belonged to the dark-haired man. Doria Luce would never have carried a partially loaded weapon.

He threw it over the side, thankful for inefficient gunmen. It was the sort of oversight that could cost you dear. The dark-haired man and Doria Luce had paid the price. Perhaps the man had not been a true professional; more an armed crewman. He had been slow to react when Gallagher had first come aboard, much slower than Doria Luce had been.

Gallagher wasted no more time thinking about it. He had to find Rhiannon. Valuable seconds had passed. He hurried below, not wanting to ponder upon how much longer he had before the boat blew up about them.

"Rhiannon!" he yelled. *"Rhiannon!"*

The launch had been refurbished to take two private cabins, as well as a four-sleeper. She was not in the larger one. The private ones were locked. Christ.

"Rhiannon!" he bawled once more.

The boat thundered about him, on its way to oblivion.

"Rhiannon!" Oh Christ oh Christ oh Christ.

He thought he heard something. He smashed at

the door he believed was the likely one. It didn't budge. The bloody thing was solidly built.

Sweet raving. . . .

He needed a fireaxe. Would there be one on this boat? Knowing Nellis's reputation for wanting everything just right when going to sea, there was bound to be one somewhere.

The bridge. He hadn't noticed one; but then, he hadn't been looking. He hurried back up, and saw it almost as soon as he entered. It was directly above where Doria Luce had fallen.

He did not look at her as he grabbed the axe and returned below to attack the cabin door furiously. After five savage blows, it flew open.

She was there, on the bunk, tied hand and foot, a gag about her mouth.

He put the axe down, looked for something to get at her bonds with. Whoever had done the trussing had carried out a good job. The boat would probably be blowing itself to smithereens while he was wasting time trying to untie her. As he searched, Rhiannon's anxious eyes followed him.

Then, in a drawer, he found what he'd least expected: a cut-throat razor. The things people sometimes carried around with them. He wondered whose it was, as he swiftly cut at the ropes that bound her; but it didn't matter now. Nothing mattered except getting off this hurtling one-way ticket with its cargo of dead.

He dropped the razor and removed her gag.

"Oh, Gordon . . . !" she began.

He shushed her with a fleeting kiss on the lips. "No time. We've got to get off this thing. It's likely to blow any moment."

Her eyes jumped with fear but, thankfully, she

did not waste valuable time by asking pointless questions. He warmed to her for that.

She followed him out, massaging her arms and legs as she stumbled after him.

From entry to exit, no more than a minute could have passed, but to Gallagher it had felt like centuries.

They made it to the wheelhouse just as the charging boat was leaving Daymer Bay, heading for Trebetherick Point and the more open waters of Padstow Bay.

Rhiannon saw the bodies, gave a sharp intake of breath, but said simply: "I'm glad."

He knew she was thinking of Alicia Davenport, and of her brother, whom she would have known by now to be dead.

"Come on, love," he said gently. "We're going for a swim. Someone is waiting to pick us up." He hoped. "Take off your jeans and your shirt. We'll wrap everything in my jacket."

They stripped, and Gallagher wrapped everything into a tight bundle. Despite the situation, he couldn't help thinking how magnificent she looked. They went out on deck, making for the stern. The wind and spray lashed at them.

"I want you to throw yourself over," he said loudly in her ear, "going diagonally off the stern. Throw yourself as far as you can. The boat will be moving away while you're still in the air. You'll be all right. Are your legs and arms OK now?"

She bit her lips, nodded vigorously.

He looked across the water and saw the red speedboat to starboard. *Good on you, Dyson.*

Dyson had obviously seen them, for the raked prow rose as it gathered speed.

"There's our pick-up!" Gallagher said to Rhiannon. *"Jump!"*

She went without hesitation and launched herself in a shallow, flying dive. She had covered a lot of distance by the time she hit the water, and was well away from the launch.

Gallagher threw in the bundle, and went after it. The water felt remarkably cold and he restrained a gasp as he went beneath the churning wake. When he'd surfaced, the white boat was speeding away from him trailing a high plume of spray, taking Doria Luce on her final journey.

The weal on his hand began to sting viciously as the salt water got to it. He had forgotten all about it in the panic; but soon it had become a background irritation.

He got to the bundle before it became waterlogged, and began swimming toward where the red speedboat had stopped to pick up Rhiannon; then it had again reared its prow and was coming toward him. Soon, he too was climbing aboard.

"Thanks for waiting, Jeff," he said as he unwrapped the bundle and passed it to Rhiannon.

She drew it about her shoulders.

They began to put on their wet jeans. The day was hot enough, and their clothes would eventually dry out.

Dyson said: "It's not every day I get threatened with a gun by somebody who wants to rescue a young lady." He grinned, motioned to Gallagher, who went up to him. "She's worth it," Dyson added conspiratorially.

"Thought you'd approve," Gallagher said, smiling, and went back to his seat.

A sudden, vibrant roar made them all look. The white boat had blown up in a most spectacular manner. A great orange fireball flared vividly upon the surface of the water, before collapsing into a pall of dense black smoke that rose skyward, etching Doria Luce's epitaph in a writhing shape which Gallagher thought looked unnervingly like a cobra.

He felt a soft touch, turned to see Rhiannon looking at him.

"Thanks for coming," she said in a quiet voice.

"Nothing would have stopped me."

The golden eyes searched his. "Nothing did." She smiled. "I saw the way you looked at me on the boat, just after we'd stripped. It made me feel good."

"You're a hussy," he said. "A Welsh pudding." He smiled at her, at last able to show how relieved and pleased he was to see her again.

Just then a new sound intruded. Again, all three looked; this time, upward.

The helicopter came swooping toward them, then hovered to one side, low above the water. Gallagher recognized Haslam peering out in their direction.

Dyson, who had been driving the speedboat slowly back to Padstow as if in deference to Gallagher and Rhiannon, looked over his shoulder to say: "Friends of yours?"

"Sort of," Gallagher said.

"Government?"

Again, Gallagher said: "Sort of."

"So you really do work for the government."

"No," Gallagher said.

And Dyson looked confused.

Rhiannon was looking at Gallagher's hand. "What happened?" she asked.

"A snake bit it," he answered.

EPILOGUE

"I would not have credited it," Fowler began, "if the evidence had not been there. Doria Luce, Naja." He shook his head slowly, in wonder. "And as for Tramm, his nationality remains a mystery."

It was a week after the incident at Padstow, and Gallagher had come to the office to return the dummy canister. He had spent most of the time with Rhiannon, helping her to get over what had happened. They were now going to have a nice long holiday together and he was looking forward to it.

Fowler said: "We checked what you said Tramm had told you, and found that many of the jobs carried out over the years did tally with their visits. Tramm, in one of his many guises, apparently ran foul of the West German police. As for Lassiter, you certainly did a job on him. It took several hours to coax him out of that hole. When he was found, he was gibbering like a baby. I don't think he'll ever be right in the head again. Which brings me to that canister. Do you recall my asking you about the gas and how you came to know about it? You never answered. Understandable, of course. You got it from Jameson, who in turn had got from someone who had been briefed by us."

Gallagher stared at him.

"That's right," Fowler said. "They are *all* dummies."

"All the stockpile? The whole shooting match?"

"The lot."

"I don't believe you."

"Do you seriously think we'd hide chemical weapons down there?"

"I still don't believe you."

Fowler's eyes gleamed behind their glasses. "Suit yourself."

Gallagher stood up. "My God. All those innocent people who died. . . . Those two divers. . . ."

"They were mistaken for Naja's people. We had not yet quite finished preparing the trap. The men involved were slightly overzealous."

"Is that what you call it?" Gallagher said in disgust. "And what about Alicia Davenport and Jack Moone and all the rest?"

Fowler said nothing.

"Do you ever get to sleep?" Gallagher asked in a hard voice. "Your dreams must be terrible."

"I sleep quite well. Naja and her people took out a substantial number of souls in their time. Miss Jameson would have gone the same way too. Remember that."

"Not if she hadn't been involved."

"Don't be naïve, Gordon."

"So now I'm naïve."

"No, Gordon. You're someone rather special." Fowler actually smiled. "Before I forget . . . we found the key to your car." He handed it over.

The intercom bleeped, stifling Gallagher's intended acid retort.

"Yes, Arundel."

"Sir John's on his way."

"Very well." Fowler shut his eyes briefly, with long-suffering weariness.

"It's a hard life," Gallagher said unfeelingly. "I don't think I can take both of you in the same room."

Winterbourne entered, saw Gallagher and said brightly: "Ah, Gallagher! Good morning."

"Goodbye," Gallagher said and walked out.

Winterbourne stared after him, then turned to Fowler. "Must you keep employing that man, Fowler?" he asked with annoyance. "He is appallingly rude."

"We don't employ him, Sir John. He's not on the Department's payroll."

Winterbourne looked as if he'd missed something.

Born in Dominica, Julian Jay Savarin was educated in Britain and took a degree in History before serving in the Royal Air Force. Mr. Savarin lives in England and is the author of LYNX, HAMMERHEAD, WARHAWK, TROPHY, TARGET DOWN!, WOLF RUN, and WINDSHEAR.

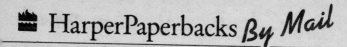

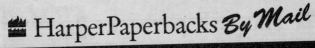

AMPBELL ARMSTRONG

gents of Darkness

spended from the LAPD, Charlie Galloway decides his
e has no meaning. But when his Filipino housekeeper is
urdered, Charlie finds a new purpose in tracking the
ller. He never expects, though, to be drawn into a
onspiracy that reaches from the Filipino jungles to the
hite House.

lazurka

or Frank Pagan of Scotland Yard, it begins with the
urder of a Russian at crowded Waverly Station, Edinburgh. From that moment
, Pagan's life becomes an ever-darkening nightmare as he finds himself
apped in a complex web of intrigue, treachery, and murder.

lambo

per-terrorist Gunther Ruhr has been captured. Scotland Yard's Frank Pagan
ust escort him to a maximum security prison, but with blinding swiftness and
utality, Ruhr escapes. Once again, Pagan must stalk Ruhr, this time into an
rth-shattering secret conspiracy.

rainfire

merican John Rayner is a man on fire with grief and anger over the death of his
werful brother. Some

y it was suicide, but
yner suspects
mething more
nister. His suspicions
ove correct as he
comes trapped in a
viet-made maze of
trayal and terror.

sterisk Destiny

sterisk is America's
ost fragile and chilling
cret. It waits some-
here in the Arizona
esert to pave the way
world domination...or
mnation. Two men,
hite House aide John
orne and CIA agent
d Hollander, race
crack the wall of
ence surrounding
sterisk and tell
e world of their
rrifying discovery.